PRAISE FOR THE
JONATHAN ARGYLL SERIES:

The Bernini Bust

"The cleverest entry yet in this deliciously literate series."
—*Kirkus Reviews*

"As charming as its title—well-paced, witty, and full of details that speak to his training as an art historian."
—*The San Diego Union-Tribune*

"Art history, literary language, and wry humor realize another auspicious combination."
—*Library Journal*

The Raphael Affair

"[As] mystery, *The Raphael Affair* is very good; as cultural explication, it is superlative."
—*Publishers Weekly*

"Presents a world the author knows well in the satisfying way Margaret Truman and Dick Francis set their mysteries in milieus they know."
—The Associated Press

"Masterful and calls for an encore."
—*The Houston Post*

continued on next page . . .

Death and Restoration

"Gleeful . . . articulate characters and erudite art commentary . . . high style." —*The New York Times Book Review*

"Pears writes delightfully witty, elegant, well-informed crime novels." —*The Times* (London)

"Pears exhibits quite a masterful touch at suspenseful story-telling . . . [he] writes clearly, persuasively, and with a hand guided by touches of sentimentality as well as mischief." —*Chicago Tribune*

"Enjoyable." —*The Washington Post*

"Pears again achieves a delicate, sure balance with a book simultaneously witty and instructive." —*Publishers Weekly*

"It is to Pears's great credit that the textured paths of modern-day mystery, ancient empires, and religious faith collide so effortlessly. Clearly, his training as both journalist and art historian make for a finely tuned duet. . . . In the end, once all the dots are connected, *Death and Restoration* leaves a memorable, satisfying imprint. We have Pears's subtle technique of mixing intrigue with intelligence to thank for that." —*The Boston Globe*

"An exciting mystery." —*The Dallas Morning News*

"The pleasure of Pears's book . . . lies in its careful . . . revelations of character." —*Houston Chronicle*

"Pears's tremendous affection for Rome comes through strongly, making the city one of the most engaging characters." —*The Sunday Times* (U.K.)

The Titian Committee

"[An] elegant mystery . . . but the real work of art here is the plot, a piece of structural engineering any artist would envy."
—*The New York Times Book Review*

"[Pears] writes with a Beerbohm-like wit." —*Publishers Weekly*

Giotto's Hand

"Fine art, quirky characters, and scenes set in Rome and an English country village add to the joys of *Giotto's Hand*. . . . A neat twist at the end is the cherry on this fudge sundae of a mystery." —*Minneapolis Star Tribune*

"Pears has a whimsical take on the scruples of the art trade, on English food and plumbing, and on Italian bureaucracy. . . . A sweet, art world 'cozy.'" —*San Jose (CA) Mercury News*

"Art, crime, and Italy mix well . . . Pears masterfully juggles his plot elements while providing delightful diversion in the contrasting manners of his English and Italian characters." —*Booklist*

IAIN PEARS

THE
LAST
JUDGEMENT

BERKLEY PRIME CRIME, NEW YORK

THE LAST JUDGEMENT

A Berkley Prime Crime Book / published by arrangement with Scribner, an imprint of Simon & Schuster, Inc.

PRINTING HISTORY
Victor Gallancz edition / 1993
Scribner edition / 1996
Berkley Prime Crime mass-market edition / October 1999
Berkley Prime Crime trade paperback edition / December 2002

Visit our website at
www.penguinputnam.com

Library of Congress Cataloging-in-Publication Data

Pears, Iain.
The last judgement / Iain Pears.
p. cm.
ISBN 0-425-18647-4
1. Argyll, Jonathan (Fictitious character)—Fiction. 2. Di Stefano, Flavia (Fictitious character)—Fiction. 3. Police—Italy—Rome—Fiction. 4. Art—Forgeries—Fiction. 5. Art historians—Fiction. 6. Rome (Italy)—Fiction. 7. Policewomen—Fiction. 8. Art thefts—Fiction. 9. Italy—Fiction.
I. Title.

PR6066.E167 L37 2002
823'.914—dc21
2002074764

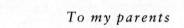

To my parents

Some of the pictures and buildings mentioned in this book exist, others are invented and all the characters are imaginary. There is an Italian art squad in a building in central Rome, but I have arbitrarily shifted its affiliation from the Carabinieri to the Polizia to emphasize that mine has no relation to the original.

1

JONATHAN Argyll stared transfixed at the scene of violence that suddenly presented itself as he turned around. The dying man, tormented by agony but bearing the pain with fortitude, lay back in a chair. On the floor beside him was a phial that had dropped from his hand; it took little intelligence to realize it had contained poison. The skin was pale and his hand, clenched into a fist, hung down loosely towards the ground. To the left was a group of onlookers, friends and admirers, variously weeping, angry or merely shocked at the sight.

It was the face, though, that grabbed the attention. The eyes were open and glazed, but it had dignity and tranquillity. It was the face of a martyr, who died knowing that others would mourn him. Death would not end his renown, but merely extend and complete it.

"Nice, eh?" came the voice at his side.

"Oh, yes. Very."

He squinted in a professional fashion. Death of Socrates, at a rough guess, complete with disciples in attendance. Just after the old buffer has been sentenced to death for corrupting youth and drinks the hemlock. Not bad stuff, on the whole, but liable to be expensive. French school about 1780, or thereabouts, and much more pricey bought in Paris than elsewhere. The thought, as so often, dampened his ardour. He looked again, and reassured himself that maybe it wasn't so desirable after all. Evidently not a well-known artist, he told himself. Needed a bit of a wash and brush up. Come to think of it, the treatment was quite cold and stiff as well. The fact that he didn't have much money to spare at the moment completed his transformation of opinion. Not for him, he decided with relief.

Still, one must make conversation. "How much are you asking for this?" he asked.

"Sold already," the gallery-owner replied. "At least, I think it is. I'm just about to send it off to a client in Rome."

"Who did it?" Argyll asked, mildly jealous to hear of anybody managing to sell a painting. He hadn't managed to unload one himself for months. Not at a profit, anyway.

"It's signed by Jean Floret. Who he was I have no idea,

but not what you might call a major figure. Fortunately that doesn't seem to bother my client, God bless him."

The man, a distant colleague of Argyll's who had taken one or two drawings off him in the past, gazed with a satisfied expression at the painting. He was not a hugely pleasant character; a bit too sharp round the edges for Argyll's taste. The sort of person where you made sure to check your pockets when leaving his company, just to make certain all the cheque-books and credit cards were still in place. Not that he'd ever done anything bad to Argyll, but the Englishman was determined to make sure he never got the chance, either. He was learning fast about the art business. People were friendly enough, and helpful enough, but occasionally came over a bit funny when money was involved.

He was standing in Jacques Delorme's gallery about half-way up the Rue Bonaparte, a few hundred yards from the Seine. A noisy, fug-filled street, lined with booksellers and print shops and the lesser sort of art dealer; the sort of people who sold cheaper paintings but knew a lot about them generally; unlike the wealthy lot in the Faubourg St-Honoré, who unloaded vastly expensive tat on gullible foreigners with more money than sense. It made them more agreeable company, even though the surroundings were less chic. Delorme's gallery was a little dingy, and outside the cars tooted their horns alarmingly close to the main entrance, this being one of those Parisian streets where pavements were more concept than reality. The weather didn't help the slightly gloomy atmosphere either;

the sky was leaden, and it had been raining more or less since he'd arrived in Paris two days before and was still splashing quietly but persistently into the gutters then gurgling down the drains. He wanted to go home, back to Rome where the sun was still shining, even in late September.

"Just in the nick of time, frankly," Delorme went on, blithely unaware of Argyll's disapproval of the northern European climate. "The bank was beginning to become very troublesome. They were muttering about the size of my loans. Reconsidering their position. You know how it is. Once I get the money for this, I should be able to fend them off for a while."

Argyll nodded as sympathetically as he could manage. He didn't have a gallery himself, but even in his low-cost, working-from-home venture, it was tough earning a decent living. The market was bad. The only thing worse was conversation with colleagues, as they managed to talk about nothing else except how dismal life was at the moment.

"Who is this man with money, anyway?" he asked. "He doesn't want any nice baroque religious pieces, does he?"

"Got a surfeit, have you?"

"One or two."

"Sorry. Not as far as I know, anyway. He particularly wants this one. The only problem is how to bring him and it into contact soon enough to satisfy my creditors."

"I wish you luck. Have you had it for a long time?"

"No. I wouldn't spend money on something like this

unless I knew I could unload it fast. Not at the moment. You know how it is . . ."

Argyll did indeed. He was in something of the same position himself. A properly disciplined art dealer would act like any other business. Small stock, high turnover. The picture trade didn't seem to work like that, somehow. Paintings just demand to be bought, even though there may be no client in sight. So Argyll had lots of them now; many had been hanging around for months, and almost no one was buying anything.

"Now, about these drawings," Delorme continued.

And so they got down to some hard bargaining. It wasn't so difficult, considering that Delorme's bank was pressuring him to sell something and Argyll was more or less under orders to buy the drawings whatever the price. It was the only thing keeping him going at the moment, his part-time post as European agent for an American museum. Without that he would have been in real trouble. It had been decided months ago that it really ought to have a Prints and Drawings collection, as it had a Prints and Drawings room with nothing to put in it. So when Argyll mentioned that he'd heard of a Boucher portfolio wandering around the Paris market, he'd been instructed to go and get it. And if he saw anything else . . .

He had. He'd dropped in on Delorme, whom he'd met a year or so back, and the Frenchman mentioned this Pontormo sketch. A quick telephone call to California and the bargaining could get under way.

The mutually enjoyable haggle ended satisfactorily;

more than the drawing would have fetched on the open market, but a decent price none the less. A little ruthlessly, Argyll exploited the fact that Delorme evidently needed the cash. One thing about the Moresby Museum, it paid fast. Business was concluded with a promise of cash on delivery, a cup of coffee, a shake of the hand and a mutual sense of well-being. All that was needed now was a rudimentary letter of contract.

The only snag was the tiresome business of getting all his drawings off to California. Argyll just about knew his way around the Italian bureaucratic labyrinth; the French one was entirely different. He wasn't looking forward to spending the next couple of days hanging around offices in Paris, trying to get all the forms signed.

Then he—maybe it was a hint from Delorme that jogged his mind—had one of those little ideas which are devastatingly brilliant in their simplicity.

"Tell you what," he said.

"Hmm?"

"That picture. Your *Death of Socrates*. How about me taking it to Rome for you, to deliver to this client of yours? In return, you could do the paperwork for these drawings and send them off for me."

Delorme thought about it. "That's not a bad idea, you know. Not bad at all. When would you go?"

"Tomorrow morning. I'm finished here. The only thing keeping me was the prospect of getting all the export licences."

The Frenchman nodded as he thought it over. "Why

not?" he said eventually. "Why not indeed? It would be more convenient than you can imagine, in fact."

"Will it need export permission as well?"

Delorme shook his head. "Well, technically, maybe. But it's only a formality. I'll deal with that, don't worry. You just take it out and I'll square it with the powers that be."

OK, so it was a little bit dishonest. But not much. It was hardly as if he were taking out the *Mona Lisa*. The only tiresome thing was that it meant Argyll would have to carry it by hand. Packers and shippers require lots of formal bits of paper with stamps on them.

"Who is the lucky buyer?" Argyll asked, ready to write the name and address down on the back of a cigarette packet. Somehow he had missed the Filofax generation.

"A man called Arthur Muller," replied Delorme.

"OK. Address?"

Delorme fumbled around—he was almost as badly or-ganized—then fished out a scrap of paper and dictated. It was a street Argyll didn't know, up in the north where the rich folk live. No great trouble; of course, it was a little below his dignity as an up-and-coming international dealer to be running around acting as someone else's cou-rier, but that didn't matter so much. Everybody's life would be made a lot simpler; and that was what counted. With the feeling that he had accomplished something use-ful on this trip after all, he wandered off into the street for lunch.

*T*HE next morning, he was sitting in the great restau-rant of the Gare de Lyon, drinking a coffee and sitting out the twenty minutes or so before his train left on the journey south. His early arrival—he'd been in the station for half an hour or so already—was due to a combination of factors. Partly it was because he was congenitally incapable of giving trains a chance to sneak off without him; he liked to have them under his eye well in advance just in case they got ideas.

Next, the Gare de Lyon was, of all the stations in the world, his favourite. It brought a touch of the Mediterranean into the gloomy, north-European air. The tracks stretched off into the distance, heading for those magical places he had adored long before he ever ventured out of his wind-swept little island to see them for himself. Lyon, Orange, Marseille, Nice; on to Genoa, through the hills of Tuscany to Florence and Pisa, then across the plains of the Campagna to Rome before heading ever further south to Naples. Warmth, sun, terracotta-coloured buildings, and an easy-going, relaxed gentleness completely alien to the lands bordering the North Sea.

The station itself reflected this in its exuberant architecture and pompous, ridiculous and entirely lovable bar, covered with gilt and plasterwork and swags and paintings, all combining to evoke the earthly paradise at the far end of the track. It was almost enough to make the most hardbitten of travellers forget he was in Paris, and that the rain was still coming down in cold, wet, autumnal torrents.

The bar was fairly empty, so he was mildly surprised when he suddenly acquired some company. With a polite

"May I . . . ?" a man in his late thirties sat down beside him. Very French, he was, with his green Alpine raincoat, casually expensive grey jacket. A very Gallic face as well, darkly handsome and marred only by a small scar above his left eyebrow that was partly hidden by the long dark hair that swept down from a high-domed forehead in the peculiar cut that France's educated middle classes seem to favour. Argyll nodded politely, the man nodded back and, the requirements of civilization satisfied, both settled back to hide behind their respective papers.

"Excuse me," said the man in French as Argyll was half-way through a depressing account of a cricket match in Australia. "Do you have a light?"

He fumbled through his pocket, fished out a bashed box, and looked in it. Then he took out his cigarettes and looked in that also. No cigarettes either. This was becoming serious.

They commiserated together for a while, and the Englishman considered the awful implications of a thousand-mile train journey without nicotine.

"If you'd guard my bag," said the man opposite, "I'll go and get some from the platform. I need a new packet myself."

"That's very kind of you," said Argyll.

"Do you know the time, by the way?" he said as he got up to go.

Argyll looked at his watch. "Quarter past ten."

"Damn," he said, sitting down again. "My wife is meant to be meeting me here at any moment. She always gets so upset if I'm not where I say I'll be. I'm afraid we'll have to go without."

Argyll thought about this. Obviously, if this man was prepared to trust him with his bags, then it should be safe to reverse the process. "I'll go instead," he offered.

"Would you? That's very good of you."

And with an encouraging smile, he promised to guard the bags faithfully until Argyll returned. It's one thing about the international confraternity of smokers. Members know how to behave properly. It's what comes of being an embattled and persecuted minority. You stick together.

Argyll was half-way out of the door when he realized he hadn't brought any money with him. All the small change he had was in the pocket of his overcoat, lying draped over the chair. So he cursed, turned round and mounted the cast-iron steps back to the bar.

As Flavia explained afterwards, not that he needed any explanation by then, it was the oldest trick in the book. Start up a conversation, win their confidence, distract their attention. Compared with someone as naturally trusting and gullible as Argyll, babies would probably put up a more spirited resistance defending their candy.

But fortune, this grey morning, decided to give him a break. He got to the entrance door just in time to see the man who was meant to be guarding his bags disappearing through the door on the far side of the room. Tucked under his arm was a brown paper package about three feet by two. Approximately the same size as paintings of the Death of Socrates tend to be.

"Oy," called Argyll in some distress.

Then he ran like fury in pursuit, appalling consequences flowing through his mind. He was sure the painting wasn't worth much; but he was equally sure he would have to refund more than his bank balance could withstand if he let it get away. It wasn't courage that made him fly across the bar, then run three steps at a time down the stairs. It was simple terror at the thought of this painting escaping him. Some dealers are insured against this sort of thing. But insurance companies, even the most amiable, do not look very sympathetically on claims for thefts committed on paintings left unguarded in bars in the company of total strangers.

Argyll was no sportsman. While not badly co-ordinated, he had never really thought it worth his while to spend much time trotting around cold, muddy fields in pursuit of inflated bladders. A decorous game of croquet he could manage, but greater athleticism was not at all to his taste.

For this reason the flying tackle he produced, running at full tilt and launching himself from a distance at the legs of the disappearing Frenchman was all the more miraculous for having no forebears. One onlooker in the crowded railway concourse even burst into spontaneous applause—the French, more than most, appreciate elegance on the rugger pitch—at the perfectly timed way in which he flew at low altitude through the air, connected with the man's knees, brought him down, did a half-roll, grabbed the parcel and stood up, clutching the prize to his chest.

The wretched man didn't know what had hit him; the violence of Argyll's assault, and the hard concrete floor, knocked the wind out of him and apparently did severe damage to the funny-bone of his right knee. Easy pickings, if Argyll had had the presence of mind to call for the police. But he wasn't thinking about that; rather he was too busy clutching the painting, relief at his success and distress at his own stupidity overwhelming him.

By the time he had recovered enough, the thief had rolled over, hobbled off and disappeared into the early-morning crowd thronging the concourse.

And, of course, when he got back to the bar he discovered that some light-fingered lad had taken advantage of his absence to lift his suitcase. But it was only dirty underwear, books and things. Nothing serious, in comparison. He almost felt grateful.

2

"ALL I can say is that you're damn lucky," Flavia di Stefano said much later on the same day when Argyll, slumped in an armchair and refilling his glass, finished telling the story.

"I know," he said, weary but content to be home at last. "But you would have been proud of me, none the less. I was magnificent. Never knew I had it in me."

"One day it'll be more serious."

"I know that too. But that day was not today, which is all that matters at the moment."

His friend sitting opposite, curled up on the sofa, looked at him with mild disapproval. It depended very much on her mood, whether she found his unworldliness comforting or profoundly irritating. This evening, because she'd been without him for five days, and because there were no serious consequences, she was in a forgiving frame of mind. It was very peculiar the way she'd missed him knocking around the place. They'd been living together for about nine months and this had been his first trip away without her. In that nine months she'd evidently got used to him. It was very strange. It was years since she'd minded being on her own, objected to having nothing to do for anybody but herself, and felt disrupted by having complete freedom to do whatever she wanted.

"Can I see the cause of this athletic zeal?" she asked, stretching herself and pointing at the parcel.

"Hmm? I don't see why not," he said, sliding off the chair and picking it up from the corner of the room. "Although I suspect it's not really your taste."

He busied himself for a few moments with knives and scissors, tore the parcel open then slid the painting out and propped it up on the desk by the window, knocking a bundle of letters, some washing, a dirty cup and a pile of old newspapers on to the ground in the process.

"Damn this place," he said. "It's like a junk-yard. Anyway," he continued, standing back thoughtfully to admire Socrates' last moments, "what do you think?"

Flavia examined it in silence awhile, offering a brief prayer of thanks that it would be in their little apartment for only a few days.

"Well, that knocks on the head the theory that it was a professional art thief," she said sarcastically. "I mean, who in their right mind would risk a jail term to steal that? It would have served him right if he'd got it."

"Oh, come on. It's not that bad. I mean, it's not Raphael, but it's fairly decent, as these things go."

The trouble with Argyll was that he did have this penchant for the obscure. Most people, Flavia had tried to explain, had simple, straightforward, tastes. Impressionists. Landscapes. Portraits of women on swings with a bit of ankle showing. Children. Dogs. That, she occasionally tried to persuade him, was how to make money, by selling things people liked.

But Argyll's judgement was more than a little out of sync with popular tastes. The more obscure the classical, biblical or allegorical reference, the more captivating he found it. He was capable of going into raptures over a rare treatment of a mythological subject, and then was constantly surprised that would-be clients looked at him as though he were crazy.

Admittedly he was getting better, learning to subordinate his obscure preferences and make some attempt to provide customers with what they actually wanted rather than what he thought would improve their attitude to life. But it was an effort that went against his nature, and given the least opportunity, his bias towards the elliptical would resurface.

She sighed. The walls of their apartment were already covered in so many swooning heroines and posturing heroes that there wasn't room to swing a cat. Argyll liked it like that; but she was beginning to find being surrounded by so many works of moral virtue a little oppressive. It was all very well his moving in to share her tiny apartment; that, somewhat to her surprise, she loved. It was just that she hadn't banked on his stock-in-trade coming as well.

"I know what you're thinking," he said. "But it's saved me a lot of trouble. And time as well. By the way," he went on as he took a step back and put his foot on an old sandwich cunningly hidden under the armchair, "have you thought about seeing whether that new flat is still available?"

"No."

"Oh, come on. We're going to have to move sooner or later, you know. Look at this place, after all. It's a positive health hazard."

Flavia grumbled. Perhaps it was a bit messy, and very overcrowded, and maybe it was a health hazard. But it was her health hazard, and she'd grown fond of it over the years. What to Argyll's objective gaze was a small, overpriced, under-lit, badly ventilated tip was home to her. Besides, the lease was in her name. Any new one would be held jointly. In Rome, considering the pressures of housing, that was more of a commitment than any formal marriage vows. Not that she didn't look on such an idea sympathetically, when she was in a good mood, it was just that she was awfully slow about taking decisions. And, of course, she hadn't been asked. No small point.

"You go and see it. And I'll think about it. Meantime, how long is it going to be before that thing is out of here?"

"If by 'that thing' you mean a most unusual treatment of the theme of the Death of Socrates in the French neo-classical style, then the answer is tomorrow. I'll deliver it to this Muller fellow and you won't have to look at it anymore. Let's talk about something else. What's been going on here in my absence?"

"Absolutely nothing. The criminal classes are getting really lax. It's been like living in a well-ordered, civilized and law-abiding country for the last week."

"How awful for you."

"I know. Bottando can always go around and fill in the time with silly meetings and lunches with colleagues. But the rest of us have been sitting and staring into space for days. I don't know what's going on at all. I mean, it can't be that the criminals are too afraid we'll catch them."

"You caught a couple a few months back. I remember it well. Everyone was awfully impressed."

"True. But that was only because they weren't very good at it."

"Considering how much you complain about being overworked, I think you should enjoy it while it lasts. Why don't you tidy up? The last time I was in it your office was even more chaotic than this place."

"What are you doing?" she asked, treating the suggestion with the contempt it deserved, as Argyll burrowed through a mound of papers and finally extracted the telephone.

"I thought I'd give this Muller fellow a ring. Set up an appointment. Nothing like seeming efficient."

"It's a bit late, isn't it? It's past ten."

"Do you want me to get rid of it or not?" he said, as he dialled.

*H*E presented himself at the door of Muller's apartment just after ten the following morning, as arranged. Muller had been delighted when he'd rung, enthused about his efficiency and consideration and could scarcely contain his anticipation. Had Argyll not protested that he was completely exhausted and could barely move a muscle, he would have been summoned round immediately.

He wasn't entirely certain what to expect. The apartment indicated a reasonable amount of money; Delorme had said that he was American, or Canadian, or something transatlantic. The marketing man for some international company. Muller ran the Italian operation. So he thought.

He did not appear to Argyll to be the epitome of the international salesman; the sort who eyes up whole portions of the world and coolly maps out master strategies for penetrating regions, grabbing market share or cutting out the opposition. For a start, he was at home at ten o'clock in the morning, and Argyll thought such people normally took off only seventeen minutes a day to do things like wash, change, eat and sleep.

Also, he was a little fellow, showing no obvious signs of hard-boiled commercialism. Across a vast middle there were all the indications of decades of eating the wrong sort of food. Arthur Muller was a model of how to die young, with the sort of weight-to-height ratio that makes dieticians wake up in the middle of the night screaming with terror. The type who should have keeled over thirty years before of clogged arteries, if his liver hadn't got him first.

But there he was, short, fat and with every sign of living to confound the medical statisticians a while longer. On the other hand, his face let the image down a little: although he looked quite pleased to see Argyll standing at his door, parcel in hand, it didn't exactly light up with glee. The habitual expression seemed almost mournful; the sort of face that didn't expect much and was never surprised when disaster struck. Most odd; it was almost as if there'd been a mismatch in the assembly process, and Muller's body had emerged with the wrong head on it.

But he was welcoming enough, at least.

"Mr. Argyll, I imagine. Do come in, do come in. I'm delighted you're here."

Not a bad apartment at all, Argyll noted as he walked in, although with definite signs of having been furnished by the company relocation officer. For all that the furniture was corporate good taste, Muller had, none the less, managed to impose a little of his own personality on the room. Not a great collector, alas, but somewhere along the way he had picked up a couple of nice bronzes and a few decent if unexceptional pictures. None of these indi-cated any great interest in neoclassical, mind you, still less in the baroque pictures cluttering up Flavia's apartment; but perhaps, Argyll thought to himself hopefully, his tastes were expanding.

He sat down on the sofa, brown paper parcel in front of him, and smiled encouragingly.

"I can't tell you how pleased I am you're here," Muller said. "I've been looking for this picture for some consid-erable time."

"Oh, yes?" Argyll said, intrigued.

Muller gave him a penetrating, half-amused look, then laughed.

"What's the matter?"

"What you mean to say," his client said, "was 'why on earth would anybody spend time looking for this very or-dinary painting? Does he know something I don't?' "

Argyll confessed that such thoughts had scuttled across his mind. Not that he didn't like the picture.

"I'm quite fond of this sort of thing," he confessed. "But not many other people are. So a friend of mine says. A minority taste, she keeps on telling me."

"She may be right. In my case, I haven't been looking for aesthetic reasons."

"No?"

"No. This was owned by my father. I want to find out something about myself. A filial task, you see."

"Oh, right," Argyll said, kneeling reverently on the floor and trying to unpick the knot keeping the whole package together. He'd been too conscientious about packing it up again last night. Another where-are-my-roots? man, he thought to himself as he fiddled. A topic to be avoided. Otherwise Muller might offer to show him his family tree.

"There were four, so I gather," Muller went on, watching Argyll's lack of dexterity with a distant interest. "All legal scenes, painted in the 1780s. This is supposed to be the last one painted. I read about them."

"You were very lucky to get hold of it," Argyll said. "Are you after the other three as well?"

Muller shook his head. "I think one will suffice. As I say, I'm not really interested in it for aesthetic reasons. Do you want some coffee, by the way?" he added as the knot finally came undone and Argyll slid the picture out of the packing.

"Oh, yes, thank you," Argyll said as he stood up and heard his knees crack. "No, no. You stay there and admire the picture. I can get it."

So, leaving Muller to contemplate his new acquisition, Argyll headed for the coffee-pot in the kitchen and helped himself. A bit forward, perhaps, but also rather tactful. He knew what these clients were like. It wasn't simply the eagerness to see what they'd spent their money on; it was also necessary to spend some time alone with the work. To get to know it, person-to-person, so to speak.

He came back to find that Muller and Socrates were not hitting it off as well as he'd hoped. As he was a mere courier he could afford to be a little detached, but he was

an amiable soul, and liked people to be happy even when
there was no financial gain in it for himself. In his heart,
he hadn't really expected tears of joy to burst forth at the
very sight. Even for the *aficionado*, the painting was not
instantly appealing. It was, after all, very dirty and unkempt; the varnish had long since dulled, and it had none
of that glossy air of well-cared-for contentment that shines
forth from decent pictures in museums.

"Let me see," said Muller non-committally, and he
completed his examination, pressing the canvas to see how
loose it was, checking the frame for woodworm, exam-
ining the back to see how well the stretcher was holding
up. Quite professional, really; Argyll hadn't expected such
diligence. Nor had he expected the growing look of disappointment that had spread slowly over the man's face.

"You don't like it," he said.

Muller looked up at him. "Like it? No. Frankly, I don't.
Not my sort of thing at all. I'd been expecting something
a bit more . . ."

"Colourful?" Argyll suggested. "Well-painted? Lively?
Assured? Dignified? Masterful? Adept?"

"Interesting," Muller said. "That's all. Nothing more.
At one stage this was in an important collection. I expected something more interesting."

"I am sorry," Argyll said sympathetically. He was, as
well. There is no disappointment quite so poignant as being let down by a work of art, when your hopes have built
up, and are suddenly dashed by being confronted with
grim, less-than-you-expected reality. He had felt like that

himself on many occasions. The first time he'd seen the *Mona Lisa*, when he was only sixteen or so, he'd fought through the vast throng in the Louvre with mounting excitement to get to the holy of holies. And, when he arrived, there was this tiny little squit of a picture, hanging on the wall. Somehow it should have been . . . more interesting than it was. Muller was right. There was no other word for it.

"You can always hang it in a corridor," he suggested. Muller shook his head.

"You make me a bit sorry I didn't allow it to get stolen," he went on cheerfully. "Then you could have claimed on insurance and got your money back."

"What do you mean?"

Argyll explained. "As I say, if I'd known you didn't want it, I'd have told him to take the thing away and welcome to it."

Somehow his attempts to cheer Muller up didn't work. The idea of such an easy solution having been missed made him even more introspective.

"I didn't realize such a thing might happen," he said. Then, jerking himself out of the mood, he went on: "I'm afraid I've put you to a great deal of trouble for nothing. So I feel awkward about asking you for something else. But would you be prepared to take it off my hands? Sell it for me? I'm afraid I couldn't stand having this in the house."

Argyll gave a variety of facial contortions to indicate the dire state of the market at the moment. It all depended on how much he'd bought it for. And how much he wanted to sell it for. Privately he was thinking dark thoughts to himself about people with too much money.

Muller said it had been ten thousand dollars, plus various commissions. But he'd be prepared to take less. As a penalty for buying things sight unseen. "Think of it as a stupidity tax," he said with a faint smile, an acknowledgement which made Argyll warm to him once more.

So a mild spot of negotiation ensued which ended with Argyll agreeing to put the picture in an auction for him, and seeing if he could get a better price elsewhere before the sale took place. He left with the brown paper package under his arm once more, and a decent cheque in his pocket for services rendered.

After that he spent the rest of the morning cashing the cheque, then went on to the auction house to hand over the painting for valuation and entry into the next month's sale.

3

IT was no good, Flavia thought to herself as she surveyed the debris all around her. Something will have to be done about this and soon. She had arrived late at her office in Rome's Art Theft Department and, after an hour, had achieved nothing.

It was September, for heaven's sake. Not August, when she expected everyone in Rome to be on holiday. Nor was one of the local football teams playing at home. She herself was rarely to be seen when Roma or Lazio were playing. What was the point? All Italian government came to an abrupt halt when an important match was on. Even the thieves stopped work for a really big one.

But today there were no excuses, and it was still impossible to get hold of anyone. She'd phoned the Interior

Ministry with an important message only to be told that every secretary, under-secretary, deputy under-secretary, everyone, in fact, from minister to floor-sweeper, was busy. And what was the excuse? Some foreign delegation in town for a beano at the public expense. Top-level meetings. International accords. Mutterings of civil servants and lawyers in dark corners on legal and financial regulations and how to get round stipulations from Brussels. How to obey the letter, and disregard the meaning. All over the continent, similar meetings were taking place. That's what unity is all about. Fiddlesticks. No wonder the country was going to the dogs.

And she'd arrived feeling enthusiastic for once, despite the lack of anything really interesting to do. Argyll had recovered from his excursion to Paris, more or less, and at last had something to occupy himself. His client had said yesterday he didn't want the picture and, as he was getting 10 per cent of the sale price on commission, he'd decided to waste today seeing what he could find out about it. Some notion about trying to up its value a little. He'd come back fired with enthusiasm from at last having a task to undertake and had scuttled off first thing to the library.

She sympathized with his efforts to find himself something to do; she was in much the same position herself. Not only was the art market in a bit of a slump; the drop in prices had triggered a knock-on effect in the world of crime as well. Or maybe all reputable art thieves had bought package tours for Czechoslovakia, the one place in Europe now where it was even easier to steal art than Italy. Only the second-rankers were still in the country, it seemed. There were the usual break-ins, and all that; but it was petty-crime stuff for the most part. Nothing to get your teeth into.

And what did that leave? Filing, as Argyll had so maliciously suggested. In her own little room she could see several dozen miscellaneous files lying around on the floor. Her boss, General Bottando, had several dozen more in various states of disarray. And across the corridor, in the rabbit-warren of little rooms occupied by the other members of staff, probably about half the contents of what was laughingly known as their archives were being used to rest coffee-cups on, prop up desks and as improvised floor-coverings.

Organization and tidiness were not her strong points, normally, and she was quite prepared to admit that she was as bad as anyone else in the building—except for Bottando, but he was in charge so could do as he liked—at putting things away. But every now and then some faint echo of house-proud zeal would rumble in her deepest subconscious and she would develop, enthusiastically if only temporarily, a passion for method and order. Perhaps Jonathan was right, she said to herself reluctantly. Maybe I should do something about this place.

So she picked all the files off the floor and stacked them on her desk, and found underneath one of them a small pile of forms requiring Bottando's immediate signature three weeks ago. No time like the present, she thought;

so, both to get this little matter seen to and to inform her boss that all pursuit of the criminal element of society would cease until the files were put into order, she marched briskly and with an air of purposeful efficiency up the stairs to Bottando's room.

"Ah, Flavia," said Bottando as she marched in, omitting to knock as usual. That was all right; she never did manage to remember, and Bottando was used to it. Some people stand on their dignity. Many a senior Polizia man would produce a freezing look and remind himself—and his subordinates—that this was a general here. Who should have his door knocked on politely. But not Bottando. It wasn't in his nature. Nor was it in Flavia's, more to the point.

"Morning, General," she said cheerfully. "Sign here, please."

He did as he was told.

"Don't you want to know what it is you've signed? It could have been anything. You should be more careful."

"I trust you, my dear," he said, looking at her a little anxiously.

"What is it?" she asked. "You've got that look on your face."

"A little job," he said.

"Oh, good."

"Yes. A murder. Peculiar thing, apparently. But we may have to stake out a minor interest in it. The Carabinieri phoned up twenty minutes ago, asking if we could send someone down."

"I'll go," she said. She didn't like murder at all, but beggars can't be choosers these days. Anything to get out of the office.

"You'll have to. There's no one else around. But I don't think you'll like it."

She eyed him carefully. Here it comes, she thought. "Why not?"

"Giulio Fabriano's been promoted to homicide," Bottando said simply, an apologetic look on his face.

"Oh, no," she wailed. "Not him again. Can't you send someone else?"

Bottando sympathized. She and Fabriano had been very close at one stage. A bit too close for Flavia's liking, and their friendship had degenerated into squabbles, fights and general dislike several years back. Shortly before Argyll had appeared on the scene, in fact. In ordinary circumstances, she wouldn't have had much to do with him, but he was in the rival Carabinieri—doing surprisingly well, considering his relatively limited intelligence, but then there wasn't a great deal of competition in the Carabinieri—and had developed the habit over the past few years of ringing her up every time he was on a case which had even the most tenuous connection with art. For example, a man has his car stolen. He once bought a picture, so Fabriano would ring to see if there was a file on him. Anything would do. He was tenacious, our Fabriano. The trouble was he also had a quite extraordinarily high opinion of himself and, as Flavia continued to keep her distance, and indeed had taken up with a ridiculous

Englishman, his tone had turned decidedly hostile. Cutting remarks. Sneering comments to colleagues. Not that Flavia particularly cared or couldn't deal with it. She just preferred not to, if possible.

"I'm sorry, my dear," Bottando went on, with genuine regret, "But there really is no one else here. I'm sure I don't know what they're all doing, but still . . ."

In a toss-up between Fabriano and filing, Flavia was unsure which was the worse option. On the whole, she reckoned Fabriano was. The man just couldn't stop himself from trying to demonstrate what a prize she'd let slip through her fingers when they'd broken up. But it seemed Bottando wasn't going to give her any choice.

"You really want me to go?"

"I do. But I don't imagine it will detain you over-long. Try and get back here as quickly as possible."

"Don't worry," she said gloomily.

*I*T took about forty minutes before it dawned on her that Fabriano's murder victim was the very same man that Argyll had been talking about the previous evening. To give her credit, thirty minutes of that delay was spent in a traffic jam trying to make her way out of the centre. Most of the remaining ten minutes was spent looking around aghast at the apartment. There was scarcely a book left on the shelves; all had been pulled off, many ripped apart then dumped in the centre of the little sitting-room. All the papers in the filing cabinets had similarly been removed and thrown on the floor; the furniture had been ripped, and the cushions cut up. Every picture had been pulled off the wall and slashed to pieces.

"Hold everything," said Fabriano with fake amusement as she walked in. "Signora Sherlock's here. Tell me quickly. Who did it?"

She gave him a frosty look and ignored the remark. "Jesus," she said, looking around at the chaos. "Someone did a good job here."

"Don't you know who?" he said.

"Shut up, Giulio. Let's keep this professional, shall we?"

"I stand corrected," he said, standing in the corner of the room and leaning against the wall. "Professionally speaking, I don't know. Must have taken several hours, wouldn't you say? To make a mess like this, I mean. We can rule out simple vandalism, don't you think?"

"Curious," she said, looking around.

"What? Do we have a blinding insight coming our way?"

"All the furniture and stuff was just shredded. Very violently, and carelessly. The pictures were sliced precisely. Taken out of their frames, the frames broken and in a pile, and the canvas cut up. It looks as though with scissors."

Fabriano delivered himself of an ambiguous gesture which was half sneer and half self-congratulation.

"And you think that maybe we didn't notice? Why do you reckon I called?"

Nice to know some people don't change. "What happened to the occupant?" Keep calm, she thought. Don't reply in kind.

"Go and look. He's in the bedroom," he said with a faint and worrying smile.

She knew from the moment he spoke that it wasn't going to be very nice. But it was much worse.

"Oh, my God," she said.

The assorted specialists who gather round on these occasions hadn't finished yet, but even after they'd tidied up a little the scene was horrific. It was like something out of Hieronymus Bosch's more appalling nightmares. The bedroom itself was domestic, cosy even. Chintz bedcovers, silk curtains, floral-patterned wallpaper all combining to give an air of comfort and tranquillity. It made the contrast all the greater.

The man had been tied to the bed, and had been treated appallingly before he died. His body was covered in cuts and bruises and weals. His left hand was a bloody mess. His face was almost indistinguishable as anything that had anything to do with a human being. The pain he had suffered must have been excruciating. Whoever had done this had taken a good deal of time, a lot of trouble and, in Flavia's instant opinion, needed to be locked up fast.

"Ah," said one of the forensics from the corner of the room, reaching down with a pair of tweezers and putting something in a plastic bag.

"What?" said Fabriano, leaning as nonchalantly as he could manage against the door. Flavia could see that even he was having a hard time maintaining the pose.

"His ear," the man replied, holding up the bag containing the bloody, torn object.

At least Fabriano turned and bolted first, although Flavia was hard on his heels in her attempt to get out of the room as fast as possible. She went straight into the kitchen and poured a glass of water.

"Did you have to do that?" she asked angrily as Fabriano came in after her. "Did sending me in there make you feel any better or something?"

He shrugged. "What did you expect? 'This is no sight for a little woman,' or something?"

She ignored him for a few seconds, trying to maintain calm in her stomach. "So?" she said, looking up at him again, annoyed that she had seemed so fragile with him around. "What happened?"

"Looks as though he had a visitor, doesn't it? Who tied him up, ransacked the house, then did that to him. According to the doctor, he was shot to death eventually."

"Reason?"

"Search me. That's why we asked you people along. As you can see, whoever it was seemed to have a grudge against pictures."

"Organized-crime connection?"

"Not as far as we can tell. He was the marketing director for a computer company. Canadian. Clean as a whistle."

It was then that Flavia got this nasty feeling. "What's his name?"

"Arthur Muller," he said.

"Oh," she said. Damnation, she thought. A complication she didn't need. She could see it now: if she said Argyll had been there yesterday, Fabriano would go straight round and arrest him. Probably lock him up for a week, out of pure malice.

"Have you heard of him?" Fabriano asked.

"Maybe," she said cautiously. "I'll ask around, if you like. Jonathan might know."

"Who's Jonathan?"

"An art dealer. My, um, fiancé."

Fabriano looked upset, which made the small untruth worth while. "Congratulations," he said. "Have a chat with the lucky man, will you? Maybe you should get him along here?"

"Not necessary," she said shortly. "I'll ring. Was anything stolen, by the way?"

"Ah. This is the problem. As you see, it's a bit of a mess. Working out what's gone may take some time. The housekeeper says she can't see anything that's gone. None of the obvious things, anyway."

"So? Conclusions?"

"None so far. In the Carabinieri we work by order and evidence. Not guesswork."

After which friendly exchange, she went back into the living-room to phone Argyll. No answer. It was his turn to do the shopping for dinner. It didn't matter; he'd be back in an hour or so. She rang a neighbour and left a message instead.

"Yes?" Fabriano said brusquely as another detective

came in, a man in his mid-twenties who had already acquired the look of weary and sarcastic disdain which came
from having worked for Fabriano for two hours. "What
is it?"

"Next-door neighbour, Guilio—"

"Detective Fabriano."

"Next-door neighbour, Detective Fabriano," he restarted rolling his eyes in despair at the thought that this
might turn out to be a long case, "she seems to be your
friendly neighbourhood spy satellite."

"Was she in during the hours of the crime?"

"Well, I wouldn't come and tell you if she wasn't,
would I? 'Course she was. That's why—"

"Good, good," said Fabriano briskly. "Well done.
Good work," he went on, thus removing from the police-
man any pleasure he might have felt at his small discovery.
"Wheel her in, then."

There must be hundreds of thousands of women like
Signora Andreotti in Italy; quite sweet old ladies, really,
who were brought up in small towns or even in villages.
Capable of labours on the Herculean scale—cooking for
thousands, bringing up children by the dozen, dealing
with husbands and fathers and, very often, having a job
as well. Then their children grow up, their husbands die
and they move in with one child, to do the cooking. A
fair bargain, on the whole, and much better than being
confined to an old folks' home.

But in many cases, the children have gone a long way
from home; many have made it big in the city, made

money on a scale their parents could scarcely even imagine in their day; *la dolce vita,* eighties style.

The Andreotti household was one such; two parents, one child, two jobs and no one in the house from eight in the morning to eight at night. The elder Signora Andreotti, who once spent her spare time gossiping to neighbours back home, was bored silly. So much so that she felt her mind going with the tedium. And so she noticed everything. Every delivery van in the street, every child playing in the backyard. She heard every football in the corridor, knew the lives of each and every person in the apartment block. She wasn't nosy, really, she had nothing better to do. It was the closest to human comradeship she came, some days.

So, the previous day, as she explained to Fabriano, she had seen a youngish man arriving with a brown paper packet, and seen him leaving again, still with the packet, some forty minutes later. A door-to-door salesman, she reckoned.

"This was what time?" Fabriano asked.

"About ten. In the morning. Signor Muller went out about eleven, and didn't come back until six. Then in the afternoon another man came, and rang the bell. I knew Signor Muller was at work, so I popped my head around the door to say he was out. Very surly look he had."

"And this was when?"

"About half-past two. Then he went away. He may have come back again, if he was quiet. I didn't hear anything, but I sometimes watch a nice game show on the television."

She explained that in the evening—the crucial time, as far as Fabriano was concerned—she was too busy preparing dinner for the family to see anything. And she went to bed at ten.

"Can you describe these men?"

She nodded sagely. "Of course," she said, and went on to give a perfect description of Argyll.

"This was the one in the morning, right?"

"Yes."

"And the afternoon visitor?"

"About one metre eighty. Age about thirty-five. Dark brown hair, cut short. Gold signet ring on the middle finger of his left hand. Round metal-rimmed spectacles. Blue and white striped shirt, with cuff-links. Black slip-on shoes—"

"Inside-leg measurement?" said Fabriano in amazement. The woman was the sort of witness the police dream about, but rarely find.

"I don't know. I could make a guess if you like."

"That's quite all right. Anything else?"

"Let me see. Grey cotton trousers, with turn-ups, grey woollen jacket with a red stripe running through it. And a small scar above his left eyebrow."

4

" _I_ N that case I suggest you get him to trot down to the Carabinieri and make a statement. Do it now, in fact," Bottando said, drumming his fingers on the desk. A definite irritant. More than many, his department had to work closely with the trade; today's witness was frequently tomorrow's defendant. It was a fine business, not to get too close to people who were, at least, liable to come under suspicion. And in the world of Italian crime and politics, accusations of corruption were easily made. The connection of Argyll and Flavia, when allied to a murder and the wrath of Fabriano, had considerable potential for trouble. What was more, Flavia knew that very well. It was perfectly understandable that she should want to keep her private life away from Fabriano's baleful gaze, but she should have known better.

"I know. I should have come clean. But you know what he's like. Jonathan would be locked up and emerge with bruises, just to teach me a lesson. Anyway, I've tried to get hold of him. He's out. But I'll see him and take a statement myself, not that there can be any connection of importance. I'll send it to Fabriano tomorrow."

Bottando grunted. Not perfect, but it would do. "Apart from that, is there anything for you to do on this case? Anything that concerns us?"

"Not obviously so, no. At least, not yet. Fabriano's going to do all the legwork. Talk to the people at Muller's office, find out his movements, and so on. Apparently he has a sister in Montreal who may come over. If anything turns up which might concern us, I have no doubt he'll let us know."

"Still as obnoxious, is he?"

"Even worse. Getting into homicide seems to have turned his head."

"I see. Good. In that case, until you talk to Mr. Argyll, you may as well amuse yourself with daily routine. Now, how do you fancy doing something with that computer?"

Flavia's face fell. "Oh, no," she said. "Not the computer."

He'd expected that. This awful machine was supposed, by the designers, to be the last word in detection techniques. The idea behind it was simple: it was to be the

Delphic oracle of art police around the world. Each force in each country could enter details of paintings and things into it, and even photographs of missing pieces. Other forces could then access this information, look through it, recognize objects that were on sale at dealers, go round, arrest, prosecute and return the stolen goods to their real owners. The committee behind it had fondly expected that art theft would dwindle away to almost nothing overnight when the forces of law and order were provided with such an awesomely sophisticated weapon.

But.

The trouble with the thing was that it was a bit too Delphic. Call up a picture of a lake by Monet, and you were likely to get a photograph of a Renaissance silver chalice. Other times it would produce rows of gibberish or, worst of all, the dreaded phrase in eight languages, "Service temporarily suspended. Please try again."

According to a technician who had been called in to look at it, it was a marvellous product of European co-operation. A perfect symbol of the continent, he said in abstract philosophic vein as the machine had, yet again, insisted that a Futurist sculpture was a long-lost masterpiece by Masaccio. Specification by the Germans; hardware by the Italians; software by the British; telecommunication links by the French. Put it all together and naturally it didn't work. Did anyone really expect it to? He left eventually, recommending the postal system. More reliable, he said gloomily.

"Please, Flavia. We have to use it."

"But it's useless."

"I know it's useless. That's not the point. This is an international venture which cost a fortune. If we don't use it periodically we'll be asked why not. Good heavens, woman, last time I went into the room the monitor was being used as a plant-stand. How would that look if any-one from the budget committee came around?"

"No."

Bottando sighed. Somehow or other he seemed to have trouble projecting his authority, despite holding the rank of general. Think of Napoleon, for example. If he issued an order, did his subordinates snort derisively and refuse to pay a blind bit of attention? If Caesar ordered an im-mediate flanking movement, did his lieutenants look up from their newspapers and say they were a bit tired at the moment, how about next Wednesday? They did not. Of course, the fact that Flavia was perfectly correct weakened his case a little. But that was not the point. It was time to exert control. Discipline.

"Please?" he said appealingly.

"Oh, all right," she said eventually. "I'll switch it on. Tell you what, I'll leave it on all night. How about that?"

"Splendid, my dear. I'm so grateful."

5

WHILE the authorities in the Art Theft Department were dealing with crucial matters of international co-operation, Jonathan Argyll spent the morning coping with more basic matters of stock management. That is, he was doing a little work on his picture. He had been struck by a good idea. That is, Muller had said the picture was one of a series. Who more likely to want to buy it than the person, or museum, or institution, who owned the others? Assuming, that is, they were all together. All he had to do was find out where the rest were, and offer to complete the set. It might not work, of course, but it was worth an hour or so of his time.

Besides, this was the bit of his trade that he liked. Dealing with recalcitrant clients, and bargaining and extracting money and working out whether things could be sold at a profit were the bread and butter of his life, but he didn't really enjoy them much. Too much reality for him to cope with comfortably. A meditative hour in a library was far more to his taste.

The question was where to start. Muller said he'd read about it, but where? He was half minded to ring the man up, but reckoned he'd have gone to work, and he didn't know where that was. Anyway, a skilled researcher like himself could probably find out fairly quickly anyway.

All he knew about the picture was that it was by a man called Floret; and he knew that because it was signed, indistinctly but legibly, in the bottom left-hand corner. He could guess it was done in the 1780s, and it was obviously French.

So he proceeded methodically and with order, a bit like Fabriano only more quietly. Starting at the beginning with the great bible of all art historians, *Thieme und Becker*. All twenty-five volumes in German, unfortunately, but he could make out enough to be directed to the next stage.

Floret, Jean. Künstler, gest. 1792. That was the stuff. A list of paintings, all in museums. Six lines in all, pretty much the basic minimum. Not a painter to be taken seriously. But the reference did direct him to an article published in the *Gazette des Beaux-Arts* in 1937 which was his next port of call. This was by a man called Jules Hartung, little more than a biographical sketch, really, but it fleshed out the details. Born 1765, worked in France, guillotined for not being quite revolutionary enough in 1792.

Served him right, as well, according to the text. Floret had
worked for a patron, the Comte de Mirepoix, producing
a series of subjects on legal themes. Then, come the Revolution, he had denounced his benefactor and supervised
the confiscation of the man's goods and the ruin of his
family. A common enough sort of story, perhaps.

But 1937 was a long time ago, and in any case the
article didn't say where any of his pictures were, apart
from hinting strongly that, fairly obviously, they no longer
belonged to the Mirepoix family. For their current
whereabouts he had to work a lot harder. For the rest of
the morning and well into his normal lunch-hour, he
trawled through histories of French art, histories of neoclassicism, guides to museums and check-lists of locations
in the hunt for the slightest hint that would point him in
the right direction.

He was beginning to get on the nerves of the librarians
who brought him the books when at last he struck lucky.
The vital information was in an exhibition catalogue of
only the previous year. It had just arrived in the library,
so he counted himself fortunate. A jolly little show, put
on in one of those outlying suburbs of Paris trying to es-
tablish a cultural identity for themselves. *Myths and
Mistresses*, it was called, an excuse for a jumble of miscellaneous pictures linked by date and not much more.
A bit of classical, a bit of religion, lots of portraits and
semi-naked eighteenth-century bimbos pretending to be
wood-nymphs. All with a somewhat overwrought introduction about fantasy and play in the idealized dream-

world of French court society. Could have done better himself.

However flabby the conception, however, the organizer was greatly beloved of Argyll, if only for catalogue entry no. 127. "Floret, Jean," it began rather hopefully. "*The Death of Socrates,* painted *circa* 1787. Part of a series of four paintings of matching religious and classical scenes on the theme of judgement. The judgements of Socrates and of Jesus represented two cases where the judicial system had not given of its best; and the judgements of Alexander and of Solomon where those in authority had acquitted themselves a little more honorably. Private collection." Then a lot of blurb explaining the story behind the painting illustrated. Alas, it was not encouraging to Argyll's hopes of finding a buyer wanting to reunite the paintings. The two versions of justice performed were out of reach, with *The Judgement of Solomon* in New York and *The Judgement of Alexander* in a museum in Germany. What was worse, *The Judgement of Jesus* had vanished years ago and was presumed lost. Old Socrates was liable to stay on his own, dammit.

And this catalogue didn't even say who it used to belong to. No name, no address. Just "private collection." Not that it really mattered. He felt a little discouraged, and it was time for lunch anyway. What was more, he had to get to the shops before they shut for the afternoon. It was his turn. Flavia was particular about that sort of thing.

It stood to reason, he thought as he lumbered up the

stairs an hour later, bearing plastic bags full of water, wine, pasta, meat and fruit, that this previous owner lived in France. Perhaps he should at least check? He could then construct a provenance to go with the work, and that always increases the value a little. Besides, Muller had said the work had once been in a distinguished collection. Nothing like a famous name as a previous owner to appeal to the snobbism that lurks inside so many collectors. "Well, it used to be in the collection of the Duc d'Orléans, you know." Works wonders, that sort of thing. And how better to go about tracking him down than to contact Delorme? Courtesy demanded that he should fill the man in about Muller's decision, and pleasure indicated the need to tell him that, because of Argyll's diligent labours in the library, he could well make more money on reselling the picture than Delorme did on flogging it in the first place.

Unfortunately, his telephone call to Paris went unanswered. Perhaps, one day, when the European Community has finished deciding on the right length for leeks, and standardizing the shape of eggs and banning everything that is half-way pleasant to eat, it might turn its attention to telephone calls. Every country, it seems, has a different system, so that all of them together make up a veritable songbook of different chirrups. A long beep in France means it is ringing; in Greece it means it's engaged and in England it means there is no such number. Two chirrups in England means it's ringing; in Germany it means engaged and in France, as Argyll discovered after a long and painful conversation with the telephone operator, it means that moron Delorme had forgotten to pay his phone bill again and the company had taken punitive action.

"What do you mean?" he said. "How can it have been disconnected?"

Where do they get them from? There is something about telephone operators—one of the universal constants of human existence. From Algeria to Zimbabwe, they are capable of imbuing an ostensibly polite sentence with the deepest of contempt. It is impossible to talk to one without finally feeling chastened, humiliated and frustrated.

"You disconnect the line," she said, in answer to his question. Everybody knows that, she left unsaid. It's your fault for having doubtful friends who don't pay their bills—that passed by equally silently. She even refrained from saying that the chances were that Argyll's line would probably be disconnected any day now as well, a shifty character like him.

Could she find out when it was disconnected? Sorry. What about if there was another line for the same name? No. Change of address? 'Fraid not.

Half enraged, half perplexed, Argyll hung up. Good God, he might have to write a letter. Years since he'd done anything like that. Rather lost the habit, in fact. Quite apart from the fact that his written French was a bit dodgy.

And so he flicked through his phone book to see who else he knew in Paris who might be persuaded to do him a favour. No one. Damn it, he thought as the phone rang again.

"Hello," he said absently.

"Am I speaking to a Mr. Jonathan Argyll?" came a voice in execrable Italian.

"That's right."

"And do you have in your possession a painting entitled *The Death of Socrates?*" the voice continued in equally bad English.

"Yes," said Argyll, a little surprised. "Well, sort of."

"What do you mean?"

It was a quiet voice, measured, almost gentle in tone, but Argyll didn't like it. Something unreasonable in the way the questions were being put, without so much as a by-your-leave. Besides, it reminded him of someone.

"I mean," he said firmly, "that the picture is currently at an auction house to be valued. Who are you?"

His attempt to regain control of the conversation went unheeded. The man at the other end—what was that accent anyway?—disregarded his question entirely.

"Are you aware that it was stolen?"

Whoops, he thought.

"I must ask who you are."

"I am a member of the French police. The Art Theft Department, to be precise. I've been sent to Rome to recover this work. And I mean to do so."

"But I . . ."

"You knew nothing about it. Is that what you were going to say?"

"Well . . ."

"That may be so. I am under instructions not to lodge any complaint against you for your role in this affair."

"Oh, good."

"But I must have that picture immediately."

"You can't."

There was a pause from the other end. The caller evidently hadn't expected opposition. "And why not, pray?"

"I told you. It's at the auction house. They're closed until tomorrow morning. I won't be able to get it until then."

"Give me the name."

"I don't see why I should," Argyll said with a sudden burst of stubbornness. "I don't know who you are. How do I know you're a policeman?"

"I would be more than happy to reassure you. If you like, I'll come and visit you this evening. Then you can satisfy yourself."

"When?"

"Five o'clock?"

"OK. Fine. I'll see you then."

After the phone line had gone dead, Argyll stood around the apartment, thinking. Damnation. It was amazing how things can go wrong on you. It wasn't much money, but at least it would have been something. Just as well he'd cashed Muller's cheque.

But the more he thought about it, the more it seemed a little odd. Why hadn't Flavia told him? She must have known there was a French picture-man wandering around

Rome. There was no need to spring a nasty surprise on him like that. Besides, if it was stolen, then he had smuggled stolen goods out of France and into Italy. A bit awkward. If he handed the picture straight back, was that an admission of something or other? Should he not consult with people who knew what they were talking about?

He glanced at his watch. Flavia should be back from lunch and hard at work in the office. He rarely disturbed her there, but this, he reckoned, was a reasonable occasion to break the rule.

"OH, I am glad you're here," she said as he marched in twenty minutes later. "You got the message."

"What message?"

"The one I left with the neighbour."

"No. What was in it?"

"Telling you to come here."

"I didn't get any message. Not from you anyway. Something awful's happened."

"You're right," she said. "Awful's the word. That poor man."

He paused and looked at her. "We're not talking about the same thing, are we?"

"It doesn't sound like it. What are you here for?"

"That picture. It was stolen. I've just had a French policeman on the phone saying he wants it back. I want to ask you what I should do."

The news was surprising enough to make her take her feet off her desk and concentrate a little harder.

"When was this?" she asked. Then, after he'd explained some more, she added: "Who was this?"

"He didn't tell me his name. He just said he would come round this evening to talk to me about it."

"How did he know you had it?"

Argyll shook his head. "Don't know. I suppose Muller must have told him. No one else knew."

"That's the problem though, isn't it? Because Muller is dead. He was murdered."

Argyll's world was already a little disordered because of this picture. This piece of information turned it into complete chaos. "What?" he said, appalled. "When?"

"Closest estimate so far is last night. Come on. We'd better talk to the General. Oh, God. And I assured him your being with Muller was simple coincidence."

They interrupted Bottando in the middle of his afternoon tea. He was greatly mocked by his colleagues for this habit, so un-Italian in style, and indeed he had adopted it many years back after spending a week with colleagues in London. He had taken to the custom. Not because of the tea itself, which Italians have never succeeded in brewing very well, but because it created an oasis of calm and reflection in the middle of the afternoon when the troubles of the world could be temporarily forgotten. He punctuated his days in this fashion. Coffee, lunch, tea and a quick drink in the bar across the piazza after work. All brief intervals when he put down his papers, sipped meditatively and stared into space, thinking of nothing.

He guarded these moments jealously. His secretary knew how to intone at such periods, "The General is in a meeting; can he ring you back?" and it was a brave subordinate who dared burst in on him in mid-cup.

Flavia was one such, but even she needed a good reason. She took the good reason in with her, and told him to sit down on the chair opposite, while she calmed Bottando's ruffled feathers.

"I'm sorry," she said. "I know. But I thought you should hear this."

Grumbling mightily, arms crossed in pique, Bottando bid farewell to his tea and meditation and leant back in his seat. "Oh, very well," he said crossly. "Get on with it."

And Argyll told his story, slowly seeing that, however reluctantly, Bottando's attention was being engaged by his tale. Eventually he came to a halt, and the General scratched his chin and reflected.

"Two things," Flavia added before he could say anything. "Firstly, when you told me to play around with the computer earlier, I typed in this picture. Just for something to do. There's no record of it being reported stolen."

"That doesn't mean anything," Bottando said. "You know as well as I do how unreliable the computer is."

"Secondly, are there any French policemen wandering about the place?"

"No," he said. "At least, not officially. And I'd be extremely upset if there were any here unofficially. It's not done. Courtesy. And, to give him his due, it's not Janet's style."

Jean Janet *was* Bottando's *alter ego* in Paris, the head of the French Art Squad. A good man, and one with whom the Italians had enjoyed cordial relations for years. As Bottando said, it was not the man's way of doing things. Besides, there was nothing to be gained by it.

"I suppose I'd better check, though. But we should assume this man on the phone is an impostor. Now, tell me, Mr. Argyll, did anybody apart from Muller know you had this painting?"

"No," he said firmly. "I tried to tell Delorme . . ."

"Who?"

"Delorme. The man who supplied it in the first place."

"Ah." Bottando jotted down a little note. "Is he dubious in any way?" he asked hopefully.

"Certainly not," Argyll replied stoutly. "I mean, I don't care for him much, but I hope I know my way about sufficiently to be able to tell who's dishonest and who's merely sharp."

Bottando wasn't so sure. He made a note to check out Delorme as well when he phoned Janet up.

"Now," the General went on, "Flavia tells me that someone tried to steal this painting when you left Paris. Is that merely another one of her coincidences, do you think?"

He said it pleasantly enough, but it didn't require a

great deal of perception to detect the slightly acidic tone underneath. General Bottando was not pleased. And, Flavia thought, with good reason. Fabriano could make a real meal out of this, if he wanted. And he probably would, as well.

"How should I know?" Argyll said. "I assumed he was just a thief spotting an opportunity."

"Did you report this to the French police?"

"No. There seemed little point and the train was about to leave."

"When you make your statement you'd better include these little details. Will you be able to give a description of this man?"

"I think so, yes. I mean, he was pretty much standard issue. Average height, average weight, brown hair. Two arms and legs. The only sort of distinguishing feature was a small scar here."

Argyll gestured to a spot above his left eyebrow, and Flavia's heart sank again.

"Oh, hell," she said again.

"What?"

"That sounds like the man seen trying to visit Muller yesterday."

Bottando sighed. That's what comes of trying to protect boyfriends. "So it seems we must at least entertain the possibility that you are going to receive a visit from a murderer. What time is he coming?"

"Five, he said."

"In which case we should be there to meet him. And

take no chances, either. If he's a killer, he's a nasty one. This picture is still at the auction house, you say?"

Argyll nodded.

"It can't stay there. Flavia, get Paolo to go down and get it. Put it in the strong-room downstairs until we decide what to do with it. Then get hold of Fabriano. A couple of armed men in the street, and another in the apartment should be enough. Discreet, eh? Make sure he understands that. When we've got hold of him, we can decide what to do next. Assuming he turns up, of course. Perhaps if we deliver a murderer we might skate over everything else."

6

*S*UCH a simple scenario turned out to be too much to hope for. They waited an hour in the small apartment and received no visitors at all. Not even Fabriano, although to Flavia's mind that was no bad thing. They had to make do with one of their own regular policemen who reluctantly admitted to knowing what end of a gun to point at a suspect; Fabriano was out on a case, so the Carabinieri said.

"When is he coming back, then?" she asked the man who answered. "This is important."

He didn't know. "Can you patch me through to his radio?" she asked impatiently.

"Patch you through?" came the mocking response.

"What do you think we are? The US Army? We're lucky if we can get the things to work at all."

"Well, get a message to him, then. It's urgent. He's to come to my apartment as quickly as possible."

"You two getting back together again?"

"Do you mind?"

"Sorry. OK. I'll see what I can do," said the voice from the other end. Somehow, he didn't inspire confidence.

If this demonstration of planning skill was less than impressive, at least Bottando had managed to get through to Janet, who informed him that he had absolutely none of his people in Italy.

"Taddeo," came the booming voice down the phone, "How could you think such a thing? Would I do something like that?"

"Just checking," Bottando reassured him. "We must do things properly. Now, tell me about this painting. Is it stolen?"

Janet said that he didn't know. He'd have to look it up. He'd ring back with the information as soon as possible.

"And now we wait," said Bottando. He looked around the apartment. "Charming place you have here, Flavia."

"You mean it's untidy and minuscule and bleak," Argyll said. "I quite agree. Personally I think that we should move."

If he had hoped for support from Bottando, though, Argyll was disappointed. Not that the General didn't agree, but the ringing of the doorbell prevented him from saying so. An expectant hush fell. Argyll turned pale, the uniformed policeman took out his gun and looked at it unhappily, Bottando went and hid in the bedroom. Unfair, in Argyll's view. He'd been planning to hide in there himself.

"OK, then," Flavia whispered. "Open the door."

And gingerly, expecting to be attacked at any moment, Argyll edged towards it, unlocked it, and retreated back out of the line of fire. The policeman waved his gun around, looking nervous. It occurred to Flavia that she hadn't actually asked if he'd ever fired one before.

There was a pause from outside, then the door swung slowly open, and a man stepped in.

"Oh, it's you," Flavia said with relief and disappointment.

Fabriano, still framed by the doorway, looked at her with irritation. "Don't sound so pleased. Who were you expecting?"

"*You* didn't get my message, either?"

"What message?"

"One of those days," she said as she explained.

"Oh. I see." He waggled his little radio. "Batteries flat," he explained. "What was it about?"

Flavia provided a brief summary. Edited version only. Some aspects of the story were covered a little fast. By the end, she'd given the impression that her relationship with Argyll was based on mutual lack of communication.

"This man's a bit late, isn't he?" Fabriano said.

"Yes."

"Perhaps because he was busy doing other things." Fabriano had that "I know something that you don't" look on his face.

She sighed. "Well? Like what?"

"Like committing another murder, perhaps." Fabriano went on. "Of a harmless Swiss tourist. Who just happened to have Muller's and your addresses written on a piece of paper in his pocket."

He explained that he'd been called out at four to the Hotel Raphael, a quiet, pleasant hotel near the Piazza Navona. A hushed and shocked manager had called to report what he said was a suicide in one of the rooms. Fabriano had duly gone along. Not a suicide, he said. That was wishful thinking on the part of the manager. There was no way the dead man could have shot himself like that. Not with the gun wiped clean of fingerprints, anyway.

"I'm afraid, my dear, that you are going to have to look at this hotel room," Bottando said. "I know you don't like bodies, but still . . ."

She agreed reluctantly, noting as she prepared to go that Bottando himself had slithered out of it. He thought he ought to go back to the office. People to telephone, he said.

Argyll wasn't so lucky. Not only did he have no desire to see this scene, he'd taken something of a dislike to Fabriano as well; largely because Fabriano had so obviously taken a dislike to him, admittedly, and he had this strong feeling it would be best to steer well clear. However, Fabriano, after eyeing him with a slight sneer of contempt around his upper lip for a few seconds, said he wanted a statement, so he'd better come too. They could deal with him later.

Flavia had described her morning in Muller's apartment and, even though she had spared him most of the worst, he had a sufficiently agile imagination to be apprehensive long before they reached the third floor room in the hotel. Fabriano, of course, was laying it on thick; so much so that, when he did finally walk into room 308, he was almost disappointed, and certainly relieved. If there were individual styles in murder, then this was one that had not been committed by the person who killed Muller.

Instead of chaotic devastation this particular scene of crime was almost domestic. The occupant's clothes were still laid out in neat piles on the table; a newspaper lay neatly folded on top of the television. His shoes were lined up and poking out from underneath the bed, which had been turned down evenly and with care.

Even the body itself conformed to this pattern. Surprisingly, there was no horror; even Argyll found it impossible to feel sick. The victim was fairly old, but evidently well preserved; even dead—a state which rarely brings out the best in people—he looked only in his sixties. His passport, however, suggested he was seventy-one, with the name of Ellman. The bullet that had killed him had done so through a neat, round hole, perfectly and symmetrically placed at the top of his bald and shiny head. There was not even much blood to get the stomach-heaves about.

Fabriano grunted when Flavia noted this, and pointed

to yet another of the inevitable plastic bags lying in the corner of the room. It was green. With quite a lot of red.

"Odd thing," he said. "As far as we can make out, the victim was sitting in the chair. His killer must have come up behind him"—here he approached the chair from the rear to illustrate the point—"put the towel around his head and shot. Right through the top of the head. The bullet went straight down; no exit wound at all, that we can find. It must have gone straight down his neck and ended up near his stomach. I suppose we'll find it eventually. So, not much mess. And as the gun had a silencer, not much noise either. Do you know this man as well, Argyll? Been selling pictures to him, too, by any chance?"

"No, I've never seen him before," Argyll said, peering at the sight with an odd interest. He decided to ignore the less than courteous way Fabriano chose to address him. "He rings no bells at all. Are you sure he wasn't the one who telephoned me?"

"How should I know?"

"So what was he doing with my address? Or Muller's?"

"I don't know that, either," he replied a little testily.

"What about his movements? Where does he come from?"

"Basle. Swiss. Anything else I can tell you? To help you with your enquiries?"

"Shut up Giulio," Flavia said. "You brought him here. The least you can do is be polite."

"Anyway," Fabriano continued, manifestly irritated at having to waste time explaining things to hangers-on, "he arrived yesterday afternoon, went out in the evening, came back late and after breakfast spent the rest of his life in his room. He was found just after four."

"And Jonathan was rung up at about two," Flavia said. "Is there a record of any calls?"

"No," said Fabriano. "He made no outside calls. Of course, he may have used the public phone in the lobby. But no one saw him leave his room."

"Visitors?"

"No one asked for him at the desk, no one noticed any visitors. We're interviewing the staff and the people in neighbouring rooms."

"So there's no reason to think either that he had anything to do with the death of Muller, or with this painting."

"The addresses, and the gun which is the same type as the one used to dispatch Muller. Apart from that, no. But it's not bad as a beginning. Although perhaps an élite specialist like yourself has some better idea?"

"Well . . ." began Flavia.

"And besides, I'm not really interested in what you think. You are here to assist me, when I ask for your assistance. And your friend here is a witness, nothing more. Understood?"

Argyll watched Fabriano's performance with interest. What on earth had Flavia ever seen in this man? he thought huffily. He had a feeling Fabriano was thinking pretty much the same sort of thing.

"You don't know who killed him, though, do you?"

Flavia went on. "Or why? Or what this picture's got to do with it? In fact, you don't know much at all."

"We will. This isn't going to be so difficult. Not when we work on it a bit," Fabriano said confidently.

"Hmmph," Argyll commented from the corner of the room. Not, perhaps, the cutting repartee he would ideally have liked, but all he could think of. Somehow being browbeaten made him dry up. A weakness, and one he had never admired in himself.

And there they all were, standing around, getting on each other's nerves. And not even accomplishing anything. Flavia decided she had better take the initiative. She would deal with Argyll's statement about the picture. If Fabriano wanted anything more, he could ask tomorrow. It was evident from the look in Fabriano's eye that he would do a good deal more than ask. But that, at least, had been postponed. So she ushered Argyll out, and suggested that Fabriano get on with whatever it was he was meant to do. She would send him round a copy of the interview when it was done.

They left to the sound of Fabriano calling down the corridor that he would call and collect it himself. And not to think he wouldn't be asking supplementary questions. Lots of them.

*T*OO much crime was making Flavia a bit callous; for some reason the evening's events had put her in an exceptionally good mood. No more mucking about with minor thefts of gilt cups from churches, or trotting about interviewing petty thieves about disappearing jewellery. No. For the first time in several months, she had something half-way decent to have a go at.

She had, in fact, been hard-pressed to stop herself humming cheerfully as she and Argyll had sat in her office, taking down a detailed statement about his role in the affair. But she was professional enough to make Argyll a little unnerved; he had not had the busy police side of her directed at him for many years and had forgotten how intimidating she could be behind a typewriter. It was the little details that bothered him; having to give her, of all people, his passport number, and recite his date of birth and address.

"But you know my address," he pointed out. "It's the same as yours."

"Yes, but you have to tell me. This is an official statement. Would you rather dictate it to Fabriano?"

"Oh, very well," he sighed and gave the information. Then there was the long process of going through the statement, his words being knocked into bureaucratically approved shape with her help. So he paid a business call on J. Delorme, picture dealer, rather than saw him; proceeded to the railway station to make his way back to Rome instead of heading for the station to catch a train. Had aforementioned person unknown attempt to abscond with said painting rather than was nearly suckered by a crook.

"So you then caught the train and travelled straight back to Rome. And that's it?"

"Yes."

"I do wish you'd reported it to the French police. Life would have been much easier."

"It would have been much easier if I'd never seen it in the first place."

"True."

"At the very least I would never have come across this Fabriano creature. What did you ever see in him?"

"Giulio? He's not so bad, really," she said absently. Why she was defending him temporarily escaped her. "In a good mood he's fun, lively and quite good company. He tends to be a bit possessive, mind you."

Argyll produced one of his non-committal grunts; the sort that indicated that he could scarcely disagree more profoundly.

"Anyway," she went on, "we're not here to talk about my youth. I must retype this thing. Keep quiet for a few minutes while I do it."

So Argyll fidgeted and looked bored while she put the finishing touches to her work, tongue between her teeth, frowning slightly, intent on making as few errors as possible.

"Now in Rome . . ." she went on. And so the enterprise continued, for nearly an hour until she had it down to her satisfaction. Eventually, she leant back, took the piece of paper out of the machine and handed it to him.

"Read this, assure yourself it's a full and accurate account," she said formally. "Then sign it, whatever you think. I'm not going to retype it."

He gave her a grimace, and read it over. There were bits missing, of course, but in his judgement they were scarcely relevant. Full and accurate seemed to be the right description. He put his mark on the dotted line and handed it back.

"Pouf. Thank God that's over," she said with relief. "Splendid. Didn't take long at all."

"How long does it normally take?" he asked, looking at his watch. It was nearly ten o'clock, they'd been cooped up for over two hours and he was getting hungry.

"Oh, hours and hours. You'd be surprised. Come on, let's go and see Bottando. He's waiting for us."

*H*E was waiting patiently and placidly, staring at the ceiling, with a pile of miscellaneous papers spread over his desk. His initial instinct when Fabriano had turned up had been to rush off himself and take on the department's end of the investigation. Reason, however, intervened. This was a Carabinieri matter and, much as he wanted to get involved, it would never do for someone as senior as himself in the rival Polizia to end up as the virtual assistant of a mere detective. So Flavia would have to do that bit. He was a bit uneasy about her clear personal involvement; hence his desire to find out as quickly as possible in her absence about Argyll's picture. If it was stolen and he, in effect, had smuggled it out of France, the matter would be clear; whoever took on the investigation it could not possibly be her. Think of the headlines in the papers. Think of the disapproving frowns on the faces of superiors. Think of the pleasure of his assorted rivals in making sure everybody knew that he had sanctioned the investigation of a series of linked offences by an officer who was the girlfriend of one of the felons.

On the other hand, the problem was how to stop Flavia investigating. What could he say? If he gave the case to someone else her reaction would be predictable and none too agreeable. If he did give it to her . . .

A conundrum. An ambiguity in the universe, and Bottando didn't like imponderables. He was thus even more irritated and perplexed when the long-awaited phone call from Paris came through and, despite his hopes, muddied the waters still further.

Was the picture stolen or not? A straightforward question, surely, and one that should produce a straightforward answer. Like yes. Or no. Either would do. What he did not anticipate, or approve of, was Janet's response.

"Maybe," the Frenchman said.

"What do you mean? What sort of answer is that?"

There was the uncomfortable sound of Janet clearing his throat at the other end. "Not a very good one. I have been trying my best, but not with a great deal of success. We did have a note from the police proper notifying us that a picture of this description had been stolen."

"Ah. There we are, then," said Bottando, clutching at the information.

"I'm afraid not," Janet replied. "You see, we were then told that no action by our department was required."

"Why not?"

"That's the problem, isn't it? It means either that it has already been recovered, or that it's too unimportant to bother about, or that the police investigating know what happened and don't require our special skills."

"I see," Bottando said, not at all sure that he did. "So what, exactly, is the status of this picture that is leaning against my desk? Does it have a right to be here or not?"

Can you give a perfectly honed and practised Gallic shrug down a telephone? Perhaps you can. Bottando could almost see his colleague delivering a masterly demonstration of the art.

"Officially, this painting has not been notified to us as stolen, so as far as we're concerned it hasn't been stolen. We have no interest in it. That's all I can say at the moment."

"You couldn't do something simple and ask the owner?"

"If I knew who the owner was, I could. But that is one of the little details that we were not given. To be on the safe side, it would be best if Mr. Argyll brought it back, but I'm not in a position to say whether we have a right to it or not."

And that was that. How very intriguing. No further on at all, Bottando put the phone down and thought. Damn picture, was all he came up with. And odd Janet. Normally the most effusive of people, but this time he had not gone out of his way to help. Normally, with any sort of request, the man swamped them with details. Usually he would put somebody on to it to dig up everything he could. But not this time. Why not? Perhaps he was just busy. Bottando knew the problem. Priorities. If you are really strapped, you can't waste too much time on minor stuff. But still . . .

Then he went and sat on his armchair, cupped his chin in his hands and looked carefully at the painting. As Flavia had said, it was decent enough, quite well done, in fact. If you like that sort of thing. But nothing special. Nothing to kill for, not that they had any real reason to think that it had been anything other than an innocent bystander, so to speak. Besides, since it had arrived in the department a couple of hours previously, a specialist from the National Museum had been summoned to examine it carefully, and concluded that it was exactly as it seemed. Nothing underneath the paint, and nothing behind the canvas and nothing hidden in the frame. Bottando sometimes had a vivid imagination in this regard. Many years ago he had caught some drug-smugglers shipping heroin hidden in holes drilled in a picture-frame, and he dearly wanted to catch someone at it again. Not in this case; despite all efforts it was resolutely still just a middling picture in an ordinary frame.

He was still looking and shaking his head when Flavia and Argyll came in.

"So? What is there to report?"

"Quite a lot, really," she said as she sat down. "This man Ellman was probably shot with the same gun that killed Muller. And you already know that he had both Muller's and Jonathan's numbers and addresses in his book."

"What about this mysterious character with the scar? No chance he was seen wandering around the lobby?"

" 'Fraid not."

"Who was he? Ellman, I mean."

"According to the documentation he had on him, he was German, naturalized Swiss. Lived in Basle, born 1921, and a retired import–export consultant. What that is I don't know. Fabriano is contacting the Swiss to find out more."

"So, we are in the position of having information without explanation."

"That's about right. Still, we can play around with some ideas."

"If we must," Bottando said dubiously. He disliked playing around with ideas. He preferred ordering facts. More professional.

"OK, then. Three events: an attempted theft and two murders, combined with the possibility that the picture was stolen. First thing we have to do is find out who the last owner was."

"Which Janet says he doesn't know."

"Hmm. Anyway. All these events are linked. The picture and the man with the scar link the first two; the gun links the second and third. Muller is tortured, and unless his killer was mad, that can only have been to find something out. His pictures were cut up into pieces, and afterwards someone phones Jonathan asking about *Socrates*."

"Yes," said Bottando patiently. "So?"

"So nothing, really," she said, a little crestfallen.

"There is also another little question," Argyll said. If the whole business was going to be complicated he didn't see why he shouldn't put in his contribution as well.

"And that is?"

"How did this man know about Muller? And how did he know I was going to be at the railway station in Paris? I didn't tell anyone. So the information must have come through Delorme."

"We will have to ask this colleague of yours," Bottando said. "And do quite a lot of other work as well. Muller's sister arrives tomorrow, I gather. And someone will have to go to Basle."

"I can go after I've seen the sister," Flavia said.

"I'm afraid not."

"Why not?"

"Ethics," he said ponderously. "That's why."

"Just a second—"

"No. *You* listen. You know as well as I do that you really ought to take a low profile in this matter. However unwittingly Mr. Argyll here may have been handling stolen goods, none the less that is what he may well have been doing. He is also a major witness and you concealed that from the Carabinieri."

"That's overdoing it a bit."

"I am merely stating what it would look like in the hands of someone like Fabriano. You cannot be seen to be involved in the investigation."

"But—"

"Be *seen* to be involved, I said. There is also another problem, which is that, for the first time in our acquaintance, brother Janet is not being entirely frank with me—and until I know why, we will have to proceed with some caution."

"What do you mean?"

"He said that it would be best if Mr. Argyll brought the picture back."

"So?"

"I never told him Mr. Argyll had the picture. Which leads me to suspect that maybe there *was* a Frenchman working here without official notice. Which I don't like. Now, Janet never does anything without a good reason; so we have to try and work out what that reason is. I could ask, but he's already had the opportunity to tell me, if he was so minded."

"So," he continued, "we must plod along methodically. Mr. Argyll, I must ask you to return that picture. I hope you won't find that too much of a burden?"

"I suppose I could manage," he said.

"Good. While there, you might arrange a tactful meeting with your friend Delorme and see if he can shed any light on this. But do not, under any circumstances, do anything else. This is a murder case, and a nasty one.

Don't stick your neck out. Do your errand and come straight back. Is that understood?"

Argyll nodded. He had not the slightest intention of doing anything else.

"Good. In that case, I suggest you go and pack. Now, Flavia," he went on, as Argyll, realizing he was no longer wanted, got up to go, "you will go to Basle and see what you can find out. I will tell the Swiss you are coming. You will then come straight back here as well. Anything else you do will be unofficial. I don't want your name on any report, interview or official document of any sort. Understood?"

She nodded.

"Excellent. I will tell you what Muller's sister says when you get back. In the meantime, I suggest you go round to the Carabinieri to deliver Argyll's statement, and see if you can persuade them to let you have a look at what they've accumulated so far. You don't want to miss something in Basle because you don't know what to look out for."

"It's nearly eleven," she pointed out.

"Put in an overtime claim," he replied unsympathetically. "I'll have all the bits of paper you need in the morning. Come and get them before you go."

7

S IX o'clock in the morning. That is, seven hours and forty-five minutes since he got in, seven hours and fifteen minutes since he went to bed. Not a wink of sleep and, more to the point, no Flavia either. What the hell was she doing? She'd gone off with the Carabinieri. And that was the last he'd heard. Normally Argyll was a tranquil soul, but Fabriano had irritated him beyond measure. All this muscular masculinity in a confined space, the sneering and posturing. What, he wondered for the tenth time, had she ever seen in him? Something, evidently. He rolled over again, eyes wide open. Had she been there, Flavia would have informed him dourly that all he was suffering from was a bad case of over-excitement, dangerous in someone who liked a quiet life.

Murders, robberies, interviews, too much in a short space of time. What he needed was a glass of whisky and a good night's sleep.

With which diagnosis he would have agreed, and indeed he had been agreeing with it all night, as he tossed and turned. Go to sleep, he told himself. Stop being ridiculous. But he couldn't manage either and, when he could no longer endure listening to central Rome's limited bird population saluting the morn, he admitted final defeat, got out of bed and wondered what to do next.

Go to Paris, he'd been told, so maybe he should. If Flavia could absent herself in such an inconsiderate way, he could demonstrate this was no monopoly of hers. Besides, it would get an unprofitable task over and done with. He looked at his watch as the coffee boiled. Early enough to get the first plane to Paris. There by ten, get the four o'clock back and be back home by six. If planes, trains and air-traffic controllers were in a co-operative mood, that is. He only hoped the nightman at the Art Theft Department had instructions to allow him to take the painting away. If he was fortunate, he could be back by evening. And then he could go and see about that apartment. If Flavia didn't like the idea, then tough.

So, his decision made, he scrawled a hurried note and left it on the table as he walked out.

*A*BOUT twenty minutes after he went out, Flavia came in. She too was utterly exhausted, although for different reasons. A long haul. It was amazing how much paper these police could generate in such a short time, and Fabriano had fought hard to avoid giving it to her. It was only when she'd threatened to complain to his boss that he reluctantly gave way. Had she been in a better mood, or less tired, she would just about have seen his point. He was working long hours on this case. It was his big chance, and he wasn't going to let it get away. He certainly wasn't going to share the credit with her if he could avoid it. The trouble was, his attitude had the effect of hardening hers. The more he resisted, the more she demanded. The more he—and Bottando, in fact—wanted to keep her out, the more she was determined to take it further. So she'd sat and read. Hundreds of sheets of paper, of interviews and documentation and snapshots and inventories.

But for all the vast quantities of information, there was little of any importance to be discovered. Meticulous lists of the contents of Ellman's hotel room produced nothing of any interest at all. Preliminary enquiries indicated no criminal record in either Switzerland or Germany; not even a driving offence to besmirch his good name. Then there was a mound of interviews, taken after they had gone back to Bottando's office. Waiters, doormen, passers-by, visitors to the hotel restaurant and bar, cleaners and guests. Starting with a Madame Armand in the room opposite who believed she may have caught a glimpse of Ellman that morning, but who spent more time complaining loudly about missing her plane than offering useful clues, right through the alphabet to Signor Zenobi

who confessed, with much guilt, that he had been entertaining a, ah, friend and didn't listen to anything and there
wasn't any need for his wife to know anything about this,
was there?

After hours of concentrated reading, Flavia gave up and
walked home to talk it over with Argyll in the short space
of time before she disappeared to Switzerland.

"Jonathan?" she called in her sweetest of voices as she
let herself in. "Are you awake?"

"Jonathan?" she said a little more loudly.

"Jonathan!" she shouted when there was still no reply.

"Oh, bugger," she added when she glanced down and
saw his little note on the table. Then the phone went. It
was Bottando, wanting her in his office as soon as possible.

*T*HE General had a problem which had surfaced almost the moment he had put the finishing touches
to his carefully considered scheme to keep Flavia and this
investigation at arm's length from each other. It was a
linguistic problem, in essence, and surfaced when Helen
Mackenzie arrived on the plane direct from Toronto. Mrs.
Mackenzie spoke English and a little French. Giulio Fabriano, who was meant to be conducting the interview,
spoke neither—a handicap he had been told more than
once might hinder his career in this age of European in-
tegration. Try as he might with cassettes and books and
lists of words, however, nothing could make any of it

stick. According to researchers, about 6 per cent of any population is incapable of learning a new language, however proficient they may be in their own. Fabriano was, unfortunately for himself, a member of that small and increasingly persecuted minority.

Bottando himself had more aptitude, but scarcely any more proficiency, although at his age and rank it scarcely mattered. He could scrape along in French, had a word or so of German, and for anything more demanding could call on the services of Flavia, who was disgustingly good at this sort of thing.

Hence his phone call, breaking his self-imposed rule within five minutes of its dawning that the interview could take weeks and be completely inaccurate unless help arrived soon. Flavia staggered in about half an hour after he called, bleary-eyed, crumpled and far from ready to conduct searching interrogations.

So matters were delayed awhile as Bottando, using his very own hands (something of a rarity but his secretary was late), made the thickest coffee he could manage, stumped off to the nearest bar for food and cigarettes, and encouraged her at least to try and stay awake. It did her stomach no good at all, but the shock treatment did at least stop the compulsive yawning.

After the twelve-hour flight from Canada Mrs. Mackenzie was scarcely in better shape, and the proceedings, when they finally began, were punctuated by yawning fits as one set off the other. She was quite a nice lady, Flavia decided. Very trim and attractive, obviously deeply upset at the death of her brother but one of the practical sort who has decided that her grieving should take place in private. For the moment, she wanted to provide as much information as possible; catching the person responsible was her first obligation now.

She was somewhat surprised when Flavia staggered in, notebook and tape recorder in one hand, coffee-pot in the other. It was not her idea of a proper police inquiry. Far too young, far too attractive, far too tired. But the young Italian, she decided, had the most charming smile and won at least the chance to prove herself by a practical account of the inquiry so far. There had been, she said, another murder, almost certainly linked to the death of Muller. She was sorry to start asking questions so quickly after the plane arrived, she went on, but they were obviously in something of a hurry.

"I quite understand," Helen Mackenzie said. "In fact I find your speed reassuring. Could you tell me, though, how Arthur died?"

Ah, Flavia thought. The last thing she wanted was to give details. Maybe the woman had a right to know. For her part, if the roles were reversed, she would rather be kept in the dark.

"He was shot," she said. "I'm afraid he was badly beaten beforehand." Leave it at that, she reckoned.

"Oh, poor Arthur. And do you know why?"

"We don't know," she said frankly. "One possibility concerns a painting. He had just bought—or almost bought one. The day before, someone tried to steal it as it was leaving Paris, and the thief was seen outside his apartment the day he died. As you may have noticed, there is rather a lot we don't know at the moment. I'm afraid that all we have are hazy ideas that need looking into. His accounts show nothing unusual, his work, his friends and his colleagues are all models of ordinariness."

Mrs. Mackenzie nodded in agreement. "That sounds like him. He lived an odd life. Very little amusement or pleasure in it. A sort of flat existence, really. He had few friends, few interests. That's why he didn't mind travelling and being posted from one country to the next year after year. He never had much to leave behind him."

"So," Flavia resumed, "this picture. He said, apparently, that it belonged to his father. We can find no trace of this. Who was his—your—father?"

She smiled. "That's two separate questions. My father was Doctor John Muller, who died eight years ago. Arthur was adopted. His father was a Frenchman called Jules Hartung."

Flavia noted this down. "When did he die?"

"In 1945. He hanged himself. Shortly before he was due to go on trial as a war criminal."

She looked up and paused for thought. "Really? I see. Perhaps you'd better tell me in greater detail. A potted history, so to speak. I don't know that it'll be relevant—"

"It may well be," the Canadian woman interrupted, "if this picture was a factor in Arthur's death. He'd been trying to find out about his father for the last couple of years. Ever since my mother died."

"Why since then?"

"Because that was when he got his parents' letters. She'd never passed them on. She and Dad didn't want to rake up the past. They felt that Arthur had enough to deal with—"

Flavia held up her hand. "From the beginning . . . ?" she suggested.

"Very well. Arthur came to Canada in 1944, after a long voyage via Argentina. He'd been evacuated from France when his parents felt it was too dangerous for him to stay. How they got him out I'm not sure. He was only four when he arrived, and didn't remember much. All he could recall was being told by his mother to be good, and everything would be all right. And being cold, hidden in the backs of lorries and carts as he crossed the Pyrenees into Spain, then a long boat ride to Buenos Aires, then moving from person to person until he was shipped off to Canada and my parents. He was frightened all the time. My parents agreed to take him in. Family and business connections. I think the idea was to look after him until peace came, then he'd go home. But peace did come, and both his parents were dead."

"What happened to his mother?"

She held up her hand to stop her. "I'll come to that." She paused to gather her thoughts, then restarted. "He had no family of any real sort who wanted him, and so my parents adopted him legally. Gave him their name, and tried to erase everything that had happened. Pretend it never had happened.

"Psychologists now say it's the worst thing you can do. That was not what they thought then. My parents were good people; they consulted everybody about what to do for the best. But children should know who they are and where they come from. They can deal better with unpleasant truths they know than with phantasms. In Arthur's case he constructed an entire fantasy world to fill out the gaps in his knowledge. His father was a great man. A hero, killed in battle defending France. He had maps showing where his father had fought, where he'd fallen surrounded by mourning comrades. Where he'd died in the arms of his devoted and loving wife. He discovered the truth when he was ten. An impressionable age. Perhaps the worst possible moment."

"And that truth was . . . ?"

"That truth was that his father was a traitor, a Nazi sympathizer and a murderer, who had spied on and betrayed members of the Resistance to the occupation forces in 1943. His wife, Arthur's own mother, was one of the people whom he betrayed. She was arrested and apparently executed without his doing a thing to save her. When he was exposed he fled the country, then came back after the Liberation. But he was recognized and arrested, and hanged himself as the case against him was being prepared. He didn't even have the courage to face his trial.

"How Arthur discovered this I don't know. And I can't

even begin to guess how some of his fellow pupils at the local school found out. But they did, as kids do, and tormented him. Children are often cruel, and this was 1950, when the memory of the war was still strong. Arthur's life was sheer hell and there was not much we could do. It was uncertain whom he hated more: his father for what he did, his fellow pupils for persecuting him, or us for concealing it. But from about then all he wanted to do was leave. Get out of the small town where we lived, get out of Canada, and go away.

"He managed it when he was eighteen. He went to university, then got a job in America. He never lived in Canada again, and never really had much contact with any of us afterwards, except for the occasional letter and phone call. As he grew older I think he accepted more that my parents had done their best; but family life, of any sort, he could never take. He never married; never even had any serious relationship with anyone, as far as I know. He wasn't strong enough or confident enough. Instead he got on with living and making a success of himself. In work at least, he succeeded."

"And then your mother died?"

She nodded. "That's right. Two years ago, and we had to clear out her house. A sad job; all those years of papers and documents and photographs, all to be got rid of. And there was the will, of course. There wasn't much; my parents had never been rich, but they still treated Arthur as though he was their son, as they always had, even though he'd gone his own way. I think he was grateful for that;

he appreciated the effort, even though he couldn't re-
spond. He came back for the funeral, then stayed to help
me clear out the house. We'd always got on well. I think
that I was as close to him as anyone ever was."

"So what happened?" Flavia was uncertain whether
this detail was necessary; but by now she was caught up
in the story. She had no idea what it must have been like
to have been Arthur Muller. But she felt for the pain and
the sheer loneliness he must have experienced. He was one
of the hidden casualties of the war; never appearing on
any balance sheet, but still suffering the consequences half
a century after the last shot was fired.

"We found some letters, as I say," she said simply.
"One from his mother, and one from his father. He'd
never been allowed to see them. He thought that was the
greatest betrayal. I tried to say that they thought it best,
but he wouldn't accept it. Maybe he was right; they had
kept them, after all, rather than throwing them away.
Anyway, he left the same afternoon. From then on, the
few times I phoned him all he would talk about was his
hunt to find out about his father."

"And the letters?"

"His mother's letter he'd brought with him; apparently
when he arrived at our house for the first time, he was
clutching it in his hand; he'd refused to let it go right the
way across Europe and across the Atlantic."

"What did it say?"

"Not a great deal, really. It was a letter of introduction,
in effect; written to the friends in Argentina he was sent

to first. Thanking them for looking after her son, and saying she would send for him when the world became safer. It said he was a good child, if a little wilful, and took very much after his father, who was a strong, courageous and heroic man. She hoped that he would grow up to be as upright and as honest as he was."

She paused and smiled faintly. "I imagine that was why he got the idea that Hartung was a hero. And why my parents hid it away eventually. It was too bitter, the way she was deluded as well."

Flavia nodded. "And the second letter?"

"That was from his father. It was written in French as well. I can still remember sitting on the floor-boards in the attic, with him kneeling down, concentrating on the paper, getting more and more excited and angry as he read."

"And?"

"It was written in late 1945, just before he hanged himself. I didn't find it enormously illuminating, as an outsider. But Arthur was predisposed to interpret anything in a positive light. He twisted the narrative until it meant what he wanted it to mean.

"I found it a cold, horrible letter. Hartung just referred to Arthur as 'the boy.' Said he didn't feel any responsibility for him, but would look after him when this little problem was resolved. This he was confident of doing, if he could get his hands on certain resources he'd hidden away before he'd left France. I suppose he thought he could buy his way out of trouble. It was a whining letter, describing the person who'd identified him back in France as having betrayed him. Considering what he'd done that was a bit much, I thought. And he said that, if nothing else, the last judgement would exonerate him. I must say, the optimism didn't carry conviction."

"You remember it well."

"Every word is engraved on my memory. It was an awful moment. I thought Arthur was going to flip entirely. Then it got worse, as he read and reread."

"Why?"

"I said he'd lived in a fantasy world as a kid. He still did, in a way, only when he grew up he'd learned to subordinate it and keep it under control. It's not surprising, as I say. Hartung was Jewish. Can you imagine what it must be like to deal with the fact—and I'm afraid it *is* a fact—that he betrayed friends to the Nazis, of all people? Arthur would do anything not to believe it, to construct an alternative truth. For years he coped by blocking it all out. Then these letters provided him with the opportunity to go back to fantasy.

"The first thing he latched on to was the reference to judgement. Jews don't believe in that sort of thing, he said—not that I knew that—so why the reference? Hartung may have got religion in his last days, but not that sort of religion. Therefore the reference must mean something else. Then he switched to this hidden treasure Hartung thought would buy him out of trouble. He never got hold of it; it was hidden where no one would find it. Obviously, QED, the reference to treasure and the reference to judgement were linked. Madness, isn't it?"

"Maybe. I don't know."

"Then Arthur left again, and all I got was the occasional progress report from around the world. All his spare moments he devoted to hunting down his father. He wrote to archives and ministries in France to ask for records. He contacted historians and people who might have known his father, to ask them. And he tried to crack the puzzle of his father's treasure. He got more and more obsessed with that. He said he was building up an enormous file of—"

"What?" said Flavia suddenly. It wasn't that her attention was wandering, although it would have been excusable if it had. But suddenly she was much more engaged. "A file?"

"That's right. That and the two letters were his two most treasured possessions. Why?"

She thought hard. "There was no file that we saw. No letters either. I'll get them to check again to make sure." Somehow she thought it wasn't going to turn up.

"I'm sorry," she went on. "I interrupted. Please continue."

"I don't have much else to say," she said. "My contacts with Arthur were few and far between. I think I've told you all I can. Does any of it help?"

"I don't know. Maybe. In fact, almost certainly. Although I think you've given us as many new problems as you've solved."

"Why is that?"

"It may be—and this is only a guess, which may be

wrong—that this is where the picture comes in. You said he became convinced that this reference to the last judgement was a clue."

"That's right."

"OK. This picture was part of a series of paintings. Of four paintings on legal themes. Of judgements, in fact. This was the last one to be painted."

"Oh."

"So it may well be that your stepbrother believed that the painting contained what he was looking for. Only—"

"Yes?"

"Only it didn't. Either he was wrong and you are right about him constructing fantasies or, just perhaps, somebody had already found whatever it was. Either way, Jona—the dealer who delivered it said that Mr. Muller was very excited when the picture first arrived, then became disappointed and decided he didn't want it. That only makes sense if he was after not the picture itself, but something in or on the picture. Which wasn't there.

"Then he was murdered, and we have not noticed this file among his possessions. There is evidently something about this painting we're missing."

She was musing again, and beginning to fantasize herself now, the sleepiness returning and taking her mind off formal matters. With a bit of an effort, she concentrated on the interview. She would be grateful, she said, if Mrs. Mackenzie could come back in the afternoon to read over the statement and sign it. Muller's company was seeing to all the practical matters of dealing with his effects and arranging the funeral. Was there anything she needed?

Mrs. Mackenzie said there wasn't, and thanked her. Flavia escorted her to the door, then went up to discuss matters with Bottando.

"So what is this, a treasure hunt?" Bottando said. "Is that it?"

"Just an idea," she said. "It does fit."

"If your interpretation of the reference to the Last Judgement is correct, and if Muller thought the same. Which may be doubted. On the other hand, he did want that picture."

Bottando thought a moment. "Can I see Mr. Argyll's statement?" he continued. "Do you have it on you?"

Flavia rummaged in her file and handed it over, then sat while Bottando read. "It says here that when he delivered the painting, he unwrapped it, then went into the kitchen to pour himself a coffee. Beforehand, Muller was excited. When Argyll came back Muller said he didn't want it."

"So he did."

"So we have three possibilities, don't we? One that whatever he was after was not there; he discovered this, realized he'd been wrong and got rid of the thing. The second is that he was right, and removed whatever it was while Mr. Argyll was in the kitchen."

"But in that case," Flavia said reasonably, "he wouldn't have seemed so downcast. Unless he was a good actor."

"And the final possibility, of course, is that this whole story is merest moonshine and there is a better, simpler and more correct explanation."

"Perhaps he missed something," she said. "Perhaps we did as well. I think we should have another look at it."

"A bit late for that. Your friend Argyll picked it up this morning and took it back to Paris."

"Damnation. I forgot about that. I was so tired I didn't think. He's going to give it to Janet, is he?"

Bottando nodded. "I assume so. At least, I do very much hope he's not going to stick his nose in where it isn't needed."

"Do you think I ought to take another look at this thing? Go on to Paris after Basle? You could ask Janet to look up some stuff for me to pick up when I get there."

"Such as?"

"Anything on this man Hartung, in essence. It would also be nice to know where this picture came from. We need more background on Ellman as well. Perhaps you could ask the Swiss . . . ?"

Bottando sighed. "Oh, very well. Is there anything else?"

She shook her head. "No, not really. Except that you could forward a copy of the interview to Fabriano when it's been typed out. I want to go home, shower and pack a bag. There's a flight at four to Basle, and I don't want to miss it."

"Whatever you say, my dear. Oh, and by the way . . ."

"Hmm?"

"Don't get too carefree. Muller died in a very nasty fashion, Ellman in a neat one. I don't want you—or even Mr. Argyll—to suffer either fate. Watch yourself. I intend to say the same thing to him when he gets back."

"Don't worry," she said reassuringly. "This is perfectly safe."

8

ESPITE his love of trains, dislike of aircraft and acute shortage of money, Argyll had decided to fly to Paris. It showed how seriously he was taking this business, that he was willing to foist on to his Visa card a debt that he had little immediate ability to pay off. But that was what the horrid things were there for, and if the credit-card company was prepared to trust him, who was he to doubt their judgement?

However awful they were, aircraft were at least a little bit faster than trains; he was in Paris as expected by ten. From then, the disadvantages became clear, and what he had fondly hoped would be a quick day trip became rapidly bogged down in hitches. With a train, you turn up with your ticket and hop aboard. Sometimes you may have to stand, or camp out in the guard's van, but generally you get on. Not so with planes. Considering that they increasingly resemble aerial cattle-trucks, the fuss made about tickets is extraordinary. In brief, every flight that evening for Rome was booked solid. Not a seat available. Sorry. Tomorrow lunch-time, fine.

Cursing airports, airlines and modern life, Argyll booked a seat, then tried to phone Flavia to tell her he would be delayed getting back. Not at home and, when he used up even more money to call the department, the obnoxious character who answered the phone informed him a little coolly that she was conducting an important interview and couldn't be disturbed. Then he phoned the headquarters of the Paris Art Squad to announce his imminent arrival with the picture. But they didn't know anything about it and, it being a weekend, there was no one around to ask. Nor were they prepared to find someone to ask. And no, he couldn't deposit his picture. It was a police station, not a left-luggage depository. Come in on Monday, they said.

So back to the airline desk to change his reservation, and into Paris to find a hotel. At least here he had some luck in that the usual place he stayed at grudgingly admitted to having a spare room, and even more reluctantly allowed him to have it. He tucked the painting under the bed—not an inspired hiding-place, but it wasn't the sort of hotel that had strong-rooms—then sat and wondered how to fill in the time. He tried Flavia again, but by this time she'd left. Wherever it was, she hadn't gone home. It was one of those days.

Shortly after, he hit another hitch, when he went down to Jacques Delorme's gallery to ask a few direct questions about the painting and its origins. He was less than happy with his colleague who, after all, had landed him in a not inconsiderable amount of trouble. Several choice phrases, carefully translated into French, had been lined up on the plane and Argyll was keen to go and deliver them before he forgot them. Nothing worse than moral indignation in the wrong gender. He didn't want to deliver a fiery speech of outrage and have Delorme giggle because he'd fluffed a subjunctive. The French are fussy about that sort of thing, unlike the Italians who are much more easy-going about the beginner's tendency to use the scatter-gun approach.

"I have a bone to pick with you," Argyll said stonily as he walked in through the door, and Delorme greeted him cheerfully. First mistake. Something wrong with the dictionary of idiom. He'd have to write and complain. Evidently Delorme thought he was inviting him out for dinner.

"What?"

"That picture."

"What about it?"

"Where did you get it from?"

"Why do you want to know?"

"Because it may have been stolen, it may have been

involved in a couple of murders and you certainly got me to smuggle it out of the country."

"Me?" he said indignantly. "I didn't get you to do anything of the sort. You offered. It was your idea."

Well, true. Argyll reckoned he'd better gloss over that one. "Whatever," he said, "I've had to bring it back to give to the police. So I want to know where it came from. Just in case they ask me."

"Sorry. Can't say. Frankly, I can't remember."

There is something about the word frankly, Argyll thought in passing. It's a sort of verbal grunt which is an effective shorthand for "I'm about to tell a lie." A prefix signifying that the sentence that follows should be understood in the negative of its spoken meaning. Politicians use it a lot. "Frankly, the economy has never been in better shape," which means, "If there even is an economy this time next year I, for one, will be very surprised." Thus it was with Delorme. Frankly (to use the term in its proper sense), he could remember perfectly well, and Argyll hinted subtly that he knew this.

"You liar," he said. "You have a picture in your gallery and you don't know where it comes from? Of course you do."

"Don't get upset," Delorme said in an irritatingly patronizing fashion. "It's true. I don't know. Now, I know it's because I didn't want to know—"

Argyll sighed. He should have known better: "Tell me the worst, then," he said. "What is it?"

"I know who delivered the painting. He told me that

he was acting for a client. All he wanted me to do—and it was a generous commission—was to organize its delivery. Which I did."

"No questions asked."

"He assured me there was nothing improper in what I was doing."

"Leaving out the question of whether there was anything improper in what *he* was doing."

Delorme nodded. "That was his problem. I checked in the latest police list of stolen art and it wasn't there, which is all I was required to do. I'm in the clear."

"But I'm not. I'm stuck with the thing."

"Sorry about that," Delorme said. He seemed as though he might almost have meant it. He wasn't a bad soul, really. Just not very trustworthy.

"I think," said Argyll ponderously, "that you knew damn well, or suspected, anyway, that there was something very dodgy about this picture. You wanted to get rid of it and unloaded it on me. That wasn't at all nice of you."

"Look, I'm sorry. I really am. But I did keep my side of the bargain. I sent those drawings off to California for you."

"Thank you."

"And I needed the money. I'm really scraping along here. Dealing with that painting kept the wolves at bay, at least for a bit. It was simple desperation."

"You could always have sold the Ferrari." Delorme's

penchant for red cars so small you could barely get into them was a weakness well known in the trade. Argyll had never understood it.

"Sell the—Oh, a joke," the Frenchman said, worried for a moment. "No, I needed the money fast."

"How much were you paid?"

"Twenty thousand francs."

"For transporting a picture? And you're going to stand up in court and say you never suspected for a moment, your worship, that there was anything wrong?"

Delorme looked uncomfortable. "Well . . ."

"And, now I come to think of it, you were in an unseemly haste to get that picture out of the country. Why?"

Delorme rubbed his nose then cracked his knuckles, then, just to be sure, rubbed his nose again. "Well, you see . . ."

Argyll looked patient.

"Come on."

"The owner—that is, the man dealing with the painting for a client—um, got arrested."

"Oh, God. It gets worse."

Delorme smiled, a little nervously.

"Who was this man? Has his name popped into your memory yet?"

"Oh, if you insist. His name is Besson. Jean-Luc Besson. An art dealer. Impeccably honest, as far as I know."

"And when this impeccably honest man was rounded up by the boys in blue your first thought was to get rid of any tangible evidence of a connection with him. Not that you suspected anything at all, of course. Just in case the police turned up."

More embarrassment.

"They did," Delorme said.

"When?"

"About an hour after you collected the picture and took it away. The man wanted it back."

"And you denied ever having seen it."

"I could hardly do that," he said reasonably. "Seeing that Besson had said he'd given it to me. No. I told them you had it."

Argyll stared at him open-mouthed. So much for honour amongst dealers.

"You what? You said, 'I know nothing about it but I do know a shady character called Argyll is at this moment about to smuggle it out of the country?' "

A watery smile indicated this was about right.

"And you told them about Muller?"

"He already seemed to know."

"Who was this policeman?"

"How should I know?"

"Describe him."

"Quite young, not a regular in the Art Squad that I know of. Thirties, dark brown hair and quite a lot of it, little scar—"

"Above his left eyebrow?"

"That's the one. Do you know him?"

"Enough to know that he's probably not a policeman. Did he show you any identification?"

"Ah, well, no. In fact he didn't. That doesn't mean he's not one."

"No. But the next day he tried to steal the painting at the train station. If he really was a policeman, he'd have just whipped out a warrant or something and arrested me. You were quite lucky, really."

"Why?"

"Because after failing to steal the painting from me, he then went and tortured Muller to death. Then he shot someone else. Somehow I don't think you would have enjoyed that."

And, leaving Delorme satisfactorily pale at his apparently narrow escape—which in Argyll's view would have been no more than he deserved, considering his behaviour—he left to see what he could do about this Besson character.

*A*T approximately the same time that Argyll was being appalled by the potential for duplicity contained in the human frame, Flavia was standing in a queue at Basle airport to change some money and buy a map of the city. She was raring to go. Her blood was up, in fact, and she had only briefly considered the possibility of finding a hotel, having a bath, getting changed and settling down for a meal and an early night. No sooner thought of than dismissed. She had work to do and she wanted to get this done, then go straight to Paris to have another look at this painting. Damned nuisance, but nothing to be done about it.

Her decision to go to Switzerland had been reinforced by the careful perusal of the papers accumulated by the Carabinieri the night before. As Fabriano had said, they were methodical; a model of how to do it. The trouble was, they hadn't had much time, and getting information via the Swiss police inevitably involved an awful lot of paperwork and delay. Not the fault of the Swiss, just the way it was.

She had toyed with the idea of ringing ahead to Ellman's apartment to give warning that she was on her way, but decided against. If the housekeeper Fabriano's report mentioned wasn't there, that was a pity. She'd have a wasted journey, but it wasn't a long one, only around fifteen minutes by taxi. When she had arrived at the destination, she stood and examined the street. It was a nondescript line of apartment blocks, all around thirty or forty years old. Comfortable enough, in decent repair and with the streets as immaculate as they always were in Switzerland. A respectable neighbourhood, but not in any way a wealthy one, so she reckoned.

The entrance to Ellman's block was similarly anonymous but worthy in appearance; clean, tidy, the walls covered in little notes reminding tenants to make sure the doors were firmly closed and the rubbish sacks secured to stop the cats getting at them. Muller himself had lived on the fifth floor, and Flavia took the well-maintained, comfortably carpeted lift to get there.

"Madame Rouvet?" she asked in French as the door opened, having desperately checked her file at the last moment to make sure that she remembered the name properly.

"Yes?" She was probably ten years younger than her employer had been, and didn't seem at all like a housemaid. Very well dressed, with an attractive face spoiled only by a thin, puritanical mouth.

Flavia explained who she was, and where she had come from, showing her Italian police identification. She had been sent up by the Rome police to ask a few questions about Mr. Ellman's death.

She was allowed in without any awkward questions being asked. Like, isn't it a bit late? And don't the Swiss authorities insist on accompanying foreign policemen when they investigate on their patch? And where is your written authority to be here?

"You've come from Rome today?" she asked.

"That's right," Flavia replied as she carefully looked around to get a feel of the place. The instant impression was of a home that was as proper as the block that contained it. Modestly furnished, with nothing exceptional. Inexpensive modern furniture, a preference for bright colours. No pictures on the wall except for a couple of popular prints of paintings. A vast television dominated the little sitting-room, and the air of meticulous cleanliness was spoiled only by the faint smell of cat.

"I arrived about half an hour ago," she continued as she took all this in. "I hope you don't mind me just turning up like this."

"Not at all," Madame Rouvet said. She looked properly, but far from excessively, distressed at her employer's death. One of those people whose period of grief would be fitted into the day's schedule, somewhere between the shopping and the ironing. "How can I help you? I'm afraid this has all come as rather a shock to me."

"I'm sure," she replied sympathetically. "A dreadful thing to happen. And I'm sure you understand, we want to find out what happened as soon as possible."

"Do you have any idea who killed him?"

"Not really. Bits and pieces, hints and clues, and lines of enquiry. But I must tell you that at the moment we need all the information we can gather."

"I will, of course, be eager to help. I can't imagine who would want to kill poor Mr. Ellman. Such a nice, kind, generous soul. So good to his family, and to me, as well."

"He has family?"

"A son. A good-for-nothing, frankly. Idle and grasping. Always coming here with his hand out. Never had a decent job in his life." She looked disapproving at the mere mention of the son.

"And where is he?"

"On holiday. In Africa, at the moment. He's due back tomorrow. Typical of him. Never around when he's needed. Always spending. Always other people's money.

And his poor father could never say no. I would have, I can tell you."

The conversation paused for a moment while Flavia jotted down details of the son and where he was. You never knew. Greedy son, dead father. Will. Inheritance. Oldest motive known to man, more or less. But somehow she thought it wasn't going to be that easy. Already, this case did not seem the sort that had money at the bottom of it. A pity; those were always the easiest. Even Madame Rouvet was sceptical; she may have disliked the son, but she didn't think him capable of murdering his own father. Largely because he was too spineless, in her opinion.

"And his wife?"

"She died about eight years ago. A heart attack, just as poor Mr. Ellman was about to retire."

"And he was in the, ah, import-export business?"

"That's right, yes. Not rich, but hard-working, and as honest as the day is long."

"And the company name?"

"Jorgssen. It trades in engineering parts. All over the world. Mr. Ellman was always flying off somewhere, before he retired."

"Did he have any interest in paintings?"

"Good heavens, no. Why do you ask?"

"Just that we think he may have gone down to Rome to buy a painting."

She shook her head. "No, that's not him at all. Mind you, he still did some business, occasionally, when they needed him."

"And where was that?"

"South America. He went there last year. And he went to France at least three or four times a year. He still had contacts there. He had a long phone call from there only the day before he left."

A slight contact, here, but nothing to get excited about yet. Flavia noted down the name of Jorgssen. She would need to have it checked out.

"This phone call. Was he planning to go to Italy before?"

"I don't know. He certainly didn't tell me he was going away until just before he left."

"Did you happen to hear what this call was about?"

"Well," she said, reluctantly, anxious not to give the impression of someone who made a habit of listening in on her employers's conversations. "A little."

"And?"

"Nothing out of the ordinary. He said very little. At one stage he asked, 'How important is this Muller deal to you?' and—"

"Whoa, there," Flavia said. "Muller. He said Muller?"

"I think so. Yes. I'm sure."

"Does the name mean anything to you?"

"Not at all. Of course, Mr. Ellman had so many business acquaintances—"

"But it's no one you've heard him mention before?"

"No. Anyway, then he said he was sure it could be done with no trouble and mentioned some hotel."

"The Hotel Raphael?"

"Maybe, yes. Something like that. I mean, he didn't say much. Listened, mainly."

"I see. And you don't know who made the call?"

"No. I'm afraid I'm not being much help."

"You're doing fine. Most helpful, in fact."

She brightened at that, and smiled.

"How do you know the call came from France?"

"Because he said that it would have been simpler to have organized things better in Paris first."

"Ah."

"And the next morning, he said he was off to Rome. I told him not to get tired, and he said that it might well be the last time he ever did one of these trips."

He was right there, Flavia thought. "Meaning what?"

"I don't know."

"Was he a rich man, Mr. Ellman?"

"Oh, no. He lived off his pension. It was enough but not a lot. He gave a lot of money to his son, of course. Far more than he should have done. Ungrateful hound. Do you know, when the cheques didn't arrive promptly enough for him last year, he even had the nerve to come here and bawl his father out? I would have sent him packing, myself. But Mr. Ellman just nodded his head and did as he was told."

Madame Rouvet did not like this son.

"I see. And when did he get Swiss citizenship?"

"I don't know. He came to live and work in Switzerland in about 1948; but when he became a citizen I'm not sure."

"Does the name Jules Hartung mean anything to you? He died a long time ago."

She thought carefully, then shook her head. "No," she said.

"Did Mr. Ellman have a gun?"

"Yes, I think so. I saw it once, in a drawer. He never took it out, and the drawer was normally locked. I don't even know if the gun worked."

"Could I see it?"

Madame Rouvet pointed to a drawer in a cabinet in the corner. Flavia went over, tugged and looked in. "It's empty," she observed.

Madame Rouvet shrugged. "Is it important?"

"Probably. But it can wait. Now then, what I would like to do is look at any files or accounts Mr. Ellman may have had."

"Might I ask why?"

"Because we need to make a list of business acquaintances, colleagues, friends, relations. All people to interview to build up a picture. Who did he know in Rome, for example? Did he go there often?"

"Never," she said firmly. "Not in the eight years I've worked for him. I don't think he knew anyone there."

"But still. Someone knew him."

With evident reluctance, she agreed to this, then led her out of the sitting-room into a small room, a cubicle almost, just big enough for a desk, a chair and a filing cabinet. "There you are," she said. "It's not locked."

With this Madame Rouvet remembered herself and

went off to make some coffee. Flavia initially refused it, but then she reflected how long it had been since she last slept. She felt OK at the moment, but you never knew. Besides, it got the woman out of the room.

She started at the front of the filing cabinet and worked her way through to the back. Tax forms, gas bills, phone bills—no calls to Rome over the past year—electricity bills. Letters to landlords—he rented the apartment rather than owned it. All the stuff of a decent, middle-class, professional life, with not the slightest hint of impropriety.

The sheaf of bank statements was also of no major interest. Meticulously balanced every month; Ellman was a man who lived within his income, and judging by the figures, that income was as modest as his tax forms suggested.

Which made the one piece of paper at the back even more strange. It was an annual summary of a bank statement, in Ellman's name. Dating to the previous year. Every month there was a credit of five thousand Swiss francs. Transferred from something called Services Financieres, not that the name meant anything either. Flavia, never brilliant at arithmetic, screwed up her eyes to help her perform the calculations. Sixty thousand Swiss francs a year was, she reckoned, no small amount. None of it declared for tax. She carried on rummaging and came up with a cheque-book, again in Ellman's name. Several of the stubs referred to sums made out to Bruno Ellman. Quite a lot of money, in all. The son, presumably.

Madame Rouvet returned.

"Bruno Ellman? That's the son?"

She nodded, lips pursed to indicate disapproval. "Yes."

"He's flying in to Basle tomorrow? Zurich?"

"Oh, no. To Paris. He flew from Paris three weeks ago, and comes back to Paris as well."

Another good reason for going there, she thought. She had a fit of the yawns all the way down the stairs, waves of exhaustion coming across her. She was still yawning half an hour later as she paid for a sleeping-compartment on the 12:05 train to Paris, and only stopped when she fell fast asleep at 12:06.

9

By the time Flavia's dormant body was passing horizontally through Mulhouse, Argyll was coming to the end of a tumultuous evening. Not that anything notably dramatic had happened, but he had ended up in a somewhat shaky and uncertain state.

After he'd finished with Delorme, he had the problem of not having anything in particular to do. What, after all, can you do in Paris? If, that is, you're not exactly in the right mood for relaxing. Somehow an evening all alone in a restaurant, however good, or watching a movie, however fascinating, did not appeal. And it was still raining, so long walks were out as well.

That left doing something about the picture under his bed. But what, exactly? There were two obvious lines of enquiry; one being to go and have a little conversation with this man Besson, who had caused all the trouble in the first place. Not that he was assuming that Besson had stolen the thing, but he was inclined to think that, at the very least, he had some explaining to do.

On the other hand, Besson was a bit of a danger. Somebody, after all, had informed this omnipresent man with the scar that the picture was to be found at Delorme's. And who might that have been? He didn't really want to have a chat with Besson and then find unpleasant characters with antisocial tendencies turning up on the doorstep an hour later. For Besson, he thought, he needed a bit more support. Like half a dozen burly French policemen on either side. Better still, leave it to them entirely.

That, of course, was another problem. The police had already arrested the man, hadn't they? Or maybe not. Janet hadn't mentioned it, and he should have, really, when Bottando made his enquiries. And he'd forgotten to ask Delorme how he knew all this anyway. Altogether, it was most curious.

Anyway, he reckoned that Besson had better go in the pending tray for a while. And that left the owner of the picture. Eighteen months ago in a private collection. Now under his bed, and had moved around a lot in the meantime.

That exhibition catalogue had only said the painting was in a private collection. A usual device, to indicate that the picture was not in a museum, without giving the name of the owner and telling thieves where to look. Another point to be noted, he thought to himself. The thief, who-ever it was, hadn't needed any help.

What good fortune, he thought as he left the hotel and hailed a taxi, that I am such a well-trained and consci-entious researcher. In the library in Rome, he'd written down the name of the man who had organized the exhi-bition and now he remembered that he worked at the Petit Palais. It was cutting it fine: the chances of this Pierre Guynemer being there were slight and he should have tele-phoned. But he had just enough time, had nothing else to do, and felt like at least putting on a display of action.

For once, luck was on his side. While the woman on the admissions desk of the museum was far from happy about seeing him, it being nearly closing-time, and openly dismissive of his suggestion that perchance Monsieur Guy-nemer might be in the building, she did agree to make enquiries. Then he was sent off through the vast echoing exhibition rooms of the museum, into the back corridors where the staff offices were located and where he was ac-costed by a man who again asked what he wanted. This obstacle overcome, he went wandering down more corri-dors, peering at names on doors as he went, until he came to the right one. He knocked, a voice told him to come in, and that was that. Simple beyond belief.

So simple, in fact, that he hadn't actually prepared him-self for the possibility that he might find the man, and consequently didn't know what he should say. Still, when in doubt, lie through your teeth. That was always the best policy.

So he concocted and simultaneously delivered a bizarre and none-too-convincing tale to explain what he was doing in this man's office at nearly five o'clock on a Saturday evening. It was a logical tale in its way, but not very well expressed; Argyll believed that its style rather than its substance was the main reason for Guynemer's slightly raised eyebrows and sceptical look.

Also, the trouble was that the curator was one of those people you take a liking to the moment you meet them, so Argyll felt bad about being duplicitous. He was a broad fellow, just the right side of overweight, comfortably ensconced in his desk chair, with an open face and cheerful expression. About Argyll's age, give or take a year or so. Which meant that he was either very bright or very well connected. Or both, of course. Unlike most museum curators, unlike most people, in fact, he seemed perfectly unsurprised at the unexpected arrival and quite willing to countenance being disturbed. Generally, if a total stranger turns up on your doorstep spinning a yarn, you chuck them out, or at least mutter about being too busy. Not this one; he sat Argyll down and heard him out.

Argyll's tale was something along the lines of his doing research into pre-Revolutionary neoclassicism, of his being on a brief and unexpected stopover in Paris until Monday afternoon, and wanting to take the opportunity to do something about these pictures by Jean Floret so that they could be included in a forthcoming monograph.

Guynemer nodded understandingly and, very irritatingly, launched into a monologue about the pictures and what he knew about them, mentioning, among other things, the article in the *Gazette des Beaux-Arts* and a host of other references which Argyll, for the sake of appearances, duly wrote down.

"So," the Frenchman said when he finished, "could you tell me, Mr. Argyll, why it is that you say you have never heard of the *Gazette* article when you've read my exhibition catalogue which refers to it several times? And how it is that you say you are in the fourth year of writing a book on neoclassicism and still know next to nothing about the subject?"

Damnation, Argyll thought. Must have said something wrong again.

"Just stupid, I guess," he said abjectly, trying to look like a particularly slow student.

"I don't think so," said Guynemer with a brief smile, almost as if he felt apologetic for bringing up such a tasteless topic of conversation. "Why don't you just tell me why you are really here? Nobody likes to be made a fool of, you know," he added a little reproachfully.

Oh, dear. Argyll hated the reasonable ones. Not that the man didn't have good reason to feel a little annoyed. Telling lies is one thing; telling bad ones is quite another.

"OK," he said. "Full story?"

"If you please."

"Very well. I'm not a researcher, I'm a dealer and at the moment I am providing a little practical assistance to the Italian art police. At the moment I have in my possession a painting by Floret entitled *The Death of Socrates*.

This may have been stolen, no one seems sure. The buyer was certainly tortured to death soon after I brought it to Rome; another man interested in it was also murdered. What I need to know is where the picture came from, and whether it was stolen."

"Why don't you ask the police in France?"

"I have. That is, the Italians have. They don't know."

Guynemer looked sceptical.

"It's true. They don't. It's a long story, but as far as I can see they are as mystified as anyone else."

"So you come to me."

"That's right. You organized this exhibition with the picture in it. If you won't help, I don't know how else to go about it."

Appeal to the human side. Look pathetic and pleading, he thought. Guynemer considered the matter awhile, clearly wondering which was the least likely, Argyll's first story or his second. Neither, in truth, was exactly straightforward.

"I'll tell you what," he said eventually. "I can't give you the name. It's confidential, after all, and you don't exactly inspire confidence. But," he went on as Argyll's face fell, "I can ring the owner. If he is willing, then I can put you together. I shall have to go and find out the details. I didn't actually do that section of the exhibition myself. That was Besson's part."

"What?" said Argyll. "Did you say Besson?"

"That's right. Do you know him?"

"His name wasn't in the catalogue, was it?"

"Yes. In small print at the back. A long story, but he left the project half-way through. Why do you ask?"

It seemed time to be open and honest about things; weaving tangled webs had got him nowhere, after all. But it might well turn out that Besson and Guynemer were bosom buddies and he would be thrown out on his ear in a matter of minutes if he were straightforward. In which case it would be a case of so near and yet . . .

"Before I say, can I ask why he left?"

"We decided that he was not suitable," Guynemer parried back. "A clash of personalities. Your turn."

"This picture, if it was stolen, subsequently turned up in Besson's hands. I don't know yet how it got there."

"Probably because he stole it," Guynemer said simply. "He's that sort of person. That's why he wasn't suitable. When we found out. We hired him as an expert in tracking paintings down and getting their owners to lend them. Then we discovered that we were in effect helping to introduce a wolf into a sheep pen, so to speak. The police got wind of it and came to warn us. Once I saw the dossier on him—"

"Ah."

"So, if I may take it one stage further for you, he would have known where this picture was, and may well have visited the house where it was kept. Draw any conclusions from that you want."

"Right. Did you not like him?"

The subject of Besson did nothing for Guynemer's amiability. Clearly he had a lot to say, but decided against saying it. However, he indicated that they were not close.

"But I think I should go and find out about your picture, do you not?"

And he disappeared for about five minutes, leaving Argyll to stew silently.

"You're in luck," he said when he returned.

"It was stolen?"

"That I couldn't tell you. But I spoke to the owner's assistant, and she is prepared to meet you to discuss the matter."

"Why couldn't this woman just say?"

"Possibly because she doesn't know."

"Is that likely?"

Guynemer shrugged. "No more unlikely than anything you've told me. Ask yourself. She will meet you at Ma Bourgogne in the Place des Vosges at eight-thirty."

"And now can you tell me who is the possible owner?"

"A man called Jean Rouxel."

"Do you know him?"

"*Of* him. Of course. A very distinguished man. Old now, but immensely influential in his day. He's just been awarded some prize. It was in all the papers a month or so ago."

RESEARCH is the secret of the good dealer; this was the little motto that Argyll had adopted in the few years since he had taken up the business. It wasn't necessarily true; at least, it was clear that he knew an awful lot about pictures he hadn't managed to sell, while colleagues unloaded others so fast they wouldn't have had time to find out about them even if they'd been so minded.

Clients were a different matter. However philistine some dealers may be—and many take a very jaundiced view indeed of the things they sell and the people they sell to—all believe that the more you know about a client the better. Not about the ones who wander in off the street, see something they like and buy; they don't matter. It's the private clients who deserve this treatment, the ones who, if you work out their tastes and inclinations properly, may come back again and again. Such people vary from the idiots who like to say loudly at dinner parties "My dealer tells me . . ." right through to the serious, judicious collector who knows what he wants—ninety-nine out of a hundred collectors are men—and will buy if you provide it. The former type is lucrative, but no pleasure to deal with; a good relationship with the latter can be as enjoyable as it is profitable.

So Argyll set to work on Jean Rouxel, not in the hope, this time, of selling him anything, but merely to know what he was getting involved in. For this task he had to go to the Beaubourg, which houses the only library in Paris regularly open after six o'clock in the evening. Fortunately it was not raining; the place becomes strangely popular when it's wet, and queues form outside the door.

Merely being in the place put him in a bad mood. Argyll

liked to think of himself as a liberal sort, open to modern ideas and a fully paid-up believer in the notion that education was a good thing. The more people had it, the better the world would be. Stood to reason, although in the twentieth century the available evidence seemed to contradict the idea. Many academics he'd met didn't help the argument, either.

Being on the fifth floor of the Pompidou Centre, however, made Argyll's belief wobble. The building itself he loathed: all that dirty glass and peeling paintwork on pipes. Classical buildings can take grime; a bit of weathering even improves them sometimes. The high-tech look just seems battered, sad and miserable when it stops being squeaky-clean.

Then there was the library itself, a haven of popular learning. The trouble was that it was the intellectual equivalent of a fast-food outlet. It was the reverence Argyll missed. Just another consumer temple, offering information instead of clothes or food. Take your pick; Socrates or Chanel, Aristotle or Asterix, they all become of equal value in the Beaubourg.

Listen to me, he thought as eventually he made his way to a vacant plastic desk with a pile of reference books. Worse than my grandfather. I don't know what's coming over me.

But at least it had some of the books he needed, so he tried to take his mind off the surroundings, and concentrate instead on the reason he was there. Rouxel, he said to himself. Find out, then get out. He worked his way through the material to find out about Jean-Xavier-Marie Rouxel. From a good Catholic family, he thought to himself, with brilliant insight.

Born 1919, the French *Who's Who* assured him, which made him around about seventy-four. No chicken he. Hobbies: tennis, collecting medieval manuscripts, time with his family, poetry and duck-breeding. So, a well-preserved all-rounder. Address: 19 Boulevard de la Saussaye, Neuilly-sur-Seine, and Château de la Jonquille in Normandy. A *rich* well-preserved all-rounder. Married Jeanne Marie de la Richemont-Maupense, 1945. Oh, ho, he thought, going up in the world, eh? Daughter of the aristocracy. Bet that helped the career. One daughter, born 1945, quick work. Wife dies 1950, daughter dies 1963. École Polytechnique, graduating 1944, in the middle of the war. Board member of Elf-Aquitaine, the French oil company. Then chairman of Banque du Nord. Then Axmund Frères stockbrokers; Services Financiers du Midi; Assurances Générales de Toulouse; no end to it. Still on the board of some. Deputy in the Assembly, 1958 to 1977. Minister of the Interior, 1967. A high-flyer, thought Argyll. Didn't agree with him though. No more politics after that. Legion d'Honneur, 1947. Croix de Guerre, 1945. Hmm. High-ranking war-hero type. I wonder when he fitted that in. Must have joined up at the Liberation. Member of war-crimes tribunal 1945. Private practice for a few years thereafter before the leap into industry and politics. Then a list of clubs, publications, jobs held, honours given. Standard stuff. A model citizen. Even lends his pictures for exhibitions, although after this experience I doubt if he'll do it again.

Other volumes fleshed out the picture but added few new facts. Rouxel was not a very successful politician, it seemed. He had been popular with colleagues but somehow or other had got up de Gaulle's nose. He was given a trial run for only eighteen months in government then was chucked out and never succeeded in attracting attention again. Or maybe it was the other way round and he didn't like high office; perhaps the pay wasn't good enough or he was more of a backroom man than a fast-talking minister type. Whatever, he still did the odd job—committees here, advisory boards there, governing bodies all over the place. One of the great and the good, the old regulars who pop up time and again in every country, serving the public and keeping their well-manicured hands firmly, if discreetly, on the reins of power in the process. Doing well by doing good; reading between the lines, Rouxel did not come from a wealthy family. He had certainly made it now.

Unfair, thought Argyll as he left. Mere jealousy because you will never be asked to do anything like that. Or just because you're in a bad mood from that library. Such were his thoughts as he marched boldly along the Rue de Francs-Bourgeois to his rendezvous with what he gloomily expected would be a spinsterish, twittering type of personal assistant; the sort who was good at writing letters but not exactly a live wire. Didn't even know if her employer had been burgled. He might well have to spend an entire evening doing his best to be charming and gallant to this woman and would get nothing useful out of it at all. Had he been consulted, he would have pleaded a previous engagement and held out to see Rouxel himself. But he was stuck with it now, he thought morosely as he rounded the corner at last into the Place des Vosges. Might as well get on with it.

So with scarcely a pause to admire the scenery—which showed what a bad mood he was getting into, it being his favourite bit of the city—he surveyed the crowd inside the restaurant. Little elderly lady, sitting on your own—where are you?

No luck. No such person. Typical. So incompetent she couldn't even show up on time. He checked his watch.

"M'sieur?" said a waiter sliding up alongside. Odd about Parisian waiters, how much they can squeeze into one word. Their most simple greeting can exude so much contempt and loathing it can quite put you off your food, and inspire foreigners with terrors of cultural inferiority. In this case, what the waiter meant was "Listen, if you're just a gawping tourist, clear off and stop blocking the way. If you want to sit down and eat, say so, but get a move on, we're busy and I don't have time to waste."

Argyll explained he was meant to be meeting someone.

"Is your name Argyll?" said the waiter, with a passable stab at wrapping his tongue round the surname.

Argyll admitted it.

"This way. I was asked to show you to madame's table."

Oh-ho. Must be a regular, he thought as he followed. Then his thoughts stopped in their tracks as the waiter pulled out a chair at a table opposite a woman sitting quietly smoking a cigarette.

Jeanne Armand was not little, she was not old, she was not spinsterish and, though technically she might have had nephews and nieces, she was not in the slightest bit auntie-ish either. And if Argyll spent the rest of the evening doing his best to be charming and gallant, his efforts were not forced; he couldn't help it.

Some people are blessed—or cursed, depending on how you look at it—with being beautiful beyond the ordinary. Flavia, now, had very definite opinions on this. She was very attractive herself, even though she put little real effort into it. But not devastating in the way that can cut off conversation and reduce grown and articulate men to gibbering wrecks. She counted this as good fortune; people instinctively liked her because of her appearance, but they did not ruin her life because they could not take their eyes off her. Even in Italy, she could get people to listen to what she said. Except, of course, Fabriano, but this was a basic defect in his make-up.

Jeanne Armand, however, was one of those who makes even the well-balanced and mature type act a bit oddly. Women often make very sneering comments about male responses in this area, but it is most unfair. Many men are, for the most part, quite good at keeping control and conducting themselves with decorum in strained circumstances. But sometimes, in very exceptional cases, there is nothing to be done; it is as simple as that. A sort of hormonal autopilot takes over which causes hot flushes, trembling hands and a tendency to stare with all the intelligence and sophistication of a rabbit hypnotized by car headlights.

This woman, or more particularly her Raphael face, her beautiful brown hair, delicate hands, perfect figure, soft smile, green eyes, exquisitely chosen clothes—and so on, and so on—was one of those people who triggers such a reaction that the continuance of even moderately civilized behaviour is an almost superhuman triumph of the will, for which those who manage it should be complimented for their strength rather than criticized for their weakness. Somehow or other she managed to combine a gentle tranquillity with just a hint of wildness. Madonna and Magdalen all in one, gift-wrapped in Yves Saint-Laurent. Potent stuff.

The element that pushed him over the edge was that the woman spoke to him in English, having discerned instantly that his French, while serviceable, was hardly up to the Racine level of eloquence. It was the accent; the woman even sounded beautiful.

"What?" he said hazily after a while.

"Would you like a drink?"

"Oh. Yes. Gosh. Super."

"What would you like?" she continued patiently. It may well be that she was used to this sort of thing.

By the time that Argyll's *pastis* had been ordered, he had totally lost control of the proceedings. While he had complacently anticipated an evening of gentle probing, careful pumping and subtle interrogation on his part, instead he was the one who was probed, pumped and interrogated. And loved every minute of it.

Unusually for someone who much preferred to listen to others, he told her about life in Rome, and the difficulties of selling pictures, and his recent tangle with this painting.

"Let me see the picture," she said. "Where is it?"

"Ah. Didn't have time to go and get it," he said. "Sorry."

She looked displeased with that, and being who she was, Argyll would have crawled on his hands and knees all the way to the hotel and back if it would have made her forgive him. A small, very small part of him was still conscious enough to be profoundly grateful that Flavia was several hundred miles away. He could almost visualize the look of lofty disdain on her face.

"Could you describe it, then?"

He obliged.

"That's the one. It disappeared about three weeks ago."

"Why didn't Monsieur Rouxel report it to the police?"

"He did, initially. But then decided not to pursue the matter. It wasn't insured, there was no hope of getting it back and there seemed little point in wasting everybody's time. He decided to treat it as the cost of not locking his house up properly and forgot about it."

"Still—"

"And now you've not only recovered it, you've found

out whose it is and you've brought it back. Monsieur Rouxel will be so grateful . . ."

She smiled at him in the sort of fashion that melts pig-iron. He looked down his nose modestly, and felt a bit like St. George after he has successfully sliced up a dragon or two.

"That is, if you're willing to let him have it back."

"Of course. Why not?"

"You might insist on some form of remuneration for your time and effort."

Well, he might. But in the interests of chivalry he was prepared to waive the matter.

"So," she went on as he adopted the pose of someone with so much money that any reward would be a trivial matter, "tell me how you got hold of this painting."

In great detail, he did. About Besson and Delorme and men with scars and train stations and Muller and Ellman and the police and libraries and museum curators. Nothing left out. She was fascinated, staring at him with wide-eyed attention all through the discourse.

"So. Who did it? Who was responsible?" she asked when he finished. "Who is on top of the police list at the moment?"

"I haven't a clue," he answered. "I'm hardly privy to their innermost thoughts. But from what I can gather no one is, really. There's this man with the scar, of course. But as no one has a clue who he is, it seems unlikely they will catch him. Unless they've made progress in my absence, they don't even know why Muller wanted the picture so badly. I mean, it belonged to his father, but so did many other things. And that's no reason to steal it anyway. Do you have any idea?"

"None," she said, shaking her head to give the word extra emphasis. "I mean, I remember the picture quite well now. It's not exactly world-class, is it?"

"No. But how long has Monsieur Rouxel had it?"

"He got it when he was young. He said so, once. But where it came from I don't know."

They refilled their drinks and dropped the subject; there seemed little else to say on the matter really. Instead she turned her attention to Argyll. He retold all his little stories about the art business, his complete run of whimsy, jokes and scandal, and she looked properly shocked, impressed and amused in all the right places. Such eyes she had. Occasionally she would laugh outright, resting her hand on his arm in appreciation at well-delivered anecdotes. He told her about life in Rome, about clients, about selling pictures and buying them, about fakes and forgeries and smuggling.

The only thing about his life he didn't mention all evening was Flavia.

"And what about you?" he said, returning to the really important question. "How long have you worked for Monsieur Rouxel?"

"Several years. He's my grandfather, you know."

"Oh, I see," he said.

"I organize his life for him, and help with the running of some of the small companies he still owns."

"I thought he was a big-business type. Or a lawyer. Or a politician. Or something."

"All of the above. So he was. But since he retired he took on a couple of smaller operations. Stockbroking, mainly. More to keep himself active than anything else. That was going to be my speciality as well."

"Was?"

"I began. Then Grandfather asked me to help him sort out his papers. You can imagine how many someone like him has accumulated over the years. Judicial papers, and business papers and political ones. And he didn't want a stranger going through them. It was just meant to be for a short while, when he was ill and overburdened, but I'm still there. I finished organizing his archives years ago but he can't do without me. I used to suggest he got someone more permanent, but he says always that nobody could ever be as efficient as me. Or as used to his ways."

"Do you like that?"

"Oh, yes," she said quickly. "Of course. He's such a wonderful man. And he needs me. I'm his only family. His wife died young. Such a tragedy; it had been a brilliant match, and he'd loved her for years before they married. And my own mother died having me. So there's no one else. And someone has to stop him over-extending himself. He can never say no. They keep on asking him to serve on committees and he always says yes. Except when I can intercept the mail and say no first."

"You do that?"

"Privileges of a secretary," she said with a faint smile. "Yes. I open all his mail, after all. But sometimes they get through. There's this international financial committee he's on at the moment. Constant journeys and meetings. It exhausts him, and serves no purpose. But will he give it up and stop wasting his time? Oh no. He's so kind and so helpful he'd never have a minute to himself if I didn't stop people wasting his time."

For the first time that evening, Argyll had a rival. It wasn't just that Jeanne liked or respected her grandfather, she seemed to come close to hero-worship. Perhaps Rouxel deserved it. For her he was not only a perfect employer, he was also one of the greatest men alive. Overdoing it a bit, though, wasn't she? Trying so hard to convince him. And what did she get in return? he wondered.

"He was given the Croix de Guerre," Argyll said.

She smiled and shot him a little glance. "You've been doing your homework, I see. Yes. He was. For his work in the Resistance. He never talks about it, but I gather he was very nearly killed several times, and he dealt with all the internal squabbling. Somehow or other he emerged with his general faith in human nature intact. I don't know how he did it really."

"You have a great admiration for him," he commented. "What happened to his political career?"

"Some people's failures are greater than their achievements. He was honest. Too honest. He wanted to clear out some of the time-servers and incompetents in the ministry. Not surprisingly, they fought back. He played clean, they played dirty, he lost. Simple as that. He learnt his lesson."

"Do you like him as well as admire him?"

"Oh, yes. He is kind, generous and courageous, and has been very good to me. The sort of man who inspires affection and trust. How could I not like him? Everybody else does."

"Somebody must dislike him," Argyll commented.

"What do you mean by that?"

"Well," he said, a bit surprised by the sharp tone that crept into her voice. "He's powerful and successful. Reading between the lines he's still very influential. And that creates jealousy. No one like that is universally loved."

"I see. Perhaps you're right. Certainly he's always fought for things he thought were right. But I can honestly say I have never come across anyone who had a personal dislike of him. Universally loved, no. Universally respected, yes. I think you could claim that. That's why he'll be up there receiving the Europa prize in a couple of weeks."

"The what?"

"Have you not heard of it?"

Argyll shook his head.

"It's a bit difficult to describe. It's a sort of European Community Nobel prize for politics. Each government nominates one of its citizens and one person is chosen from the short list. It's for a lifetime's achievement. It's only been awarded a few times; it really is an extraordinary honour."

"So what does it involve? I mean, is it just a question of turning up and collecting the cheque?"

She looked disapproving, as though he weren't taking the honour seriously. "There's a ceremony at the next meeting of the Council of Ministers. Monsieur Rouxel will be given the award, and then address every head of government in the community, and the Parliament. He's been working on his speech for months. It'll be a summary of his vision for the future and, believe me, it's very good indeed. A sort of statement of his life's principles. A summing-up of everything he believes in."

"Splendid. I shall look forward to reading it," he said politely but not entirely truthfully. There was a pause as each looked at the other wondering what to do next. Argyll resolved the situation by calling for the bill and paying it. Then he helped her on with her coat and they walked out into the night air.

"It was very kind of you to see me . . ." he began.

She moved closer and rested her hand on his arm, looking steadily into his eyes.

"Why don't we go to my apartment for a drink? It's just down there," she said softly, pointing down a street to his left. That slightly wild look was back again.

One of the most popular types of picture of the late seventeenth century was the classical allegory, in which mythological subjects were used to illustrate moral issues. An enormously popular topic was entitled the Judgement of Hercules. It was painted dozens of times in the baroque era.

The subject is very simple: Hercules, the strong man of antiquity, dressed in a scanty lion-skin so that the viewer can both identify him and admire the painter's skill at depicting the male torso, stands in the middle, listening to two women. Both are beautiful, but one is dressed in often quite severe clothes which cover most of her body, and frequently carries a sword. She may be shown with the finger of one hand raised as though making a not very appealing point. She is Virtue, sometimes personified as Athene, daughter of Zeus and defender of just causes.

On the other side, often lying languidly on the ground, and always semi-naked, is another figure. She may not be doing much of the talking, but she lies there tempting Hercules by her very presence. She is the easy life, sometimes Vice, occasionally Temptation, personified as Aphrodite, goddess of love. To the left, on the side where Athene stands, is a road, quite rocky and hilly, which leads to fame and fulfilment; on the side where Aphrodite lies is a gentle path, leading past all sorts of pleasure and going nowhere.

Hercules is listening to the women's arguments, trying to make up his mind which one to choose. Generally his face would be that of the patron who paid for the picture, and he would be depicted at the very moment he plumps for the life of virtue. A handsome and decorous bit of flattery.

And to Argyll's left, as this piece of art-historical trivia passed through his mind, lay the street which led back to his hotel, and to his right lay the road to Jeanne's apartment.

Hercules at least had time to think about it, to weigh up the pros and cons, to ask supplementary questions and find out what he was letting himself in for. Argyll had to weigh Jeanne's invitation, his attraction to her, his love of Flavia, all at the same time.

"Well?"

"I'm sorry. I was thinking."

"Does it need to be thought about?"

He sighed and touched her on the shoulder. "No, not really."

And, like Hercules, he reluctantly trod the path of virtue.

10

FLAVIA'S train arrived in Paris at 7:15 the next morning, and she was ejected unceremoniously by the station porters into the cold, windy hall of the Gare de l'Est while still half asleep. It had been a rotten ride: non-stop interruptions from screaming babies, ticket-inspectors, new arrivals in the compartment and sudden, jerking stops waking her up, it seemed, every five minutes. She felt dirty, unkempt and ragged. God, just look at me, she thought as she looked at herself in a mirror. What a mess. At least Jonathan never notices. She was looking forward to seeing him; he was a reassuring person to be around and, even though he was frequently mightily irritating, she found herself pleasurably anticipating a long chat. There hadn't been much to be cheerful about recently, after all.

She was half inclined to stop and have a coffee and a proper breakfast before heading off to his hotel. What she thought was his hotel, anyway. It had never occurred to her that he might be staying in a different one. Now that it did, she realized she had a potential problem on her hands. How would she ever find him? Equally alarming, what if he'd gone back to Rome?

Worry about that later, she told herself. The more immediate problem was that no bars were yet open, she had no French money, and consequently couldn't take a taxi.

She walked down the stairway into the Métro, worked out where she was meant to be heading, then stood and watched the passers-by. About one in ten came up to the turnstiles, looked around carefully and vaulted over. Although there were official-looking types around, they paid no attention. When in Paris, do as the Parisians, she thought. Clutching her bag, she hopped over the barrier, then scampered off down to the platform, feeling atrociously guilty.

She had once stayed with Argyll in his usual hotel, and remembered it was somewhere near the Panthéon. Exactly where was more difficult: it is an area with a lot of hotels, and all Flavia could remember was that it had a very ornate door. On the fourth go she didn't find it, but at least got directions from an early-morning porter to the right place. She finally arrived at 8:15.

Did they have a Jonathan Argyll staying here?

A flipping of pages, then the man at the desk admitted that they did.

Where was he?

Room nine. Did she want him to ring?

No, it was all right. She'd just go up.

And so she did, walking up the stairs, finding the right door and knocking on it vigorously.

"Jonathan?" she called. "Open up. It's me."

There was a long silence. There was no one in. Unlike him, she thought. Not one of the world's early risers.

She stood outside the door for a few moments, wondering what to do next. Of all the possibilities she'd considered, the idea that he might be out had never crossed her mind.

Fortunately, she did not have to resolve the problem of what to do next on her own. A clumping of feet up the stairs—Argyll was no ballet-dancer—indicated that the decision was made for her.

"Flavia!" Argyll said as he appeared, in much the same tone as you'd expect from a stranded mountaineer greeting his favourite St. Bernard as it turns up with a keg of brandy.

"There you are. Where have you been at this ungodly hour?"

"Me? Oh, nowhere, really. Just to get some cigarettes. That's all."

"Just after eight on a Sunday morning?"

"Is it? Oh. I couldn't sleep. I'm so pleased to see you. Here."

And he wrapped his arms around her and hugged her with a vehemence she had not noticed in him before.

"You look really beautiful," he said, standing back and looking at her admiringly. "Quite wonderful."

"Is anything the matter?" she asked.

"No. Why do you ask? But I had an awful night. Tossing and turning."

"Why was that?"

"Oh, nothing. I was thinking."

"About your picture, I suppose?"

"Eh? No, not about that. I was thinking about life. Us. That sort of thing."

"What?"

"It's a long story. But I was wondering what it would be like if we split up."

"Oh, yes?" she said, a little perturbed. "What makes you think of that?"

"It would be awful. I couldn't face it."

"Ah. Why is this in your mind at the moment?"

"No reason," he said brightly, thinking about the previous evening and his decision about apartments. She was going to take some persuading. The old charm was going to be needed. Not that he mentioned any of this, with the result that Flavia was forced to conclude that he was going slightly wobbly on her. This sort of gushing he normally kept to himself. He was English, after all.

"Do you have any money?" she asked eventually. No point in pursuing this bizarre mood of his, after all. And it was early.

"Yes. Not much."

"Enough to buy me breakfast?"

"Enough for that, yes."

"Good. So take me somewhere. Then you can tell me what you've been doing in the few minutes I have before I fall asleep for ever."

"*T*HAT'S not bad at all," she said, two coffees and a measly croissant later. A bit patronizing really, but she was too tired for subtlety. "If I grasp it right, you think that Muller may have contacted Besson after this exhibition, Besson pinched the thing and delivered it to Delorme. Then Besson gets arrested, Delorme panics and unloads it on to you. The man with the scar talks to Delorme pretending to be a policeman, finds out that you have the thing, and tries to pinch it at the Gare de Lyon. He then trails you to Rome, goes to Muller and wham. Exit Muller."

"An exemplary summary," Argyll said. "You should have been a civil servant."

"I, meanwhile, have discovered that Muller had been obsessed by this picture for the past two years, believing it contained something of value. He thought it belonged to his father who hanged himself. The trouble is this Ellman character. Why would he come to Rome as well? The Paris phone call could have come from your man with the scar, but why would both of them turn up in Rome?"

"I don't know."

"There's no chance the phone call came from Rouxel?" she went on.

"Not according to his granddaughter, no. That is, she'd never heard of Ellman and deals with all Rouxel's mail and stuff. Besides, she said he'd given up hope of finding the picture. Wasn't even looking."

She yawned mightily, then looked at her watch. "Oh hell, it's ten o'clock."

"So?"

"So I hoped to have a bath and a lie-down, but there isn't time. I have to get to the airport by midday. Ellman's son is due back. I want to have a little chat with him. Not that I'm looking forward to it."

"Oh," said Argyll. "I was hoping to spend some time with you. You know. Paris. Romance. That sort of thing."

She looked at him incredulously. His sense of timing was sometimes so bad it defied the imagination.

"My dear demented art dealer. I have had four hours' sleep in the past two days or something. I have not had a bath for such a long time I don't know if I could remember how to run the water. People sitting next to me on the Métro get up and move away. I have no clean clothes, and a lot of work to do. I am not in the mood either for romance or sight-seeing."

"Ah," he said, continuing the monosyllabic style he had settled on. "Shall I come with you to the airport?"

"No. Why don't you take that picture back?"

"I thought you wanted to examine it?"

"I did. But you tell me there's nothing to examine . . ."

"There isn't. I've been sharing a bed with Socrates for the past day or so. I know it inside and out, up and down. There ain't nothing there."

"I believe you," she said. "You're the expert. And I thought, now if you took it back, you might get to talk to Rouxel. See if he knows anything that might be of help. Ask him about Hartung. Ellman. Somebody must connect these two somehow. You know. Probe."

Then, looking at her watch again and tutting about how late she was, she ran off, leaving Argyll to pay the bill. She came back a few moments later, just for long enough to borrow some money off him.

*G*ETTING to Charles de Gaulle is not the sort of thing you do in a taxi if your boyfriend has only grudgingly given you two hundred francs to last the day. Admittedly it was nearly all that he had on him, but not princely. So she took one as far as Châtelet, then wandered around, getting increasingly anxious, in the semi-lit subterranean corridors, wandering where, in this vast underground mausoleum, they actually kept the trains. By the time she'd tracked the right one down, hidden cunningly among the booths and leather-goods stalls, and got on board, she was in no mood to be soothed by the music which wafted across the platform to her ear-drums. She was in a sweat of anxiety which, considering her state, wasn't a good idea. If she didn't have a bath soon, she'd have to burn these clothes.

She got to the airport about twenty minutes after Ell-man junior's plane was due to land, and then had to wait for a bus to get to the right terminal. Then she ran all the way up to Arrivals, anxiously scanning the notice-boards. "Baggage in hall," she was told, damn it. There was not much point in just standing and staring at the tired and weary passengers as they trooped past, so she ran to the enquiries desk and got them to put out a message.

Then she stood around, stifling another fit of yawns, and waited. It wouldn't be a disaster if she missed him, so she thought. But it would be a great shame, and involve not only her having to go back to Switzerland, but also subjection to Bottando's ironic looks when he examined her expenses, coupled, no doubt, with muttered comments about attention to detail.

She was still thinking along these lines when she noticed the man on the desk pointing her out to a newly arrived traveller. She had formed a picture of Bruno Ellman from the description given by the housekeeper. Not a flattering one at all, despite her attempts to keep an open mind. A playboy type, was what she'd come up with. Expensive khaki trousers, safari gear, a large Nikon. Sunburnt, ex-travagant and bit of a parasite.

What she got instead was very different. For a start, he was in his forties, if only his early forties. A bit paunchy, with too much starch in his diet. Rumpled clothes whose condition could not be attributed solely to an overnight flight in an aircraft. Hair thinning on top, with what re-mained turning a little grey.

Must have made a mistake, she thought, as the man came up and introduced himself and proved her wrong. It was Bruno Ellman.

"I'm so glad you heard the message," she said in French. "I was afraid I'd missed you. Is French OK?"

He inclined his head. "French is fine," he replied with a better accent than hers. "And here I am. Standing before you, and at something of a disadvantage."

"I'm sorry," she said, and introduced herself, producing her identity card for good measure. "I'm afraid I have some bad news. Could we go somewhere quiet to talk?"

"What bad news?" he asked, standing his ground.

"It's your father."

"Oh, no," he said with the air of someone almost expecting it. "What is it?"

"I'm afraid he's dead. Murdered."

Now this was curious. On first impression—of which Flavia was particularly fond—Ellman held up well. The sort of person you'd trust to give you directions if you were lost. The type who would be a good son, whatever that was. The sort who would be upset to hear of his father dying, and devastated to hear of his being murdered.

But this was not the reaction. Ellman pursed his lips as he digested the information, but produced no further response at all. "You're right," he said. "We should go somewhere quiet to talk."

And he led her off to the bar on the ground floor of the vast concrete building, then disappeared to get coffee.

If he was in any way disconcerted by the sudden fashion in which he was given the news, he had put himself back together by the time he returned. "Right," he said in a businesslike way. "Perhaps you'd better tell me what's been going on."

Flavia had no reason not to, so she produced a fairly full account, followed by her increasingly standardized set of questions. Was his father interested in pictures? No. Did he know someone called Muller? No. Or Hartung? No. What about Rouxel?

"Not such a rare name," he said non-committally.

"It strikes a chord?"

"Tell me about him."

"Jean. A businessman and politician, in his seventies," she said succinctly.

"French?"

"Yes."

"Has he been in the news recently?"

"He was awarded something called the Europa prize. It's quite a big deal, so I'm told, so it was probably reported."

"Yes," Ellman said. "That's the one." He thought for a moment, trying to pin the memory down. "That's right," he said eventually.

"Go on."

"There's nothing else to say," he said apologetically. "I heard about it on the news."

"That's all? No connection with your father?"

"Not as far as I know. My father was not the sort of

person someone like Rouxel would ever associate with, I think. I didn't myself, normally, except when there were money problems."

"Like your allowance being late."

He looked at her with surprise, noting the faint tone of disapproval that had crept in. "You have been doing your work. Been talking to Madame Rouvet as well, I see."

She nodded.

"Yes, my allowance, if you want to call it that. Did Madame Rouvet tell you what I do, by the way?"

"No."

"I suppose you got the standard story. Good-for-nothing lay-about. Well, if you like . . ."

"OK then. What do you do?"

"I work for a charity. It sends aid to Africa, mainly francophone. Africa and areas with problems. I've been in Chad for the last couple of weeks. There's an epidemic there."

"Oh."

"Not on safari, if that's what you were thinking. My, ah, allowance funds an orphanage for kids so starved they become brain-damaged. If there's nothing else to be done, we bring them out and try to do what we can in Switzerland. A drop in the bucket, and the money I get from my father—*got* from my father in fact, as I've no doubt it'll all go to his housekeeper now—was a mere molecule in the bucket."

"I'm sorry," she said. "I got the wrong impression."

"At least you're honest about it. Thank you. Apology

accepted. I wouldn't have brought the subject up at all . . ."

"Except for the fact that you thought maybe I was wondering whether you had organized your father's death for the money."

He nodded. "If it helps you can see my passport. The village I was in was so out of the way that it would have been impossible to sneak out, kill my father and sneak back in anything under five days. My main defence is that he didn't really have enough money to be worth killing."

"I believe you," said a chastened and somewhat surprised Flavia. "Do you know anything about your father's finances?"

"Not a thing. Nor do I want to know."

"There was a bank statement and cheque-book in his apartment with monthly payments of money. Quite a lot of money. Where did it come from?"

Ellman sighed. "I really don't know or care. I just know that when it was late, last year, I mentioned it and he said not to worry, he was going to sort it out the next day. The next day I rang and Madame Rouvet said he'd gone on a trip. Sure enough, the money came in regular as clockwork after that. That's all I can tell you. We barely communicated, except when we had to.

"My father and I did not get on too well," he said. "In fact, we hated each other. He was a vicious and mean man. A monster in his small-minded way. He didn't even have the grandeur to be a big monster. He as good as killed my mother through his neglect and cruelty, and I remember my own childhood as being one long nightmare. He sucked people dry. I loathed him."

"But you asked for money, and he gave it."

"And didn't he hate it."

"But if he was as bad as you say, why did he give it?"

Ellman gave a smile which Flavia thought initially was apologetic, until it became clear that it was a smile of pure pleasure at the memory. "Because I was blackmailing him," he said.

"Pardon?"

"I was blackmailing him. The Swiss are very punctilious people, and my father concealed certain matters when he got his citizenship. Like what his real name was. Had they found out, he would possibly have been prosecuted, and would certainly have lost his citizenship and his job. About a decade ago I found out about it, and suggested then that he started contributing to my charitable work. By way of recompense."

"You did that to your own father?"

"Yes," he said simply. "Why not?"

"But why did he change his name?"

"Nothing terrible, you know. He wasn't a bank-robber on the run or anything. At least, I don't think so."

He said it with the tone of someone who had almost certainly made some enquiries. It's the way it was, it seemed; people wanting to find out about their fathers, the good and the bad. What a lot of trouble it caused.

"It was the need for a job. The original Ellman was a comrade killed in the war. A childhood friend, I gather, although it's difficult to imagine my father having friends. My father was the town layabout and thug, Ellman was the studious, hard-working type. Before they both went into the army, my father drank and chased girls, Ellman studied and got a degree. He was killed, so when he came to Switzerland in 1948 my father assumed his name, and the degree, and got a well-paid job on the basis of it. Jobs were short after the war. He reckoned he had a right to all the help he could get. He was like that."

"What was his original name?"

"Franz Schmidt. About as common a name as you can get, really."

"I see," she said. A new variety of family life, she thought. Which was worse, a father like that, or a son like him? Maybe they deserved each other. Ellman seemed untroubled by what he said; he lived in a topsy-turvy world where bad means corrupted good ends and he was incapable of noticing. What made such a man tick, she wondered after she'd ended the interview and gone back to the train. Did he end up working for an African charity to cancel out his father? Didn't it occur to him that maybe he was re-creating his father behind a smoke-screen of virtue? It would have been so much easier had he been a simple, straightforward, no-nonsense playboy she could have disliked.

*B*y the time Argyll got back from his errand, Flavia was making up for lost time. She'd bathed, collapsed on the bed, and was so profoundly unconscious she could well have been in advanced rigor mortis. Argyll found her, breathing softly, her mouth open, her head resting on her arm, curled up like a hamster in full hibernation and, much as he wanted to prod her and tell her his little stories, he let her be. Instead, he watched her awhile. Watching her snooze was a favourite occupation of his. How you sleep is a good indication of what you are like: some people thrash around and mutter to themselves, constantly in turmoil; or regress to childhood and stick their thumbs in their mouths; some, like Flavia, manifest a deep-seated tranquillity that is often disguised when they are awake. For Argyll, watching Flavia sleep was almost as restful as sleeping himself.

As spectator sports go, however, it could command the attention for only a short time, and after a while he left to go for a walk. He was feeling quite pleased with himself. See if you can talk to Rouxel, Flavia had instructed and, obedient as he was, that was exactly what he'd done. When he'd left Jeanne Armand, he'd promised to bring the picture round the next day; the implication was that he would take it round to her apartment. But there was no reason why he shouldn't indulge himself in a little misunderstanding so, taking the picture, a taxi and what money he had, he'd gone out to Neuilly-sur-Seine.

A suburb just outside Paris proper, Neuilly is very much a place for the rich middle classes who have the funds to indulge their tastes. Apartment blocks began to spring up in the 1960s, but many of the villas built there still survive, small monuments to France's first flirtation with the Anglo-Saxon ideal of gardens and privacy and peace and quiet.

Jean Rouxel lived in one such villa, an 1890s' rusticated art nouveau affair, surrounded by high walls and iron gates. When he arrived, Argyll rang the bell, waited for the little buzzer indicating that the gate had been unlocked, then marched up the garden path.

Rouxel had taken the possession of a garden seriously. Although the English eye could fault the excessive use of gravel and look a little scornfully at the state of the lawn, at least there was a lawn to look scornfully at. The plants were laid out with care as well, with a distinct attempt at the cottage-garden look of domesticated wildness. Certainly there was none of the Cartesian regimentalism with which the French so frequently like to coerce nature. Just as well; however geometrically satisfying, there is always something painful to the English eye about French gardens, creating a tendency to purse the lips and feel sorry for the plants. Rouxel was different; you could tell at a glance that the owner was inclined to let nature take its course. It was a liberal garden, if you can attribute political qualities to horticulture. Owned by someone who was comfortable with the way things were, and didn't want to tell them how they should be. Good man, thought Argyll as he crunched up the path. It is dangerous to form an opinion about someone merely on his choice of wistaria, but Argyll was half inclined to like Rouxel even before they'd met.

He was even more so inclined when he did. He found Rouxel outside, around the side of the house, looking pensively at a small flower-bed. He was dressed as people should be on a Sunday morning. As with gardens themselves, there are two schools of thought on this: the Anglo-Saxon, which prefers to slope around looking like a vagabond, in old trousers, crumpled shirt and sweater with holes symmetrically located at both elbows. Then there is the Continental school which dons its best and presents itself to the outside world in a haze of eau-de-Cologne after hours of preparation.

However much he was the epitome of French values, Rouxel belonged, sartorially, on English territory. Or at least on an offshore island: the jacket was a bit too high-quality, the trousers still had a crease in them and the sweater only had one, very small, hole in it. But he was trying, no doubt about it.

As Argyll approached with an amiable smile on his face and Socrates under his arm, Rouxel grunted, bent over—stiffly, as you'd expect from a man in his seventies, but with signs of suppleness none the less—and pounced on a weed, which he ripped out and eyed with triumph. He then placed it carefully in a small wicker basket hanging on his right arm.

"They're a devil, aren't they?" said Argyll walking up. "Weeds, I mean."

Rouxel turned round and looked at him puzzled for a moment. Then he noted the package and smiled.

"You'll be Monsieur Argyll, I imagine," he said.

"Yes. Do forgive me for disturbing you," Argyll said as Rouxel looked placidly at him. "I hope your granddaughter told you I would be coming . . ."

"Jeanne? She did mention she'd met you. I didn't realize you'd be coming here, though. No matter, you're most welcome. Let me just get this little one here . . ."

And he bent down again and resumed the attack on his incipient bindweed problem. "There," he said with satisfaction when this too had been consigned to the basket. "I do love my garden, but I must confess it is becoming a bit of a burden. A brutal occupation, don't you think? Constantly killing, and spraying and rooting out."

He had an impressive voice, mellow and well modulated with an underlying vitality of considerable power. Of course, he had been a lawyer, so it was probably part of the job; but from the voice alone, Argyll could see why a run at politics had been tempting. It was the sort of voice that people trust—as well as being the sort of well-honed instrument that could change in a flash to threat, anger and outrage. Not a de Gaulle voice; not the rolling oratorical style which gains your whole-hearted support even if, like Argyll when he first heard one of the General's speeches, you don't have a clue what he's talking about because it's all in French. But certainly a match for all modern French politicians Argyll had ever heard.

So while they both looked carefully for any more weeds, Argyll apologized once more and explained that he'd wanted to return the picture as soon as possible so he could get back to Rome. As he'd hoped, Rouxel was delighted, considerably surprised, and, as any well-brought-up gentleman should, responded by insisting, absolutely insisting, that dear Mr. Argyll should come in and take a cup of coffee and tell him the whole story.

Mission accomplished, Argyll thought as he settled himself down in an extremely comfortable stuffed armchair. Another point in the man's favour. Of all the houses Argyll had ever been in in France, this was the first one to have even remotely comfortable furniture. Elegance, yes. Style aplenty. Expensive, in many cases. But comfortable? It always seemed designed to do to the human body what French gardeners liked to do to privet hedges, that is, bend and distort them out of all recognition. They just have a different idea of what relaxation is.

And on top of that, Argyll even approved of his pictures. He was in the man's study, and it was lined with a comfortable jumble of paintings and photographs and bronzes and books. By the large glass doors leading on to the garden was further evidence of Rouxel's enthusiasm for gardening: an impressive array of healthy, and no doubt well-sprayed, house plants. Faded Persian rugs on the floor, evidence of a large dog from the excessive amounts of moulted hair scattered around. One wall was covered in mementoes of a career in and out of public service. Rouxel and the General. Rouxel and Giscard. Rouxel and Johnson. Rouxel and Churchill even. Pictures of awards, records of honorary degrees, this and that. Argyll found it charming. No false modesty, but no boasting either. Just a quiet pride, hitting exactly the right tone.

The pictures were an electric jumble, from Renaissance to modern; no masterpieces but nicely done. Apparently hung at random but, in fact, with a distinct pattern to them. A tiny little Madonna, Florentine school probably, matched by what looked suspiciously like a Picasso drawing of a woman in pretty much the same posture. A seventeenth-century Dutch interior paralleled by an impressionist interior. An eighteenth-century version of Christ enthroned in Glory with Apostles, which Argyll studied carefully for a moment, and alongside it—a bit blasphemously, really—a socialist-realist painting of a meeting of the Third International. Evidently the owner had a slightly impish sense of humour as well.

As Argyll was looking around, Rouxel rang a small bell by the side of the marble fireplace. In due course it produced Jeanne Armand.

"Yes, Grandfather?" she asked, then saw Argyll. "Oh, hello," she said, a bit flatly. Argyll was surprised by this; considering the way they'd hit it off the previous evening, he expected her to be as pleased to see him as he was to see her. Evidently not. Maybe *she* hadn't slept well, either.

"Coffee, please, Jeanne," Rouxel said. "Two cups."

Then he turned his attention back to Argyll, and his granddaughter left without saying another word. Again, Argyll found this a little perplexing. There was a brusqueness, almost an impoliteness, which contrasted strangely with the way the charm suddenly returned as the old man indicated a chair for his visitor on one side of the fireplace and settled himself into another one nearby.

"Now, dear sir, do tell me. I'm dying to hear how this painting has come back to me in such an unexpected fashion. Has it, by the way, been damaged at all?"

Argyll shook his head. "No. Considering that in the past few days it's been hurled around train stations and hidden under beds, it's in perfect condition. Please examine it, if you want."

So Rouxel did, and expressed satisfaction once again. Then he gently probed the entire story out of Argyll.

"Besson," Rouxel said half-way through the rendition. "Yes. I remember him. He came to the château to measure up and take it away for the exhibition. I must say, I didn't take to him at all. Although I never would have suspected—"

"It is only a suspicion, you understand. I wouldn't want the police—"

Rouxel held up his hand. "Goodness, no. I have no intention of bothering the police. I did have a word with one I knew when it was stolen and he told me, frankly, that it would be a waste of time to try and get it back. Now I *have* got it back, it would be perfectly pointless."

Jeanne re-entered, bearing a tray with a pot of steaming coffee, milk, and sugar. And three cups. Rouxel looked at the tray with a frown.

"What's this?" he said. "I said two cups."

"I want a cup myself," she said.

"Oh, no. I'm sorry. But you know how pressed I am. Stop being a gossiping woman and get back to your work.

Those letters really must be finished today. Please attend to them."

She retreated once more, flushed with humiliation at the publicly dismissive tone of his order. Argyll could well understand why. It hardly matched up with the glowing portrait she'd sketched out the previous evening. Far from being the highly valued, indispensable organizer of his life, the devoted and doted-on granddaughter, it seemed that in reality she was little more than a secretary. A bit awkward to have her fantasies unveiled in such a way.

Rouxel carried on as though this small domestic scene had not happened, returning to the conversation as though there'd been no break in it at all. The charm was back in full force.

Then the litany of questions, buried in the running account of the case so far. And at each point, Rouxel shook his head. Muller didn't ring a bell. Nor Ellman. But at the mention of Hartung, he nodded.

"Of course, I remember the name," he said. "It was quite a *cause célèbre*. And as I was involved with the prosecutor's office in Paris at the time I knew of the case."

"What happened?"

He spread his hands. "What can one say? He was a traitor, who caused the death of many, many people. He was arrested and would have been tried. And, I've no doubt, found guilty and guillotined, had he not killed himself first. A bad business, all around. There was a hysteria in the air then. Lots of old scores to be paid off, many collaborators and traitors to be rooted out. Fortunately it died down quickly, but we French are still a little sensitive on the question of what happened during the war. It was not a happy time."

Now *there* was an understatement, Argyll thought.

"So what are your conclusions?" he asked with a smile. "You seem to have done a considerable amount of hard work on my behalf over this."

"The only thing which makes sense is that Muller was completely potty," he said. This was a bit disingenuous, but he had decided he didn't wholly like or trust the old man. Just prejudice, and he certainly didn't have the full facts, but he was almost shocked by the way Rouxel had spoken to his granddaughter. Families have their own little ways, of course, and it is a foolhardy outsider who rushes to pass judgement on them. But Argyll did not approve of the contrast between the cold family man and the warm, charming version being presented to him. Too much of the politician, there.

"And you have no idea what Muller was after?"

"All I know is that somebody else took it seriously enough to kill him. And you now have the picture. It's none of my business, I know, but I would beg you to be a little more careful. I would never forgive myself—"

Rouxel waved his hand dismissively. "Pah. I'm an old man, Mr. Argyll. What possible point could there be in killing me? I shall be dead soon enough anyway. I'm sure I'm in no danger at all."

"I hope you're right," Argyll replied. Then he got up to leave, an exit accompanied by a satisfying jousting between Rouxel who wanted to ply him with cheques for having been so kind and helpful, and Argyll who, desperately as he needed the money, felt it would spoil his gesture if he accepted. He parted instead with a heavy hint that, if ever Rouxel wanted to sell some pictures and needed an agent . . .

Back in the garden, after he had left Rouxel, he spied Jeanne Armand again. She was clearly waiting for him, so he gave her a wave and waited for her to come over.

"How are you this morning," he asked breezily, noting that she didn't look so happy.

"Quite well, thank you. I wanted to explain."

"You don't owe me any explanations, you know."

"I know. But it's important to me. About Grandfather."

"Explain away, then."

"He's under enormous pressure at the moment. What with the preparations for the prize, and being on this international financial committee and all the rest. He overdoes it, and that reminds him that he's getting old. So he gets ill-tempered sometimes."

"And takes it out on you."

"Yes. But we really are very close. He's such a great man, you know. I . . . I just didn't want you to get the wrong impression. I'm all he has. His one close relative. Close enough to be irritable with."

"Right," said Argyll, thoroughly mystified by why she felt obliged to tell him this.

"And of course he's never really forgiven me."

"What for?"

"For not being a grandson."

"You're not serious?"

"Oh, yes. It was important to him. He wanted to found a great dynasty, I think. But his wife gave him a daughter and then died. And his daughter produced me. And I'm divorced. He hated it when I left my husband. I think it makes him wonder what it's all been for. Of course, he never says that," she went on quickly. "But I know he thinks it sometimes."

"It's ridiculous."

"Just old-fashioned. That's all. He's an old man."

"But still."

"And he never refers to it, and never really holds anything against me. And is generally the kindest and most loving of grandfathers."

"Fine," Argyll said. "Whatever you say."

"I didn't want you to get the wrong impression."

"No."

And they smiled distantly at each other, and she let him out of the gate.

11

"You look wonderful," he said intently from the other side of the table, by way of continuing his charm offensive.

There really was no accounting for people, Flavia reflected. She could spend ages getting herself up in her finery and he would not notice—or at least not pass any comment. And now, dressed as she was in crumpled shirt and battered jeans, he was going on as though she was the Venus de Milo. It made a pleasant change; but she would still like to know what had brought it on. Something very fishy going on here.

"Thank you," she said, even more surprised by his sudden devoted attentiveness. "And I appreciate the comment. But if you stare into my eyes much longer you're going to get soup down your jacket."

They were in a restaurant in the Rue du Faubourg St-Denis, called Chez Julien, one of Argyll's favorites. Covered in art nouveau plasterwork and mirrors and hatstands. You could eat and be cultivated simultaneously, he pointed out. It saved a great deal of time if you were in a hurry. Food wasn't bad either, although technically it was breakfast. Without even trying, Flavia had slept straight through until seven in the evening; then she had woken and complained loudly about being hungry. Argyll's credit card had generously offered to take both of them out to dinner.

Argyll summarized first, talking about Rouxel and Rouxel's granddaughter. He downplayed her charms, and instead concentrated on the factual material he'd garnered.

"It was odd," he said musingly. "She was so insistent that I should understand that Rouxel was really such a doting grandfather. I wouldn't have bothered. I mean, it was no business of mine."

"Family pride," Flavia said, as she gazed enraptured at the plate of escalope de foie gras that the unusually amiable waiter delivered. "No one likes those little cracks in the edifice to be shown to the public. You try to cover them over. Common enough, isn't it? Think how embarrassed you get when we have a fight in a restaurant."

"That's different."

"Not really. Are you sure we can afford this?"

"The meal?" he asked, dragging his mind off Jeanne Armand. "Of course we can't. I'm relying on your expense account to race to the rescue at the last moment. Do you want to tell me what you've been doing as well?"

"Naturally," she said after a long pause to allow a slice of foie gras to dissolve like butter on her tongue.

"Who knows? If we glue our two stories together we might come up with some obvious conclusion. Wouldn't that be nice? Then we could go home."

The statement stemmed from his eternal optimism that good times were just around the corner. Even he, when Flavia had finished, was forced to concede that by joining the two together, all they now had was more information which still didn't make much sense.

"What do you reckon, then?"

"I reckon, firstly, that I have to go and do the decent thing tomorrow. That is, go and see Janet. I really should not have gone out to Roissy to talk to Ellman without telling Janet first. Bad manners. He won't mind, but I'm sure he'll be a little upset if I don't go and pay my compliments. Next, we should do a little work on Besson; he might know why Muller wanted that picture, or at least how he came to the conclusion that the picture was the one he wanted."

"Splendid. What about me?"

"You can dig around with this picture. Find out how it got into Rouxel's hands. And why Muller had it stolen."

"That's easy. Wrong picture."

"So, you find the right one."

"Not so easy."

"No, but it will give your brain cells a bit of exercise. Is there any chance?"

"Maybe. There was an old dealer's label on the back of the frame. Rosier, in the Rue de Rivoli. There's not much likelihood he's still there, but I'll see."

"Good. And I'll talk to Bottando to see if any dribbles of information have come in from the Swiss or from Fabriano. I also want him to check out this Schmidt/Ellman a bit more closely. And finally—"

"Whoa. I think that's quite enough," Argyll said. "Your food will get cold. Eat up. Then we should have an early night."

"I slept all afternoon. I don't feel in the slightest bit tired."

"Oh, good."

No doubt about it. He was acting most peculiar these days.

*H*OWEVER distinguished a purveyor of art the Rue de Rivoli might have been seventy years ago, it was so no longer. Apart from the excessively expensive *galeries* slipped in where once there had been one of the finest hotels in Europe, the nearest thing to a decent antique you can buy there nowadays is a luminous model of the Eiffle Tower. The broad Imperial thoroughfare has gone down in the world a little in the past century. Rosier

Frères had vanished as well. Even on a sunny morning, the tawdry lines of foreign-exchange booths, postcard stands and souvenir shops are less than appealing. Thinking over what to do next, Argyll sipped his coffee—disgusting weak stuff they sold in France compared to the real Italian brew—and wondered what to do next. Flavia had vanished on her errands, he had decided to start on the great picture hunt.

How do you do that? Eliminate the impossible, so the great man had said. Or, to translate that into more acceptable terms, start with the easy bits. Which, in this case, suggested finding out as much as possible about this picture.

There wasn't much to go on here. Really famous pictures have pedigrees that can be traced back through the generations; with many, you can tell where they were at any moment during the past five hundred years. Frequently you can even say a picture was hanging on this wall, in this room, in this house, on this day, in this year. But that is the élite minority. Most pictures bumble about the world hopping from owner to owner and it is impossible to find out where they've been unless you are really lucky.

In the case of *Socrates*, all he had was the faded label on the back of the frame. The more he thought about it, the more he was certain it was his only real chance. It was impossible to say with any accuracy how old it was, but from the typeface he placed it somewhere in the inter-war period.

Phone book? he thought. A long shot, certainly, but think how pleasant if it worked. So he borrowed an old, dog-eared copy of the phone book and started hunting. And there it was. Family businesses are wonderful things. Rosier Frères still existed. Perhaps not at the same address, but a gallery of that name had an address in the Faubourg St-Honoré, with a little logo saying "Established 1882." Bingo. He looked at his map, decided it was an easy walk and set off.

A very long street, the Rue du Faubourg St-Honoré, about five kilometres long, with galleries stretched out all along it. He should have taken a cab, and he was hot and tired by the time he finally stood outside Rosier Frères, having previously nipped round the corner, straightened his tie, run his fingers through his hair and tried to adopt the air of a successful dealer calling on a colleague in the trade.

He rang the bell, heard the click of the electric lock opening and went in. There were no customers. Really up-market galleries don't encourage them.

"Good morning," he said to the woman who came forward to greet him with a formal, chilly smile. He handed her his card—he rarely got the chance to do that and generally when someone wanted one he'd left them at home—and asked if the owner was in. He wished to consult him about a picture he'd bought which once passed through their hands.

So far so good. Such a request, if rarely made in person, is not so rare. Art dealers spend quite a lot of their time trying to work out where their pictures have been in the past. Realizing that she was dealing with a colleague and not with a client, the woman became almost welcoming; asked him to wait a moment, disappeared through a curtain at the back then reappeared to ask him to go through.

Despite the name, Rosier Frères was now run by a dapper little fellow called Gentilly, who brushed aside Argyll's apologies for interrupting with a sweep of the hand. Nonsense. Bored to tears this morning. Glad for the distraction. Who are you?

The aesthetic mating game interrupted business while Argyll laid out his credentials and Gentilly inspected them to see how seriously he should treat the young stranger. This is a standard routine, the artistic equivalent of dogs sniffing each other's bottom before deciding whether to chase balls together or bury a fang or two into each other's necks. What makes dogs decide to be friends rather than enemies is unclear; but no more obscure than what makes dealers decide to be co-operative or not to colleagues. In this case it was the former connection with Edward Byrnes that did the trick. Gentilly had, apparently, once done some business with Argyll's former employer, and got on well with him.

So they talked about Argyll's old boss awhile, swapped gossip, then commiserated with each other about the parlous state of the market, all by way of building up mutual trust and understanding. Then, all the preliminaries disposed of, they settled down to business. What, exactly, did Argyll want?

Leaving out some of the more interesting details, Argyll explained. He had acquired a picture which, judging by a label on the back, had probably passed through the gallery's hands. Unfortunately it was many years ago. But he wanted to find out as much as possible.

"How long ago?"

He said that it was probably sixty or seventy years. Certainly pre-war.

"Oh, dear. I don't know if I'll be of much help, then. The Rosier family threw most of the records away when they sold up, and that was thirty years ago."

He'd half expected that. Some dealers, the very old, very established ones, keep records of every work of art that passes through. Most run out of space to store the mountains of paper and sooner or later throw them out. At the very best they donate their records to archives or something; few keep such things hanging around the gallery to gather dust.

Gentilly was politely interested, at least, but Argyll had little else to tell him. He described the *Socrates* in as much detail as he could remember, but without seeing it for himself there was nothing the other man could usefully say. The only further thing he knew about it, Argyll said, was that it might have been owned by a man called Hartung. But even this was doubtful.

"Hartung?" Gentilly said, perking up. "Why didn't you say so?"

"You've heard of him?"

"Good lord, of course. Before he fell from grace he was quite a big Paris collector. An industrialist, I think."

"This gallery may well have sold stuff to him, then?"

"More than likely. From what I've heard—and it was well before my time, remember—he bought widely, and judiciously. What's more, I may well be able to tell you. Like most dealers we're extraordinarily snobbish in this firm. Ordinary clients—pouf. We throw away the records. Important ones, rich ones—ah, now that's another matter. We like to remember them. You never know when we might be able to drop their names into the conversation. Hartung, you might know, is not the sort of person one likes to remember as a client, because of his subsequent career . . . None the less, he'll be in our old Golden Book of the distinguished. Just one moment."

And he disappeared to emerge a few moments later with a ledger-book. He thumped it down on the desk in a cloud of dust and opened it up with both hands, then sneezed loudly.

"Not opened this for some time. Now then. H for Hartung. Let me see. Um."

And with much frowning and grunting, little reading-glasses perched on the end of his nose, he laboriously turned the pages.

"There we are," he said. "Jules Hartung, 18 Avenue Montaigne. First became a customer in 1921, last purchase in 1939. In all bought eleven pictures from us. Not one of our most lavish clients, but a nice selection. Very

nice, I may say. Except for some mediocre wallpaper pictures."

"May I see?" Argyll said, coming round to the other
side of the desk in his impatience and peering at the ledger
eagerly.

Gentilly pointed at a scrawled entry half-way down.
"This is the one you want, I imagine. June 1939. One
painting by Jean Floret of a classical scene, delivered to
his house. And another, same painter, of a religious scene,
delivered to a different address. The Boulevard St-
Germain. The unfashionable end."

"Good. Must have been another in the same series."

"What series?"

"There were four," he said briskly, displaying his
knowledge. "All of legal scenes. This other one must be
another one of the series."

"I see."

"Anyway, that's one little problem cleared up. Now,
how can I find out who lived at this other address?"

"You are keen, aren't you? Why does it matter?"

"It probably doesn't. Just being thorough."

Gentilly shook his head doubtfully. "I don't see how it
can be done. With a lot of work you could find out who
owned the apartment, if that's what it was. But the
chances are that it was rented. I don't imagine there's the
slightest chance of finding out who lived there."

"Oh," he said, disappointed. "That's a nuisance. What
about Hartung himself? How would I get hold of people
who knew him?"

"It was a long time ago, and he's not the sort of person people like to remember. People did bad things in the war; but he . . . Do you know the story?"

"Bits. I know he hanged himself."

"Yes. Good thing too. I believe he was quite popular in the social whirl before the war. Very beautiful wife. But you won't get many people admitting to having been his friend now. Not that there can be many left alive. It's a very long time ago. All forgotten."

"Perhaps not."

"As you say; perhaps not. But it should be. The war's over. Just history. What people did in the past."

*D*ESPITE his enhanced confidence in his ability to wheedle information out of fellow art dealers, Argyll's subsequent assault on Jean-Luc Besson was not a great success.

After he left Rosier Frères, he calculated carefully, decided that the money would just run a taxi and directed it to Besson's address. Simple and successful so far. He knocked, and Besson opened—about forty, with thinning hair pasted over the front of his scalp to spread it as widely as possible, and an unexpectedly open and friendly face.

Argyll introduced himself with a false name and, despite a none-too-convincing excuse for the visit, Besson invited him in. Coffee? Or tea? The English drink tea, don't they?

He even began chattering away as the coffee was made

without Argyll having to prompt him. He was taking a few days off, he said, as his visitor shuffled discreetly around the apartment eyeing the paintings. Not bad at all. It was a habit that both he and Flavia had. Flavia did it because she was in the police and had a suspicious mind; he did it because he was an art dealer and couldn't help making running assessments of other people's possessions. It wasn't polite, really, but it was occasionally useful. He checked quickly through the pictures, eyed up the furniture, examined the grandfather clock and was on to the collection of photographs in art nouveau silver frames before the water was even boiling. Nothing of interest there; just Besson in the company of various anonymous figures. Relations, by the look of them.

"You know how it is, I'm sure," Besson was saying as he looked up and scuttled back to his seat. "You wake up and just decide you can't face it today. All those customers coming in, looking at your pictures, then finding out the price and sucking in their breath in a disapproving fashion like you're a fairground pickpocket. Or even worse, trying to look as though they could easily afford it when you know for sure they can't. The only ones I like are the people who tell you frankly they'd love it if they had the money. But of course, you don't make an income out of them. Do you have a gallery, Mr. Byrnes?"

"I work in one," Argyll lied cautiously.

"Really? Where? London?"

"That's right. Called Byrnes Galleries."

"Are you that Byrnes? Sir Edward Byrnes?"

"Oh, no," he said, thinking that maybe it would have been better to have chosen a less prominent name. "He's my, ah, uncle. This is a Gervex, isn't it?" he said, pointing with sudden interest at a small but beautifully painted portrait of a woman.

Besson nodded. "Handsome, don't you think? One of my favourites."

"You mainly do nineteenth-century French, then?"

"Not mainly. Only. Got to specialize these days. There's nothing worse than a reputation for having broad tastes. People only think you know what you're doing if you narrow your range down."

"Oh."

"You sound surprised."

"I am. Well, more disappointed, in fact."

"Why's that?"

"Because it sort of means I've wasted my time. And yours. I've got a painting, you see, that I was told might have passed through your hands at one stage. But as it's not nineteenth-century, then perhaps I was told wrong. It's a shame, I dearly want to find out about it."

"I do occasionally handle other stuff. What is it?"

"I don't know. It's a Death of Socrates. Late-eighteenth century."

As discreetly as possible Argyll watched to see what the reaction to this was. Apart from taking a sip of his coffee, Besson appeared to cope with the surprise quite well. However, there was just a hint of a guarded tone in his voice when he next spoke to indicate that the man was a little cautious.

"Oh, yes?" he said. "Where did it come from?"

"I don't know. I was doing a trip down to Italy a couple of days ago to see what I could lay my hands on. And I bought this painting off a dealer there. Name of Argyll. Jonathan Argyll, he was called. He seemed keen to get rid of it. Very charming man."

Was there any harm in a bit of publicity? he thought to himself. After all, if you were going to lie, there was no reason not to fib to your own advantage. What was he to do after all? Make himself out to be a monster?

"Anyway, he said he was short of cash so he wanted to unload it. I've taken it off his hands. Now, I think it may be valuable, so I was wondering where it came from. I heard that you . . ."

Besson, however, was not going to be co-operative. "No," he said slowly, "never heard of it."

He went through the motions of thinking again. "Sorry. Can't even think of any of my colleagues who might have had it. Tell you what, though, I'll ask around. How does that sound?"

"That's very kind of you," he said. They were both getting into the swing of it now. Each trying to out-lie the other. Argyll was quite enjoying himself and he had a sneaking idea that Besson was as well.

"Not at all," Besson said, reaching for a pad of paper and a pen.

"Tell me where you're staying in Paris and I'll let you know if I find anything out."

Argyll had thought of that one. The last thing he wanted was to hand over the address of his hotel.

"It's OK," he said. "I'll be out all day, then I'm going back to London. You can ring me at the gallery if you find something."

Byrnes was going to be a little surprised at the sudden expansion of his family circle, but Argyll felt moderately confident he would deal with the situation with his accustomed aplomb.

"What are you doing this evening?"

"Why do you ask?"

"How about going out? I'm going to a wonderful club, in the Rue Mouffetard. Very new, very good. If you like, I could pick you up at your hotel . . ."

Some people are very persistent. Argyll gripped his leg and grimaced. "Oh, I couldn't." And slapped his leg.

Besson looked enquiringly.

"Broke it a year ago. It's still painful. I have to be careful."

"How dreadful."

Argyll got up, and shook Besson warmly by the hand. "Thanks all the same. Now, I must run."

"On that leg?"

They exchanged a knowing smile, and Argyll left, remembering to limp slightly until he was out of sight.

•   •   •

*A*S she was being ushered into Inspector Janet's office in the great, bleak building on the Île de la Cité Flavia realized that, for the first time since she'd left Rome, she felt comfortable. It was a bad sign, in her view. She was getting too settled. The station was reassuringly familiar: the desk by the entrance manned by a bored policeman; the notice-boards in the corridor full of schedules and rotas and roughly printed complaints from the union about the latest pay offer; the glossy but peeling paint. It all made her feel alarmingly at home. She was becoming too used to her job. She must watch that.

She was there largely as a matter of courtesy. A question of etiquette, really. If one of Janet's underlings was discovered galumphing around Italy without so much as a by-your-leave, Bottando would have been mightily put out. It's not done, that sort of thing. You ask first. Then you go galumphing around.

Above all with Janet; Franco-Italian relations in the matter of art thefts were delightfully harmonious, and had been for years. There was no reason at all to be deceitful, and many reasons not to damage a perfect understanding.

Nor did either Bottando or Flavia want to be deceitful. At least, they didn't want to deceive Janet. The trouble was this sneaking feeling in the back of her mind that Janet might, perhaps, be deceiving them. But she was ushered in, given a warm embrace and a cup of coffee, sat herself down on a comfortable seat just out of range of the man's halitosis and prattled on about holidays and sights and museums.

It was Janet himself who brought up the subject of a certain painting.

"Is that why you're here? Taddeo has been on the phone about it a couple of times."

"That's the one. Although the picture itself is not so important anymore. It was given back to the owner yesterday. I'm sorry I didn't tell you in advance, but—"

He waved it aside. "No matter. As I say, we weren't formally interested anyway. Where did it come from?"

"A man called Jean Rouxel."

Janet looked impressed. "Oho. How very interesting."

"You know him?"

"Oh, yes. Not that there's anything surprising in that. A very distinguished man. One of those people who've wielded influence for what seems like decades. You know he was awarded—"

"The Europa prize. Yes, I do. We're not interested in that. All I'm trying to do is put together a few bits and pieces about these two murders in Rome. When I do that, then I can go home."

"Is there anything I can do?"

Flavia smiled sweetly. "I was hoping you'd say that."

"I know. That's why I said it. I mean, this is really our patch. I think it would be much the easiest course if you just told me what you need. There is no real point in staying here, doing stuff that we can almost certainly do in half the time. I could send you the results straight to Rome."

"That's an idea. A tempting one," she said. "Well, then.

There was a phone call. To Ellman and probably from Paris. It seems to have been what sent him off to Rome. Is there any way you could find out where it came from?"

Janet looked alarmed at the idea. "I'm really not very good at this sort of thing. Can it be done? I've not a clue. I'll have to ask."

"I can give you the number dialled, and the approximate time it was made."

"That would be a help."

So she dictated and he jotted down, ending by promising to see what he could do.

"Anything else?"

"Yes. The front-runner for the burglar of Rouxel's château is a man called Besson."

Janet looked mildly put out at the mention of the name. "More than likely," he said glumly.

"You know him?"

"Oh, yes. Monsieur Besson and I go back a long way. I've been trying to look him up for years. Never succeeded, though. Come close, once or twice, but never pinned him down. What's he been up to, exactly?"

Flavia explained.

"There you are," Janet said with satisfaction. "Lots of suspicion and likelihood, but will we ever get any proof? No. You can bet your life that on the evening Rouxel's place was burgled, Besson was surrounded by admirers at a party a hundred kilometres away with at least a dozen people ready to swear blind he never left the room, not even to go to the toilet. All lying through their teeth of course, but we'll never shake them. Even if we did get your Delorme to say in court that Besson gave him the picture, Besson will claim he bought it at some country auction in outer Poland. How did he know where the picture was?"

Flavia explained again about the exhibition and Besson's suddenly leaving the organizing team.

"Ah, yes. I remember that. That was me. I heard he was attached to the thing, so gave them a little warning that he was not the sort of person to be left in a room unguarded. Once I gave the organizer a good look at his file he took the point. Petty stuff, I know, but harassing is all we can do."

"That's another thing. I was told he'd already been arrested. And his arrest seems to have prompted our suspect with the scar into action."

Here Janet shook his head. "Not by us, alas."

"Are you certain?"

He looked mildly irritated. "Of course. We manage to arrest people so rarely I always hear about it. Certainly had it been Besson. Now, anything else?"

"This man with a scar."

Janet shook his head once more. "Not a clue. If you want to spend an afternoon going through the mug shots . . . ?"

"No. Whoever he is, he doesn't sound like a regular art thief."

"Possibly not. You reckon he's the killer?"

"The best candidate. The trouble is, he seems too smart by half."

"Why?"

"He knows so much. He knew Argyll would be at the railway station. In Rome he knew where Muller lived, where Ellman was to be found, and where Argyll was. He made an appointment with Argyll, we were waiting and he didn't show up. It mystifies me how he knows all this."

"There I have no advice to offer. Anything else?"

"Hartung. Jules Hartung."

"That's going back a long way."

"I know. But he was Muller's father."

"Not much I can say. I mean, I've vaguely heard of him. War crimes, right?"

"That sort of thing."

"I was much too young. Besides, I come from the east; I didn't come to Paris until the late fifties. We didn't pay much attention to that sort of thing. So there's not much I can say."

"He was Jewish. Is there some sort of deportation documentation centre? The sort of place that might hold records? Just an idea."

"There's one in the Marais. It has mounds of manuscripts and all that on the war period. I could ring for you, if you wanted to go down. Give you an introduction. It might save you some time. Or I could send someone down myself. As I say, it would be quicker if you went back home."

But she asked him to phone for her anyway. She might have time to look in before she left. Quite possibly futile, but you never knew. She asked him to go ahead, and then left, promising to ring back in the evening to see what he'd come up with. Strange that he was so keen for her to go back to Rome, she thought as she went back into the street.

12

"AND what did you do this afternoon?" he asked when he had found Flavia again. It had been one of those afternoons. He got back, she wasn't there. He left a note saying he'd got nowhere with Besson, and went out. She came in. She went out again. They finally met at well past seven, and Argyll gave full and complete details of his inability to extract any useful information. What had she accomplished?

"I saw Janet," she said, "and then I went shopping." She was in an extraordinarily good mood, considering.

"You what?"

"I went shopping. I've been wearing the same clothes for months. And had my hair done. Just as well, too, considering what little progress you made. Just a second."

"Just a fifteen minutes" doesn't sound quite as good, and that was the time she spent in the bathroom. Even Argyll, however, no great connoisseur of these matters, was impressed by the transformation.

"Good heavens."

"Is that the best you can do?" she asked, twirling herself around and admiring the result in the mirror.

"You look very handsome."

"I do not look very handsome, young man. I look gorgeous. Absolutely devastating. It was a sale. I couldn't resist."

She admired herself some more. "Years since I had a short, black and slinky. I shouldn't have denied the world the pleasure. What about the shoes?"

"Very nice."

"I think you need a bit of practice at this sort of thing," she said sternly, still admiring herself. "I know I don't get dressed up too often, but when I do it would be nice to have a slightly more enthusiastic response. Next time, try 'wonderful.' Or 'fantastic.' Something like that."

"All right. What's your shopping got to do with my not making any progress with Besson?"

"Because I shall have to do it myself. I want to talk to him. Was he, or was he not, arrested? I'm going out for the evening."

"Without me?"

"Of course without you. I don't want you to strain your leg."

Argyll looked a little peeved. "Is it so important, really?" he asked.

"Maybe not, but we've lost another lead. That is, no calls were made from Paris to Ellman's number. I just talked to Janet. He's going to ask the Swiss nicely to see what they can do from their end. But Besson is fast becoming one of the few areas left to explore."

"I hope you're going to be careful. You don't want me to hang around discreetly in the background?"

"No. You can't be discreet, and if Besson so much as catches a whiff of you, it'll be ruined. Don't worry. I'll be fine. Must get more of these things," she said reflectively, as she put on her coat and checked to make sure she still looked as beautiful.

And she walked out the door, leaving Argyll feeling a trifle abandoned and more than a little concerned.

*B*Y the time she came back, the ebullient mood had dissipated. She walked in the door of the hotel room, clicked on the light, and collapsed in the easy chair by the window.

Argyll had, within ten minutes if he judged it right, just fallen asleep after a long, anxious but otherwise extremely dull evening, and was not amused. He looked at his watch.

"God almighty. It's one in the morning."

"I know." Her hair was dishevelled, the dress awry, and her feet dirty. She looked tired, but very stimulated.

"What on earth happened? You look as though you've been dragged through a hedge."

"Quite close. And my own fault as well. Dammit."

He sat up, shook himself awake, and looked at her more closely. "You do look a mess. I'll run you a bath."

She nodded, and he trotted next door to oblige while she searched the little fridge in the corner for something restoring.

"I've been on mineral water all evening," she complained. "I thought I'd better keep my wits about me."

When the bath was run, she dropped in with a loud sigh of relief, while Argyll perched on the toilet and pressed for an account of the evening's entertainment.

To begin with, she began, it went like a dream, if an extended one. She'd gone to Besson's street, checked he was at home, and waited. He'd emerged at nine and gone, alone, to a restaurant near by. She hadn't anticipated such a golden opportunity arising quite so soon, but who was she to throw it away? So she'd gone in, made sure Besson was eating on his own, and bribed the waiter to give her an adjoining table.

She'd given him a long sultry look from over the top of her aperitif and, within ten minutes, bingo. She was sitting at his table and the evening was off to a roaring start.

"Not only did he pay for the meal," she said parenthetically, "but he was quite delightful company. I've never had so many compliments thrust upon me in such a short space of time in my life."

Argyll grunted non-committally.

"You should try it some time," she said. "It works wonders."

Another grunt. "I have been," he pointed out. "The only response I get is warnings about spilling my soup."

"And," she went on, "if I may say so, I gave pretty good value for money as well. I laughed. I simpered. He told his little stories about the art world, and I smiled, looked grave and appalled in all the right places, and occasionally rested my hand appreciatively on his arm at particularly well-delivered anecdotes. I told him how wonderful it must be to have beautiful objects in his arms all the time, and gave him a lustful look. Such fun."

Argyll was beginning to feel uncomfortable, so he crossed his arms and listened.

"I really laid it on with a trowel. I was fascinated by his stories and, in short, behaved like a complete moron. And he fell for it. Hook, line and sinker. Really. It's amazing how gullible men can be. At least you would never be that easily taken in."

"I should hope not, indeed," Argyll said, crossing his legs for the sake of symmetry.

"The important point was that he did have this painting on his hands—he didn't say where he'd got it."

"That's not so great. We knew that."

"Patience. The only touchy moment was after the meal, when he suggested going back to his apartment. I had this horrible vision of running around the sofa protesting my virtue. And, as you point out, I still hadn't found out much. Fortunately, I remembered about the club. So I suggested we go dancing instead. I was sure someone like him knew all the best places. Can't say I was in the mood, but duty calls and all that."

"And so you did?"

"And so I did."

"So that's why you're so tired."

"Certainly not. I'm in my prime. Men may start going downhill in their thirties, but women are at their peak. I could dance all night if need be. Not that I get the opportunity with you. Besson, however, is a wonderful dancer, if a little touchy-feely."

Argyll restrained himself. He had a feeling Flavia was enjoying this. "So why the dishevelled, exhausted look?"

"I'm coming to that," she said. "I decided things were going a bit too slowly, so I did the hard-to-get act. He redoubled his efforts to impress me. And when I asked him how lucrative art dealing was, in a gold-digging fashion, he said enough, if you play it right, but of course it had other uses.

"So of course I asked what that meant. He looked all secretive and said it was a useful front."

"A front?"

"Yes. Absurd, isn't it? Anyway, so I said, don't tell me I'm dancing with a drug-dealer, and he looked upset and said, no, of course not, he was on the right side of the law."

"Oh, yes?"

"That's right. I squeaked with excitement—you would have been appalled if you'd been there—"

"I'm appalled enough already."

"—and said, 'So you're a *spy*. I *knew* there was something special about you.' All round-eyed with amazement. So he said not exactly. But he did help the Authorities—just like that, with a distinct capital A—occasionally. They knew he could be trusted.

" 'Ooh, tell me, tell me,' I said. Then, damn him, he came over all coy. He wasn't at liberty to disclose . . ."

"God almighty," Argyll said.

"Yeah, I know. In his defence I must say he was getting a little drunk by this stage, and my flattery had addled his brain. But I managed to get some hints. He'd recently played an important part in an operation. Matters of State, he said. He couldn't tell me the details even if he'd wanted to. He was just a small part and didn't know everything.

"Anyway, that's when I made my discovery. And my mistake. He was talking about his relations with the Authorities, so I took a gamble. 'What about your being arrested by the art police?' I said. 'How did you know about that?' he said. I smiled, and said I thought he'd said it. He gave me a very suspicious look and said he had to go to the toilet. I saw him on the phone, and I wasn't going to get caught like that. So I grabbed my coat and made a dash for it.

"Unfortunately—and this is where we get to the dishevelled part—his friends were rather quick. They caught up with me as I was getting close to the Métro. Jumped out of the car and grabbed me."

"But here you are."

"Of course. I haven't lived in Rome for years without learning how to deal with little things like that. I screamed bloody murder. Help, Rape, Save me. There were half a dozen winos drinking themselves into a stupor round the corner, and they picked up their bottles and ran to my rescue."

Argyll had given up making comments by this stage. He just looked at her in amazement.

"It was like the cavalry: Sir Lancelot of the Wine Lake. They charged into action, swinging their bottles round their heads and beat the very hell out of them. It only took a couple of minutes, and there they were, lying on the pavement, out cold. Everybody was very jolly about it, for a while.

"And," she went on, "one of them had a little scar above his left eyebrow."

"Are you sure?"

"Yes. Absolutely. Of course, his face was a bit mussed up by then. But that scar, you know. Seemed a bit much of a coincidence."

"So who is he?"

"I didn't have time to find out. A police car came round the corner; my gallant defenders picked up their bottles, shook my hand, and melted into the background. I decided I ought to do likewise."

"Why?"

"Because it stinks to high heaven. Janet was lying; at

least I found that out. So, I thought, if I've just beaten up a copper, I'm in real trouble here."

"Stop," said Argyll, thinking that this had gone on for too long. "This is getting absurd. Three days ago I was a humble art dealer, doing my best to earn a modest living. Now, thanks to you, I'm associated with people who push bottles into policemen's faces."

"What do you mean, thanks to me?"

"I didn't hit him, did I?"

Flavia looked at him appalled. "How ungrateful can you get?" she asked. "I'm not doing this for my benefit, you know."

"Whose, then?"

"You were the one who started all this with that picture."

"I didn't do any of the rest, though. Besides, it's all over."

"What do you mean?"

"I've been thinking. This is getting too complicated and dangerous. If Janet is going out of his way to obstruct us, we're wasting our time. Go home, hand it all over to Bottando and let him deal with it. This needs a higher authority."

"Wimp," she said, feeling more than a little betrayed by this correct but irritating opinion.

"So why don't we go home? A job well done."

"Because of Ellman."

"Carabinieri. Your friend Fabriano. Let him sort it out."

"And we don't know why it was stolen."

"So? I don't care. People steal all sorts of things. Do you have to draw up a psychological profile every time something goes missing? The world is full of lunatics."

She sat on the bed and made a face. "I'm not happy," she pronounced. "I don't feel as though I've got to the bottom of this. Do you really want to go home?"

"Yes. I've had enough of this."

"Off you go, then."

"What?"

"Off you go. Go back home and sell pictures."

"What about you?"

"I shall carry on with my work. With or without the help of you. Or Janet."

"That's not what I meant."

"Tough. That's the way it is. You want to go, you go. And I will do my job, filling up any spare hours thinking of you anew as a rotten, treacherous, cowardly toad who'd abandoned his fiancée in dangerous circumstances."

Argyll thought about that. "Did you say fiancée?"

"No," she said.

"Yes, you did."

"No, I didn't."

"You did. I heard you."

"It slipped out by accident."

"Oh. What I meant was, anyway, that we should both go back to Rome. But, if you're staying, I shall stay too.

I wouldn't dream of leaving my fiancée in such a pickle when I'm needed."

"I'm not your fiancée. You've never asked me. And I'm not in a pickle."

"Have it your own way. I'm not going. But on one condition."

"What's that?"

"If you ever do consent to go back home, we go and look at a new apartment."

"You drive a hard bargain."

He nodded.

"Oh, very well, then."

"Wonderful. What a nice fiancée you are."

"I'm not your fiancée."

"Have it your own way."

And, both of them feeling they had struck an acceptable, if expensive, deal, they went to sleep.

13

"*I* think," she said in the morning, "we'd better think of changing hotels."

"Why?"

"Because someone is looking for us and I don't think I'd like him much. It takes time to track people down in hotels, but when I go back to Rome I want to go with my intestines in working order, not scattered around the landscape like a plate of spaghetti."

"I'm eating my breakfast. Do you mind?"

"Sorry. But you get the point. We change hotels, we find one a little bit more down-market that doesn't get you to fill out little forms, and we use a different name. OK?"

"How exciting."

"Good. Let's go."

Flavia's notion of somewhere a bit less obvious was an entirely disreputable establishment in a dingy alley off the Boulevard Rochechouart. It probably hadn't been painted since it was built and, when they checked in, the man on the desk leered at Argyll through his three-day stubble and demanded cash in advance. But at least Flavia was correct in thinking that he wasn't going to waste precious time getting them to fill in registration forms for the police. It was not that sort of hotel. They signed in under the name of Smith. Argyll had always wanted to sign into a hotel under the name of Smith.

The room was even worse than the lobby. The wallpaper was a horrible shade of pink with little flowers on it, stained with damp and peeling off in several places. The furniture consisted of a bed, a hard chair and a metal table with a plastic top. There was an air of damp and misery about it that gave both of them the shivers.

"I can't imagine anybody would want to stay long here," Argyll commented as he looked around their new and, he hoped, very temporary home.

"I think that most customers are in and out of here so fast they don't notice the wallpaper. Besides, they've probably got other things on their mind. I must say, I never thought of you as a person who went to hotels for loose women."

"I never realized you *were* one. Come on, the sooner we're out of here the better. Didn't you say something about ringing Bottando?"

So she had. She'd rather hoped he'd forgotten about that. With great reluctance, she went to a telephone booth in the nearest post office and dialled.

"I was wondering when you'd turn up," the General said when he picked up the phone. "Where are you?"

She explained. "Jonathan reckons that everything is all sorted out and we should come home. I want to keep on plugging."

"Obviously, if you want to curtail your holiday, that's fine by me. It may well be that you're wasting your time there."

"How's Fabriano?"

"Him? Oh, getting nowhere, I gather. Vast piles of information which add up to nothing. Although he has established that the same gun killed Muller and Ellman. And that it belonged to Ellman. Which, I must admit, doesn't surprise me. He has eliminated dozens of people from his enquiries, which I suppose is negative progress. How are you doing?"

Flavia summarized, and Bottando drew in his breath.

"Look, my dear, I know what you're like, but you must be more careful. What on earth are you doing approaching these people on your own? You could have got very badly hurt. Why don't you just get Janet to pull Besson in? Be simple and straightforward for once."

"Because."

"Because what?"

"Because Janet is playing silly buggers, that's why."

"Do you want me to talk to him?"

"No. I don't want him to know what I think. You can fight with him later, if you want. He wants me to go home. So does Jonathan. In fact, I'm the only one who really wants to give this a bit more time."

Bottando thought. "I don't know that I can advise you. The Carabinieri need help, even though Fabriano refuses to acknowledge it, and this is a double murder. But whether or not you are wasting your time I can't tell you. All I can say is that if you decide to come home you can; then we can tell Fabriano that we've done our bit and he's on his own. Or do you want to show him you're better at this than he is?"

"That's a very unfair question."

"It just crossed my mind."

"I want to get to the bottom of this."

"In that case you'd better hang on. Anything I can do?"

"One thing," she said, looking at the meter ticking away. "A phone call to Ellman. It didn't come from Paris, apparently. I asked Janet to contact the Swiss, but could you put a bit of pressure on them as well?"

"Fine," he said. "I'll take care of it."

"Well?" asked Argyll as she emerged.

Flavia thought carefully. "He's absolutely adamant that I should carry on. Very keen to continue the investigation," she said. "Absolutely essential, he reckons."

"Oh," he replied, a bit disappointed. There was an auction sale just outside Naples the next day he'd been hoping to get to. "So I suppose we do, then."

"Yes. No choice. Sorry."

"We are running awfully short of money, you know."

"I know. We'll just have to improvise."

"How do you improvise about money?"

"I'll think about it. Meantime, I want to go to this documentation centre. You coming?"

So they walked south, back into the proper, tourist, *Guide Michelin* part of the city, away from the run-down streets, the hordes of lost and sad-looking inhabitants, across and through the sweat-shop district of overworked women from Asia on whose shoulders rests the city's reputation for *haute couture,* and then again east into the ever more elegant Marais, long since shorn of the down-at-heel occupants who once gave the area its charm.

In this part of the world lay the Jewish documentation centre, because that was where the Jewish quarter once was, until the combined efforts of Nazis and, more recently, property developers reduced it to a couple of streets.

The Rue Geoffroy-l'Asnier was not a major street in the tourist itinerary. One building of considerable beauty, a concrete memorial to the deported of the war, and that was about it. The rest had been flattened to make way for something. No one seemed too sure what it was. Even in the sunlight it seemed forlorn and half abandoned.

There was a minor debate as the pair of them stood outside, trying to decide who should take on the task of going inside and searching for useful information. Flavia particularly wanted to go in; she felt as though she should turn her mind once more to the attempt to give form to this hodge-podge of miscellaneous information.

"So, you or me?" she said, when her train of thought petered out. "Personally, I think I'd be better."

"OK. I've thought of something else to do anyway. I'm off to see about paintings. See you later."

*F*LAVIA went into the building next to the monument to the deported, checked that Janet had, after all, phoned to say she was coming, signed in and then began making earnest enquiries. The woman at the desk was perfectly happy to help—there was almost nobody else in the building, after all—and she was shown to a vast cabinet full of filing cards. The name Jules Hartung was there, and a dossier number, which she wrote on a request form and handed back in. At the same time, the archivist recommended another series of dossiers on confiscated and looted property. If Hartung was rich and dispossessed, then there might well be some account of him, if only a brief one, in that as well.

She thanked the woman, sat down and waited, filling up the time by reading a pamphlet the dear lady brought to her on the confiscation of property during the occupation. She read it with considerable attention, having half formed in her mind the theory that Hartung's art collection might be at the bottom of this somewhere.

It was a reasonable hypothesis, after all. Since the Berlin

Wall had come down, long-lost treasures had been popping up in the basements of obscure East-European museums like mushrooms. Hundreds of paintings, looted in the war and never seen since, were now giving curators major headaches and exercising the minds of diplomats. Was it possible, she thought as she read, that all this business was stimulated by the possession of a major art collection?

Not that she knew anything about it, she realized as she ploughed her way through the pages. She'd never conceived that the looting was so well and bureaucratically organized. Extracts of letters from a secretary at the German embassy in Paris detailed how a special art force, the Einsatzstab Rosenberg, methodically arrested people, searched houses, confiscated goods and transported the product of their labours to Germany. An interim report of 1943 announced that it had confiscated more than 5,000 paintings. By the time its labours were interrupted by the untimely arrival of the Liberation, it had shifted nearly 22,000 articles to Germany. With the diligence of the committed thief, the plunderers made meticulous notes of their labours. None the less, the article concluded by announcing that a large proportion had never been seen again.

"Here you are, mademoiselle," said the archivist, dragging Flavia from her reading and temporarily confusing her before she realized she was being addressed. The woman handed over a bulky file.

"Confiscated goods. I hope you read German. We'll bring you the other document you ordered in a while."

Flavia's face fell as she opened the dossier. Bad German handwriting was her idea of a nightmare. Still, she wasn't there to enjoy herself, so screwing up eyes with concentration, and with the library's best German dictionary by her side, she did her best.

It wasn't as bad as she feared. The names of the previous owners were at the top of the sheet, so in most cases she merely had to check them off, and head on for the next document. Even so, it took two hours of hard work, and a depressing experience it was, skimming through dozens of lists of rings, jewels, prints, drawings, statues and paintings.

She found it at half-past one. Hartung, Jules; 18 Avenue Montaigne. List of goods confiscated on 27 June 1943, pursuant to orders given under Operation Razor on the twenty-third of the same month.

A rich haul, judging by the size of the list. Seventy-five paintings, 200 drawings, 37 bronzes, 12 marbles and 5 boxes of jewellery. Not bad for a morning's work. A nice collection, she thought, if the objects really were what the inventory claimed. Rubens, Teniers, Claude, Watteau, they were all there.

But nothing by this Floret man, even though she checked twice. Nothing matching the title. Damnation, she thought. There goes another theory. And, if, this was something to do with the man's collection, why concen-

trate on a minor painting when there were all these good-
ies to be had?

"Mademoiselle di Stefano?"

She looked up again. "Yes?"

"Would you come and see the director, please?"

Not again, she thought, eyeing the fastest route to the
door as she stood up. If I have to take to my heels again
I shall scream.

But the librarian still seemed friendly enough, almost
apologetic in fact, and led her across to an office at the
far end of the room without the slightest hint that she was
preparing a trap. I'm getting paranoid, she thought.

"I'm delighted to meet you," said the director, extending his hand in greeting as he introduced himself as Fran-
çois Thuillier. "I hope you've been getting what you
need."

"So far, yes," Flavia replied, still a little cautious about
all this. In her experience directors of archives did not
personally welcome each customer, no matter how bad
trade was. "I'm still waiting for another file, though."

"Ah, that'll be the one on Hartung, no?"

"That's right."

"I'm afraid we have a problem there."

Oh, I get it, she thought. I knew life was a little too
easy this afternoon. Just saving up the little sting in the
tail.

"It's very embarrassing to have to admit it, of course,
but I'm sorry to tell you that we can't seem to lay our
hands on it at the moment."

"You've lost it?"

"Ah, yes. That's right."

"That's a pity."

"It's just not in place. I assume that it wasn't put back after the last reader—"

"What last reader? When was this?"

"I really don't know," he said.

"And it disappeared?"

"That's right."

"Is it such a popular file?"

"No, not at all. I'm dreadfully sorry, but I'm sure it will turn up soon."

Flavia was not so certain, but she smiled her most plaintive smile, and explained her problem. She was running out of money, had little time . . .

Thuillier smiled sympathetically. "Believe me, in the last hour or so we've tried very hard. I think it must have been put back in the wrong place. I'm afraid we have no choice but to wait until it turns up. However, if you like I am able to tell you what I know of this case. I can do that, at least."

She stared at him. What was going on here? she wondered. Thuillier looked very upset about something, and she had an idea she knew what it was.

"When were you told not to let me see this file?" she asked.

He spread his hands hopelessly. "I can't answer that," he said. "But it's true that we don't have it."

"I see."

"And I shouldn't have said that," he went on. "But I don't like interference. So, I will tell you what I can, if you want to hear."

"You know what's in it?"

"Not word for word, obviously. But occasionally if someone asks for something I have a quick look. We had an enquiry about six months ago about the Hartung family and I looked through the file. Unfortunately the man in question never contacted us again."

"What was his name?"

The director frowned. "I don't know whether I should tell you."

"Oh, please do. After all, this man might be able to help me as well. You don't like interference, remember. Nor do I."

"True. Just a moment."

And he rummaged in his desk for a diary and flicked through the pages. "Ah, yes," he said. "Here we are. His name was Muller. With an address in Rome. Have you heard of him?"

"Oh, yes. I know him well," Flavia said, her heart beating a little faster at the news. So she wasn't wasting her time after all.

"And, as I say, I had a look at the file."

She waited, and he smiled at her.

"Well? Go on, then. Please tell me."

Thuillier placed the tips of his fingers together in scholastic mode. "You must remember," he began cautiously, "that it is far from being a full account. For that you would need the judicial dossiers prepared in advance of his trial."

"Where can I get those?"

He smiled. "I very much doubt that you can. They're classified. Not to be released for a century."

"I can ask."

"You can. All I can say is that I think you'd be wasting your time."

"I think you're right."

"Tell me, how much exactly do you know about this period? Or about Hartung?"

Flavia confessed that she didn't know much. What she'd learnt at school, mainly, together with what she'd found out about Hartung in the investigation.

"Hartung's son was trying to find out about him. I suppose that's natural, but it did lead to his death. He was some sort of industrialist, wasn't he?"

Thuillier nodded. "That's right. Chemicals, mainly, but many other things as well. Very large family firm, founded about the turn of the century. He was the second generation and was the main figure who built it up. None of this, by the way, is in the files. It's just what I know."

"The more the better. I think I may find out more by listening to you than I would have by reading. I'm quite glad now the file's lost."

Thuillier smiled and, suitably encouraged by her perfectly genuine appreciation, went on.

"Well then. He was born in the 1890s and his family was a long-established part of the Jewish community in

Paris. Even before Hartung et Cie took off they were wealthy, from various sorts of trade. Hartung was both a capitalist and a liberal. Workers' housing projects, educational schemes, all the usual sort of thing you find in the more enlightened entrepreneurs of the day. He was one of the few employers to support the idea of statutory paid holidays for workers in the 1930s. He fought in the First World War and, if I remember correctly, was injured and decorated. I could find out the details if you want . . ."

"No, no," she said, holding up her hand. "Perhaps later if it's needed."

"As you wish. From the 1930s onwards, his career took on a new aspect. Like many French Jews, he had relations in Germany and, unlike many, he was perceptive enough to realize that the rise of Hitler was not something that would just go away if he kept his head down. So he appears to have embarked on a double-edged policy. On the one hand, helping Jews in Germany, and on the other keeping up contacts with the authorities there and with the French Right.

"Now, with hindsight, it is clear that this was opportunism, playing the market both ways, so to speak. His lack of principle is obvious—now. Then, it was less clear. Lots of people were doing exactly the same; many were far more open in supporting the Right than he was. As in many crises, a lot of people merely wanted to keep themselves and their families safe, and would do whatever was necessary."

"But Hartung was different."

"Not really. He wanted to keep safe, and to keep his factories going. And he was successful; his factories were left surprisingly alone. He said, I believe, that this was due to his skill, the fact that they produced essential goods and his ability to pay vast bribes to fend off confiscation. Certainly he talked more and more about running out of funds.

"He had a wife, very much younger than himself and very much more politically minded. I don't think it was a close marriage, but they observed all the formalities. She was drawn more and more into the Resistance, and he inevitably got to know something of what she was doing. He was only on the fringes, mind; he was never allowed close in. But through her, he knew much more than he would have done otherwise. This, it seemed, was a fatal mistake."

"I'm sorry to interrupt," Flavia said quickly, looking up from her note-pad, into which she had been writing as furiously and as fast as she could go. "His family. They got out?"

"That's right. His wife stayed, though. But his son was smuggled abroad at some stage."

"Yes. That checks. I'm sorry. I interrupted."

"That's all right. Hartung's wife was associated with a Resistance cell code-named Pilot. Do you know about those?"

"A little."

"They were given code-names, mainly for radio iden-

tification purposes or for bureaucratic and security reasons in England. They were strictly isolated from each
other to limit the damage if anything should go wrong. In
this case, there was some overlap with another, bigger
group called Pascal. In all, about a hundred and fifty people were involved."

Thuillier rubbed his glasses and paused for a while to
collect his thoughts. Flavia looked suitably sombre and
encouraging. She was having a hard time imagining all
this.

"There were rumours of a traitor, of course. Perhaps
that was part of the secretive life these people had to live.
It was inevitable that suspicion and mistrust should thrive.
But there was enough evidence that there was some basis
to it. Operations went wrong; saboteurs would go out to
find the Germans waiting for them. Supplies were
dropped, and the Germans were there to catch them.

"Eventually, as suspicion without proof mounted, they
set a trap. A false operation was concocted, and news of
it was given to Hartung alone. It worked: the Germans
turned up again. Hartung fled, and the Germans responded fast. He'd told them more than anyone dreamed
possible; within twelve hours, they'd swept up the whole
of Pilot. Only a small handful survived; and they provided
the damning evidence against Hartung after the war."

"And his wife?"

"She was arrested and was presumably executed. He
didn't even try and save her. He had, apparently, made a
bargain; he passed on what he knew and the Germans left

him alone. When he fled, he told them and they swooped down before their information became too old to be useful."

Flavia looked at him for a long time, nodding to herself and chewing this one over. "And most of what you've just told me came from the missing file?"

"A lot of it, yes."

"Not from the material assembled by the prosecutor?"

"Not directly. That was bound to be confidential until any trial—which of course didn't happen. But I imagine it would have covered a lot of the same ground, and there were leaks and newspaper reports at the time."

"What happened to Hartung? I know he came back and was arrested."

"Perfectly simple, I think; he was interrogated by the prosecutor's office. It must have become increasingly clear that the case against him was overwhelming, and what the verdict would be. He had a choice of waiting and being guillotined, or cutting short the agony and committing suicide. He chose the latter."

"And there's no doubt that he was a traitor?"

"Absolutely none. We also conduct our interviews, to build up our dossiers of material; we talked to some people ourselves about what happened."

"What did they say?"

Thuillier smiled. "There you are pressing my memory too far, I'm afraid. It was a long time ago and I haven't read those statements. All I can supply there is the names. Not that they will be of much use."

She smiled at him, and asked for the names. He led her out of his office to a bank of card-index drawers. "This may take some time," he said.

So she wandered off to the desk by the entrance. There was one other thing which she needed to do before she left.

"I know it's a little bit irregular," she began when the librarian lady smiled apologetically and asked what she needed. "But would it be so dreadful to know who else is interested in my files. Just paranoia, I know. But if the documents don't turn up, I might be able to approach him and see if he has any notes . . . ?"

"We don't normally do that, you know," she said. "But in the circumstances, I'm sure we could bend the rules a bit."

She rummaged under the desk and took out a book. "No computerized technology here, I'm afraid. We just write it all down in this book. Let's see. A few months back, I'm told. I was on holiday then, otherwise I'd be able to help you."

Flavia flicked through the pages, frowned, then flicked through them again. There was Muller's name, bold and clear. She tore the page out and stuffed it in her handbag. It probably wouldn't be there if she came back for it.

Then she wandered back to Thuillier, still labouring with the file cards. "Oh, dear," he said. "I'm being less help than I hoped. After all that, I can only find one name. The others also seem to have been mislaid."

"What a pity," she said drily.

He handed over an old file card, with a hand-written annotation on it. H. Richards, it said. With an address in England.

"And who is this?"

"I've no idea. I imagine he must have been a liaison officer in the British army or something like that. We have an awful lot of cross-references to material in other libraries and centres. This one, you can see from the reference number, is to papers in the Justice Ministry. It wasn't with the rest, which is why it's still there. I assume that it was testimony collected for the trial. And that means, of course, that it is confidential."

"So you have no idea what's in it?"

"Not a clue. And I doubt you'll be allowed to look. In fact, I know you won't."

"And you don't know if this man is still alive?"

"I'm afraid not."

14

*B*y the time he got to the café in the Rue Rambuteau where he was meant to meet Flavia, Argyll was feeling pleased with himself. He'd spent a quiet afternoon in the Bibliothèque Nationale, doing valiant battle with the microfiche machines, and had emerged victorious. No small thing. His eyes might never recover from being screwed up for four hours, but he had something fascinating to report, and he was looking forward to a pleasant evening out with Flavia telling her all about it, and hearing her tell him how clever he was.

She wasn't there, so he sat in a corner, ordered an aperitif and hummed quietly to himself, staring into space and trying to get his eyes back in full working order. A few minutes into his drink, a hand tapped him on the shoulder. He turned round with a welcoming smile.

"Oh, good, you're back . . ."

The words died on his lips. Standing next to him by the table was the man who had stolen his painting, who had tried to nobble Flavia and, he assumed, already had a murder or two to his credit. He'd read somewhere that if you've murdered once it's easier the second time round. Third time round must be about as exciting as going to the supermarket. For some reason the thought didn't make him any happier.

"Good evening, Mr. Argyll," said this presence. "Do you mind if I sit down?"

"Make yourself at home," he said a little nervously. "I'm afraid we haven't been introduced, though."

Nor, it seemed, were they going to be. The man with the little scar settled himself awfully politely on the chair by the window, and looked apologetic.

"Would you mind my asking when your, ah, friend will be returning?" he said, very much, to Argyll's mind, with the air of someone fully in charge of proceedings.

"Why do you ask?" Argyll said cautiously.

"So that we can have a little conversation. We seem to have been running into each other so often that I thought it might be an idea to swap notes. So far, every time we meet, someone hits me. Frankly, I'm getting a little tired of it."

"Sorry about that."

"Hmm. We also seem to share a common interest in a painting. Your interest I am beginning to find tiresome."

"Are you, indeed? Why is that?" Argyll said perkily, thinking that maybe it wasn't such a good idea to say it had been returned to its owner. If this man was going to such a lot of trouble to get it, he might be distinctly peeved to discover he was now, thanks to Argyll, back at square one again.

"I think for the time being it would be best if I ask the questions."

"Right-ho. Fire away."

"You are an art dealer, is that correct?"

"Yes."

"And your friend? What is her name?"

"Flavia. Di Stefano. Flavia di Stefano."

And there the conversation lapsed into a temporary silence, rather as with two people at a tea-party who feel constrained in each other's presence. Argyll even found himself smiling encouragingly at the other, in the hope it might stimulate him to say something. It didn't. Maybe he was just concentrating on his injuries. Poor man. A bad bruising from Argyll's tackle, then being kicked in the ribs and hit over the head by a bottle thanks to Flavia. He rubbed the plaster over his eye.

"Guess what?" said Flavia as she bounded through the door.

"Do tell," said the Frenchman.

"Oh shit," said Flavia.

One thing about her, nothing wrong with her reflexes.

The moment she saw him, she swung round and hurled her handbag in his direction. She kept enough emergency rations in it to last a month, so the weight and speed were impressive. The bag hit the man on the temple and, in the few half-seconds he was off balance, Flavia picked up the tiny vase on the table and brought it crashing down on him. He groaned loudly and rolled on the floor, clutching his head. Flavia looked triumphantly at Argyll. Saved him again. What would he do without her?

"It's like living with a Rottweiler," Argyll said, beginning to run out of the door of the café with her. "He was being very peaceful, you know."

"Follow me," she yelled back in high excitement as she disappeared into a milling throng of tourists. Not Germans, she thought as he elbowed his way after her. Too many to be Dutch, this would be about the entire country. Czechs, maybe. Whoever they were, they were very good at obscuring the couple's tracks for them. Even though the pursuer was commendably quick, Flavia and Argyll emerged on the other side of the throng with a good five-second lead, and thundered off down what looked like a sort of pedestrianized street a good seventy metres ahead of him.

But he was in rather good shape, and made distinct gains: one of the sort who take care of their bodies. Exercise bikes. Neither Flavia nor Argyll were much into that sort of thing, and while both could put on a decent show of speed in bursts, keeping it up was another matter. Their pursuer kept on gaining.

Then he made his mistake. "Police," he screamed. "Stop them."

One of the most endearing things about the French is that they, especially adolescent Parisians, are so very public-spirited. The Revolutionary tradition of fraternity lives on in them. Policemen—even pretend ones—inspire particular feelings of dislike; no sooner had the man opened his mouth than the entire street was on the alert, watching what was going on, assessing the situation, seeing that the putative fugitives from justice were being steadily overtaken.

With that sense of brotherly concern which they seem to imbibe with their mother's milk, everybody in close proximity moved to assist. Flavia didn't see clearly, as she was otherwise engaged, but the snatched glance over her shoulder was just enough to reveal four different legs extending themselves to intercept their pursuer. He successfully leapt the first two but tripped on the third; the owner of the fourth, perhaps dismayed at being cheated, instead kicked him sharply in the ribs as he went down hard on the pavement.

But he was resilient, no doubt about that. He rolled over and was up almost immediately. Resuming the chase, he again began to gain ground.

There was one chance and Argyll, taking the lead once more, grabbed it and Flavia simultaneously. They were running through that part of Paris which once contained Les Halles, the most beautiful food market in Europe. But in the spirit that gave the world the Beaubourg Centre, this was flattened and replaced with a cheapjack and now increasingly tatty shopping mall which dives ever deeper into the damp and often putrid ground near the Seine. About as good a hiding-place as you can imagine; on the few occasions Argyll had ever ventured into its underground streets, he hadn't even been able to find himself, let alone anyone else.

And access was by escalators, which were edged by flat, smooth, shiny metal sections. The sort of thing that kids love to slide down, despite the best efforts of the authorities to stop them. Flavia had once accused Argyll of having an almost absurd tendency to indulge in childhood pleasures, and now he demonstrated that an infantile sense of fun could have its uses. He hopped on to the side of the escalator and let go, whistling down the incline several times faster than the stairs progressed. Had the situation not been so serious, he would have been tempted to let off a whoop of pleasure. He hadn't done that for years.

Flavia followed him down, thanking heaven she had chosen to wear jeans that morning, then ran with him to the escalator that took them down to the second level. By the time they got there, they were a good way ahead of their pursuer.

"Where now?" she asked.

"Don't ask me. Where do you want to go?"

"Gloucestershire."

"Where?"

"It's in England," she explained.

"I know where . . . oh, never mind. Come on."

And they ran off down the corridor, turning left, right, left, taking short cuts through clothes stores and fast-food outlets, anything to confuse the scent.

It seemed to work. The ominous pounding of feet behind them was no more to be heard, and eventually, slowly coming to believe that they had shaken off the pursuit, they eased up to get their breath back.

Still puffing, but feeling much better, they rounded another corner and realized firstly that they were back where they'd started, and secondly that their pursuer was about six feet in front of them. He had an almost amused smile on his face as he began to run in their direction.

An abrupt about-turn and they disappeared down the next escalator, but this time they were followed closely; they started running again at the bottom with their lead cut to about a second.

It seemed they were in the Métro station; there were tunnels leading off at various places, and a bank of turnstiles directly in front of them. Flavia led the way this time. With the grace of an Olympic athlete in the 400-metre hurdles, she took the turnstile on the run, vaulting over its projecting metal arms with a stylishness that produced ironic cheers from a group of disreputable-looking youths in one corner and a loud protest from a ticket-inspector in another.

Argyll, less elegantly but just as effectively, followed half a second behind her, with the pursuer just behind him. Fortunately, it was at this stage that the forces of law and order decided they had had enough. There was not much to be done about the woman, who was already disappearing down a corridor on the far side of the barrier. The second culprit was heading in the same direction.

But three in as many seconds was too much. With a cry of triumph, the ticket-inspector leapt forward and fastened a powerful hand on the shoulder of the last miscreant, throwing him off balance and making him catch his foot on the stile.

As Argyll in turn vanished down the corridor, he heard the shouts of frustration and furious protest as their pursuer was placed under arrest for trying to avoid paying his 6 franc 20 centimes Métro fare.

*I*N the two hours before the next boat-train left for England from the Gare du Nord, Argyll's opinion of Flavia underwent a major revolution. He'd known her for years, after all, and tended to think of her as one of those upright citizens who keep on the right side of the law. Especially as, in most cases, she was its appointed embodiment and defender. She was, after all, someone who paid her taxes—most of them, at least—and didn't leave her car in no-parking zones unless there was really nowhere else to put it.

However, as Flavia pointed out, it was not her fault she was on the run from a bunch of lunatics. Or that Paris seemed a little too dangerous for them to contemplate with equanimity the prospect of remaining there. Or that this case very inconsiderately scattered its witnesses the length and breadth of Europe.

True enough, but she did seem to take to her new role with more relish than was seemly.

There was, for example, the problem of tickets, it being unreasonable to expect that both of them could get all the way to London without being asked to produce one at some stage. To buy a ticket you need money, and between them they had about thirty-five francs left. Argyll would have just whipped out his Visa card, but Flavia pointed out that the sign at the ticket-office clearly said that all tickets for the nine o'clock departure were sold.

So she stole them. Argyll was appalled, and quite lost his power of speech when she turned up after a ten-minute absence with two tickets in her hand and a smug look on her face.

"You picked someone's pocket?" he squeaked as she explained with a slight giggle.

"It's very easy," she said imperturbably. "You just sit down in the café—"

"But—"

"Don't worry. He was very affluent-looking. He can afford to buy new ones. I also relieved him of a couple of hundred francs."

"Flavia!"

"It's OK. It's in a good cause. I'm sure he had plenty left. Besides, I took his entire wallet; if you insist I can send him a refund when we get back to Rome. I mean, if you want to give your ticket back and wait for our friends to turn up . . ."

Argyll had a tough time with his conscience, but ultimately agreed that, now the deed was done, there was no point in thinking about it too much. So Flavia led the way to the train, they found themselves seats and sat, both nervously hoping that the train would pull out of the station before anyone came looking for them.

It did, although the wait was one of the most anxious either of them had ever spent. Both kept on fabricating reasons for getting up and popping their heads out of the door, scanning the platform with wary eyes just in case a familiar face hove into view. Both fidgeted mercilessly, to the point of provoking irritated looks from the more placid characters ranged alongside them. Both heaved an enormous sigh of relief as the train, with familiar screeching of wheels and jerking movements, lurched forward and slowly gathered speed.

"Now what do we do?" Argyll asked as the bleak northern suburbs of Paris began to rattle past.

"I don't know about you, but I'm going to eat. I'm starving."

They trooped off to the restaurant car and grabbed themselves an early seat. By this time Argyll was beginning to enter into the spirit of things as well: considering what they had been going through in the past few days, rude letters from credit-card managers seemed minor stuff. He ordered two champagne cocktails to start off. Flavia had not only stolen tickets, she'd even managed to steal first-class ones.

"Did that card give an address?" Argyll asked as Flavia's account drew to a close and they launched into supplementary questions.

"Yes. But it's about forty years old. I mean, the chances of this Richards man being still alive are a bit small. The address is in Gloucestershire. Where is Gloucestershire?"

Argyll explained.

"Have you really only got seven francs left? I have twenty. Plus the two hundred I . . ."

Argyll converted it into lire. "We're going to have fun in London with that. What do you fancy, a bus ride and a glass of water? Flavia? Flavia?" he prompted again.

"Hmm? I'm sorry. What was that?"

"Nothing. I was just prattling. What were you thinking about?"

"Janet, mainly. I'm very upset. He was Bottando's closest colleague. Still, it's not my fault. What were you up to?"

"Me?" he said lightly. "Just making a major advance in this business, that's all. Just catching Rouxel in an enormous lie. Nothing serious really, I suppose . . ."

She gave him the sort of look his complacency merited.

"I read through old newspapers, back in 1945 and 1946. It took hours."

"About Hartung?"

"Yup. His return, arrest, and suicide. It caused quite a stink, the whole business, even if it's mainly forgotten now. Fascinating stuff; I was quite engrossed when I finally latched on to it. But the main thing is that it made clear something we already knew."

"And that is?" she asked patiently.

"And that is Rouxel worked for some war-crimes commission early in his career."

"I know. He told you that."

"Not only that, he had the job of assembling evidence against people."

"Including Hartung?"

"Above all Hartung. He was the last person to see the man alive. The papers said so. He interviewed him in his cell one evening and Hartung then hanged himself during the night. And it had slipped his memory. 'I knew of the case,' he said. Seems to me he knew a damn sight more than that."

"Maybe he just doesn't like talking about it."

"Why not?" he went on insistently. "He didn't do anything wrong. On the right side all the time. What could he have to hide?"

She pushed away her plate, suddenly feeling exhausted. There'd been too much crammed into too short a time. Now that they were on their way to what they hoped was safety, or at least a respite, the effects were sweeping over her. She shook her head once more when Argyll asked if she wanted coffee, and said she'd prefer to go back to their seats and sleep.

"No point asking me. I want a few hours not thinking about this," she said as they made their way back. "Perhaps we'll find the answer in Gloucestershire."

15

*S*HE slept like a lamb all the way, content to half-rouse herself when Argyll nudged her at Calais, and to follow in his wake as he steered her around the station to get on the boat, then off it on the other side. The customs and immigration people at both ends were admirably lax, staring blank-eyed and uninterestedly as the troop of weary travellers filed past them, scarcely even bothering to look at their passports, let alone examine them with any care. Either the people chasing them in Paris weren't police, or they hadn't worked out where they might be going, or official liaison channels were silted up again.

"Sleep well?" he asked gently at six o'clock the next morning as he prodded her awake.

She prised open one eye and cautiously looked around her, trying to remember where she was.

"Well, yes. But not for long enough. What's the time?"

"Far too early. But we'll be at Victoria in twenty minutes, or thereabouts. We have to decide what to do next."

"This is your country. What do you recommend?"

"We need transport and we need money. At the moment I also need a friendly face and a bit of reassurance."

Flavia looked disapproving. "You don't want to go and visit your mum, do you?"

"Eh? No. I thought we might drop in on Byrnes. He might be good for a loan. I'm not having you wandering about London acting like something out of Oliver Twist until we have enough."

"Very well. I hardly think he'll be in his gallery waiting for customers at six o'clock in the morning, but we can go and see if you like."

"I doubt if he'll be in the gallery at all. He's not a shopkeeper, you know. I think we should blow our final cash on a taxi and go to his house. If I can remember where it is."

Changing their remaining crumpled notes into sterling was a bit of a difficulty, of course: Victoria Station only has some thirty thousand foreigners passing through every day and sees no reason why it should fuss unduly about helping them to get money. Still, the task was done after a while and Argyll led the way to the taxi stand.

Fortunately, considering the time of day, they did not

get one of those cheerful cabbies that guidebooks talk about so much. A rather taciturn man, in fact, who said not a word to them all the way along Park Lane, down the Bayswater Road, past Notting Hill and into the white-stuccoed elegance of Holland Park.

"Art dealing seems to be a more lucrative business in London than it is in Rome," Flavia observed as they got out at what Argyll vaguely remembered as Byrnes's house. "His garden shed is bigger than our apartment."

"All the more reason to get a new apartment."

"Not now, Jonathan."

"I know. I've often wondered how he does it. Maybe he's better at art dealing than I am."

"Perish the thought."

One of the advantages of being a highly successful, well-established dealer approaching those sunset years when most of the serious work can be safely left to sub-ordinates is that you no longer have to rise at dawn to get on with the business of making money. As other people are downing rapid cups of coffee, you are still safely doz-ing in bed. As they are rushing off to the tube station, you are sitting down at the kitchen table for a leisurely break-fast. As they are frenziedly getting into their work, you are contemplating the letters page of the newspaper.

And when bedraggled fugitives ring your doorbell at 6:45 in the morning you are, normally, sound asleep and not at all happy when you are awakened.

Nor, for that matter, is your wife, who gave the new arrivals a very frosty reception when, after Flavia had leant on the doorbell for several minutes, she finally opened up. First impressions were of vagabonds or worse: while both Argyll and Flavia thought of themselves as being moderately presentable with honest, open faces, the sort you trust instantly, Lady Byrnes saw two very scruffy, haggard people in need of a damned good wash. What was more, there was a distinctly furtive look about both of them; and the woman, who might have been attractive had she combed her hair and changed her clothes, had that unfocused, hazy look that Lady Byrnes, like all right-thinking folk who lament declining social standards, instantly associated with drugs or worse. Whoever they were, they looked the sort who were going to ask for money. Here, of course, she was quite correct.

"Hello," Argyll said in a tone which suggested he was expected for tea. "You must be Lady Byrnes."

Drawing her dressing-gown more closely around her for protection against sudden attack, she cautiously admitted this was the case.

"We've never met," said Argyll, stating the obvious. "I used to work for your husband until about a year ago."

"Really?" she said coolly. As far as she was concerned, even had he been her husband's fairy godmother that was no excuse for turning up at such an hour.

"Is he in?"

"Of course he's in. Where do you expect him to be at this time of day?"

"It is a bit early, I know," Argyll persisted. "And I know he likes his sleep, but we would like to see him.

This, by the way, is Flavia di Stefano of the Rome art police. She nearly arrested your husband once."

Why he thought this piece of information would convert a frosty reception into a warm embrace was unclear, but having delivered the partial anecdote, he stood back like someone waiting to be welcomed into the bosom of the Byrnes household. And Elizabeth Byrnes, well-brought-up lady that she was, who had always done what was expected, stood back and said:

"You'd better wait inside while I wake Edward, then."

All was serenity. They had been ushered into a small sitting-room with velvet curtains, chintz sofas and loudly ticking clocks. The weak morning sun shone through the French windows, the paintings on the walls and the statues on their plinths looked well established and secure. The air was full of the scent of flowers and pot-pourri. It all seemed awfully safe, an entire universe away from the past couple of days.

"Dear God. Just look at you two," came a quiet, cultivated but somewhat sardonic voice from the door. Sir Edward Byrnes, swathed in his silk dressing-gown, yawned mightily, blinked several times and looked puzzled.

"Hello," Argyll replied, more cheerfully than he felt. "I bet you didn't expect to see us here."

"Indeed not. But I'm sure you have an entertaining explanation. Could you drink some coffee?"

That was the good thing about Byrnes. Imperturbable.

In the years Argyll had known him, he'd never seen him bat an eyelid at anything. Not even a vague tremor round the eyebrows. They followed as he slid into the kitchen then watched him fuss away. Here his weak spot emerged: whatever his eminence and however sophisticated his connoisseurship, culinary matters were not his strong point. After he had puzzled for a few moments about how to switch on the coffee-pot, fretted about where his wife might keep the milk—Argyll suggested the fridge—and asked whether icing sugar would do, Flavia took control. She hated such incompetence and ordinarily would have left him to get on with it, but she was feeling desperate. She liked sleep, and became a touch short-tempered when deprived of a reasonable supply. The sight of a tubby art dealer, whether or not swathed in silk, displaying his inadequacies for all to see could well have made her brusque. And considering that they wanted to touch him for some money, that would not have been such a good idea.

"Oh, splendid," said Byrnes, lost in admiration over the way she poured the coffee into the machine.

"Just a question of practice," she said sharply.

"We, ah, have a favour to ask you," Argyll put in rapidly. "We seem to be in a bit of a pickle. You know how it is."

Byrnes didn't. In his entire life he had never been engaged in anything remotely exciting, except for that brief moment when Flavia had thought of arresting him. That, of course, had been Argyll's fault as well. On the other hand, he loved listening to other people's stories of the adventurous life, once he was awake.

"Do tell me."

It was Argyll's language, so he summarized the state of play to date, leaving out little details like Flavia's picking people's pockets. You can never tell when people are going to go all moralistic on you.

"How dreadfully complicated," Byrnes said when the tale was finished. "Someone seems awfully keen to head you off at the pass, so to speak. I wonder why? Are you sure it has something to do with this picture?"

Argyll shrugged. "I suppose it does. I mean, until I came into contact with it, my life was very routine and straightforward. Nothing untoward at all, except the usual business of paying the bills."

"Business bad, is it?"

"Very."

"Do you want a job?"

"What do you mean?"

"We can talk about it later, if you like. One thing at a time. Tell me, what would happen if you went back home and forgot all about this?"

"Nothing at all. But Flavia here is in one of her stubborn moods."

"I've heard of Rouxel," Byrnes said meditatively. "Wasn't he awarded—"

"Yes," said Flavia wearily. "That's him."

"And you've established that he wasn't telling the entire truth."

"Yes. Of course, there's no reason why he should. He wasn't under oath."

"And if possession of this picture leads to a nasty demise, there's every reason why he might think that a small falsehood would be excusable," Byrnes went on. "After all, if my wife took Argyll here for a miscreant, isn't it likely that Rouxel might think the same? If I had a painting stolen, and all of a sudden some total stranger turned up asking if I wanted it back, my first reaction would be to wonder whether he'd stolen it himself. And if he then came out with some story about murders, I might wonder whether he was delivering some oblique threat."

Argyll was not impressed by this. "And if I'd wanted to kill him, I could have done it then and there."

"So he doesn't know what you're after. He's confused, and perhaps a little alarmed. Somebody is behaving threateningly, it seems to be something to do with him and his picture, so the best course is to deny it. After that—"

"After that any sane and sensible person calls the police," Flavia said. "Which he didn't do."

"But you do get a visit from this man with the scar, and you tell me he may be a policeman after all. Or is it a murderer he's meant to be? I assume he can't be both."

"We don't know," said Argyll miserably. "But there was this man Besson, you see, who was arrested, and a couple of days later this man turns up at Delorme's gallery in the Rue Bonaparte. That sort of indicates—"

"That he was a policeman after all," Flavia said reluctantly. "But."

"But what?"

"But he was in Italy without asking permission; Janet denied all knowledge of him . . ."

"Different branch?" Byrnes suggested.

"When he approached Argyll at the Gare de Lyon he didn't try to arrest him, which would have been the obvious thing to do. If he is a policeman, he's acting in a very odd way."

"No need to get heated with me," Byrnes said. "It was only a suggestion."

"Yes. I'll bear it in mind. Meanwhile . . ."

"Meanwhile you'd better tell me to what I owe the pleasure of this unexpected visit. Nice as it is to discuss such exciting matters with you."

"I was hoping to ask you a favour," Argyll said.

"Obviously."

"We're a bit short of money. A loan, you understand, to be replaced when Flavia can fill in an expenses form."

Byrnes nodded.

"And a car. I was going to rent one, but neither of us brought our driving licences." He smiled wanly.

"Oh, very well. But on one condition."

"What's that?"

"It's a clean car. Before you get into it, you have a bath,

go and buy some fresh clothes. Then you eat and rest. Otherwise, you can't have it."

They agreed to this. Byrnes bustled off in search of keys and cash, and the pair of them sat and finished off their coffee.

"What an obliging man," she remarked, after Byrnes had returned and also agreed to phone Bottando and tell him where they were.

"Isn't he. He may look like a complacent, pompous old connoisseur, but he's got a heart of gold really."

He also, unfortunately, had a Bentley, a vast, shiny thing which he showed them as they went out with some of the Byrnes fortune clutched in their hands to buy some clean clothes. It made Argyll decidedly nervous. A scratched door would probably cost more to repair than his annual earnings. How about a Mini? A Fiat Uno? A Volkswagen? he suggested. Something a bit less ostentatious? More in keeping with Argyll's modest position in the social hierarchy?

"It's all there is, I'm afraid," Byrnes said. "Don't worry. I'm sure you'll grow into it. It's an awfully useful runabout."

Some people, Argyll thought as he backed nervously out into the street a few hours later, just don't live in the real world.

"*W*HAT is this place we're going to, anyway?" Flavia asked once Argyll was calm enough to resume conversation.

"Upper Slaughter? Just a cute little Cotswold village."

He translated into Italian. "How appropriate," she said. "Is it big?"

"Tiny. I just hope there'll be a pub or restaurant near by. Maybe in the next village. We can stop there first. Get the lie of the land."

"What's the next village?"

"Lower Slaughter, of course."

"Silly me. How far is it?"

"About eighty miles. A hundred and twenty kilometres. About five days, at the rate we're going."

But eventually the jam eased a little, and Argyll's conversational powers ebbed. It was a long time since he'd driven in his own country, and it frightened the life out of him. The expense of making a mistake with Byrnes's car made him even more nervous. The fact of being on what he now regarded as the wrong side of the road, combined with a wildly different national style of driving, caused him to grip the steering-wheel with white-knuckled hands, grit his teeth and exert all his mental faculties to resist a Roman-style flourish in his conduct that would undoubtedly have caused a major pile-up. By the time they left the motorway at Oxford he was sweating less obviously and as they drove along the road west—still in heavy traffic, but at a more genteel pace—he almost began to enjoy himself. Not at all like Italy, he thought, but with a rolling charm all of its own. Tranquil and safe. Apart from these damned cars all over the place.

But even these last remaining commuters were left behind eventually as they turned off to head north, Flavia navigating as best she could, Argyll beginning to remember bits and pieces of scenery from his youth.

"Six miles and we're there. All we have to do is find a pub."

Even that proved surprisingly easy. There is nothing like a little money—especially someone else's—to bring out the best in a quiet part of the English countryside; the next village along had a good but enormously expensive hotel; the sort of thing that Argyll's own income would not have managed. But as Flavia had a penchant for comfort and they were both tired, it did quite nicely. It even had a restaurant where the food was edible and a bar which Flavia, a sucker for local colour, immediately visited while Argyll fretted about parking Byrnes's car.

As it was the sort of thing she thought she ought to do in English pubs, she perched herself on a stool by the counter, surveyed the scene with approval, ordered a pint in her best English, and beamed at the taciturn man who served her.

"On 'oliday, are yer, miss?" he asked, for want of anything better to do rather than because he felt like conversation. The tourist season was nearly over. Rotten year this year, anyway.

That was correct, she said. They were driving around, just visiting places. Yes, she thought it was very beautiful.

Thus satisfied, the barman became positively loquacious.

"From abroad?"

That's right. Although her friend was English.

"Ar. Don't look foreign, him."

"No. English," she replied, finding that her sentences were becoming almost as short as his were. They nodded at each other, Flavia trying to think of a way to open up the conversation a little, the barman waiting for an opportunity to end it so he could go and polish his glasses down the other end of the bar.

"Get a lot of foreigners round here," he said after a while, so she wouldn't think him too rude.

"Oh yes?" she replied brightly.

"Ar," he said, evidently thinking this wasn't, after all, so interesting a line of discussion that it deserved pursuing.

Flavia sipped her beer, which she found an unusual brew, to say the least, and wished Argyll would hurry up.

"We're visiting a friend," she said.

"Ar," he said, with real fascination.

"At least we think we are. Jonathan—that's my friend—knew him years and years ago. We just hope he's still alive. It's a surprise visit."

The barman didn't seem to approve of surprise visits.

"Perhaps you know him," she went on doggedly. It seemed fair enough to try. There weren't that many people living around here.

"Richards is his name."

"Is that Henry Richards?"

"That's right."

"Doctor Richards, that is?"

"Very possibly."

"Turville Manor Farm?"

"Yes," she said, with growing excitement. "That's the one."

"Dead," he said with a tone of finality.

"Oh, no," she said with real disappointment. "Are you sure?"

"Carried the coffin at the funeral."

"Oh, that's awful. Poor man. What happened?"

" 'E died," replied the barman.

She was obviously upset by his information, so he felt he couldn't just forsake her, no matter how much he wanted to polish his glasses.

"Surprised you knew him, considering."

"Why? Considering what?"

"Oh, 'e must have died—when was it, now?—oh, at least twelve years ago. Family friend, was he?"

"Sort of," she said, also losing interest in the conversation now.

"His wife's still alive. You might visit 'er. An odd one, she is. Doesn't get too many visitors, that I know."

"What do you mean, odd?"

The barman shrugged, put down his glass-polishing towel and came back towards her end of the bar. She offered him a drink to lock him in place.

"What they call a recluse," he said. "Don't go out. Nice enough lady, but an invalid. And she's never been right since he died. Devoted, they were."

"What a shame. Were they married long?"

"Ar. Long time. 'Course, she was much younger than he was."

"Oh."

"They say they met in the hospital. I think they got married, let me see now, just after the war, if I remember."

"She nursed him, did she?"

"Her? No. He was her doctor, so I'm told. Beautiful, she was. Never knew what was wrong with her, but in constant pain. Didn't improve her looks."

"Her husband was in the forces, wasn't he? During the war, I mean."

Flavia's question was more for form's sake than any-thing else. Her heart, in truth, wasn't in this conversation so much anymore. It was clear that, whatever they'd hoped from this trip, their wishes were not going to be satisfied. Richards, the one tangible lead they had, was dead. And that was that. They'd have to go and see this old invalid, just in case. But whatever he'd known about Hartung, his secrets had probably died with him. If they hadn't married until later, the chances of her knowing much weren't that great.

"Him? Lor' no. Whatever made you think that?"

"Just something I was told."

"Oh, no, miss. Maybe you've got the wrong person. No, he were a doctor. A surgeon. A what-d'-you-call-it. The ones that put people back together."

They searched their respective vocabularies for the right word.

"A plastic surgeon?" she suggested after various other strands of the profession had been eliminated from their enquiries.

"That's the one. He started working on burn victims in the war. You know, soldiers. People like that."

"Are you sure?"

"Oh, yes. I remember that very well."

"So how old was he?"

"When he died? Oh, ever so old, he was. A bachelor, most of his life. Everyone was so surprised when he married her. Pleased, of course; but surprised as well."

*F*LAVIA'S conversation with the barman put both of them off their meal which, considering the price, was something of a waste.

"But we can't have made that much of a mistake, surely?" Argyll asked as he pushed his food around the plate with a fork. "Was this man certain there were no children?"

"Absolutely. Once he finally opened up, he seemed to know the life-histories of everybody within thirty miles of here. He was very definite. Richards was a pioneering plastic surgeon. He set up a specialized burns unit in Wales during the war and worked there straight through. He was also in his late forties then. He only married once, and to this woman after the war. No children."

"Not, in other words, the sort of person to be found working with the Resistance in Paris in 1943."

"No."

"Which leaves cousins, nephews, brothers and things like that."

"I suppose so. But the barman didn't mention any."

"Look on the bright side," he said as cheerily as possible. "If he was the one we were after, then he'd be dead and that would be that. As he probably wasn't, there's still a faint chance we might get somewhere."

"Do you really think that?" she asked sceptically.

He shrugged. "Might as well, for want of anything better to think. Where is this Manor Farm place? Did you find out?"

She had. It was about two miles to the west of the village. She had the directions. Argyll suggested they go out there. There was nothing else to do, after all.

16

*B*EFORE they set out, they did their best to ring in advance to give warning of their arrival. But, as the barman pointed out, it was not so easy as Mrs. Richards had no telephone. She had a permanent nurse and an odd-job man who kept the house running. Apart from those two, she saw and talked to virtually no one. He was not convinced she was going to welcome their visit. But if they were friends of her husband's—he made no attempt to disguise the fact that he found this a little unlikely—she might agree to see them.

Having little alternative, they piled in their car and drove the two miles or so to Turville Manor Farm. It was a much grander establishment than Flavia had expected from the narrow gap in the hedge and the muddy, neglected track that led away from the small road to the house. Nor was it a farm, as far as she could tell; at least, there was no sign of anything remotely agricultural.

However attractive it might have been—Argyll, who knew about this sort of thing, guessed the builders had been at work on it round about the time that Jean Floret was putting the finishing touches to his painting of Socrates—the handsomely proportioned house was not looking its best. Somebody, at some time, had begun painting a few of the dozen windows in the main façade, but had apparently given up after three of them; on the rest the paint was peeling, the wood was rotting and several panes of glass were broken. A creeper had gone wildly out of control along one side of the building. Rather than adorning the house, it showed signs of taking over entirely; another couple of windows had vanished completely under the foliage. The lawn in front was a complete wreck, with weeds and wild flowers spreading luxuriantly over what had once been a gravel driveway. If they hadn't been told the place was inhabited, both of them would have assumed it was abandoned.

"Not the do-it-yourself type," Argyll observed. "Nice house, though."

"Personally I find it thoroughly depressing," Flavia said as she got out and slammed the door. "It's confirming my already strong feeling that this is a waste of time."

Privately Argyll agreed, but felt it would be too discouraging to say so. Instead he stood, hands in pockets, a frown on his face, and examined the building.

"There's no sign of life at all," he said. "Come on. Let's get this over with."

And he led the way up the crumbling, moss-covered steps to the main door and rang the bell. Then, realizing it didn't work, he knocked, first gently, then more firmly, on the door.

Nothing. "Now what?" he asked, turning to look at her.

Flavia stepped forward, thumped the door far more aggressively than he had and, when there was again no response, turned the handle.

"I'm not going all the way back just because someone can't be bothered to answer," she said grimly as she went in.

Then, standing in the hallway, she shouted, "Hello? Anybody home?" and waited while the faint echo died away.

Many years ago it had been an attractively furnished house. No wonderful hidden treasures, certainly, but good solid furniture entirely in keeping with the architecture. Even a good dust and clean would work wonders, Argyll thought as he turned and looked around him. But at the moment the atmosphere of gloom and dereliction was overpowering.

It was also cold. Even though it was about as warm outside as an English autumn could ever get, the house had an air of dampness and decay that only long neglect can produce.

"I'm starting to hope there isn't anyone here," he said. "Then we can get out of this place fast."

"Shh," she replied. "I think I can hear something."

"Pity," he said.

There was a scraping noise coming from up the dark and heavily carved staircase; now that he stopped and listened, Argyll knew she was right. It was not at all clear what it was, though; certainly not a person walking.

They looked at each other uncertainly for a moment. "Hello?" Argyll said again.

"There's no point in standing down there shouting," came a thin, querulous voice from the landing. "I can't come down. Come up here if you have any serious business."

It was not just an old voice, but also a sick one. Quiet but not gentle, unattractive and even unpleasant in tone, as though the speaker could barely be bothered to open her mouth. Odd accent as well.

Argyll and Flavia looked at each other uncertainly. Then she gestured for him to go ahead and he led the way up the stairs. The woman stood half-way along a dimly lit corridor. She was clad in a thick, dark green dressing-gown and her hair hung in long, thin strands around her face. Her legs were encased in thick socks, her hands in woollen mittens. She was clutching on to a tubular steel walking-frame, and it was this, painfully inching its way along the wooden floor, which made the noise they'd heard.

The old woman herself—they assumed this must be the

reclusive Mrs. Richards—was breathing hard, making a rasping noise as she sucked the air in, as though the effort of walking what appeared to have been only about fifteen feet was more than she could manage.

"Mrs. Richards?" Flavia gently asked the apparition, elbowing her way past Argyll as they approached.

The woman turned and cocked her head as Flavia approached. Then she narrowed her eyes slightly and nodded.

"My name is Flavia di Stefano. I'm a member of the Rome police force. From Italy. I'm most dreadfully sorry to disturb you, but I wondered if we could ask you some questions."

Still the woman looked thoughtful, making no response at all, either by sign or speech.

"It's extremely important, and we think you may be the only person who can help."

The woman nodded slowly once more, then looked in the direction of Argyll, standing in the background. "Who's this?"

Flavia introduced him.

"Don't know where Lucy is," she said suddenly.

"Who?"

"My nurse. It's difficult for me to move without her. Would your friend get me back to bed?"

So Argyll came forward while Flavia took away the frame. She was astonished by how gentle he was with the woman; normally he was hopeless in this sort of situation; but now he just lifted her off her feet, walked back down the corridor and softly laid her back into the bed, pulling the bedclothes up around her and assuring himself that she was comfortable.

It was like a furnace in the bedroom; the air was thick with heat and the overpowering odour that goes with sickness and old age. Flavia longed to open the window, to let in some oxygen, to pull back the musty curtains and let in some light. Surely it would make the old lady feel better as well, having some cool, clean air blowing through the room?

"Come here," Mrs. Richards commanded, leaning back on the thick pile of pillows which kept her partly upright. Flavia approached and the woman studied her carefully, then ran her fingers over Flavia's face. It was hard to avoid flinching from the touch.

"Such a beautiful young woman," she said softly. "How old are you?"

Flavia told her and she nodded. "You're lucky," she said. "Very lucky. I looked like you once. A long time ago. There's a picture of me on the dressing-table. When I was your age."

"This one?" Argyll said, picking up a photograph in a silver frame. It was a picture of a woman in her twenties, her face half turned towards the camera, laughing as though someone had just told a joke. It was a face full of spring and happiness, with not a line of care or worry on it.

"Yes. Hard to credit, you're thinking. Such a long time ago."

Both of the statements were sadly true. There seemed no resemblance, not a shred, between the happy girl in the photograph and the old, lined face lying on the pillow. And in this unkempt, run-down, dirty room, it seemed like a memento from another age.

"Why are you here? What do you want?" she asked, switching her attention back to Flavia.

"It's about Dr. Richards. His experiences in the war."

She looked puzzled. "Harry? You mean about the burns unit? He was a surgeon, you know."

"Yes, we know that. It was his other activities we're interested in."

"He didn't have any, as far as I know."

"His work in France. With Pilot, I mean."

Whatever the woman might say next, Flavia was instantly certain that she knew exactly what Pilot was. And yet her reaction was odd. There was no startled look, or fumbled, amateurish attempt to pretend not to know. Rather there was a certain hooded demeanor, of almost relaxed caution. She seemed suddenly to be back on territory where she felt secure. Almost as though someone had asked her this before.

"What makes you think that my husband knew anything about this Pilot, then?"

"Apparently he gave some sort of evidence after the war to a tribunal in Paris. It's documented."

"He gave evidence?"

"His name's in the file."

"Are you sure?"

"Yes."

"Henry Richards?"

"Something like that. With this address."

"Oh."

"Is anything the matter?"

"I was wondering why all of a sudden anybody is interested in my husband. He's been dead for years."

She turned again towards Flavia, considering carefully before she spoke. "And now you mention Pilot. You're from Italy?"

"Yes."

"And you're interested in Pilot. Why, might I ask?"

"Because people are being killed."

"Who is being killed?"

"A man called Muller, and another called Ellman. Both murdered in Rome last week."

The woman's head had sagged forward as Flavia spoke and the Italian was half afraid she'd fallen asleep. But now she lifted her head up, her expression thoughtful and cautious.

"And so you came here."

"We thought your husband might be alive. There's a possibility that anyone who knows something about Pilot might be at risk."

The woman smiled weakly. "And what risk is that?" she said half mockingly.

"Of being murdered."

She shook her head. "That's not a risk. That's an opportunity."

"Pardon?"

"I am the person you are looking for."

"Why you?"

"I was the one who gave that evidence. And signed it. My name is Henriette Richards."

"You?"

"And I'm in a condition where the only thing I feel for this Muller and Ellman is envy."

"But will you help us?"

She shook her head. "No."

"Why not?"

"Because everybody's dead now. Myself included. There's no point. It's something I've spent the past half-century trying to forget. I succeeded, until you arrived. I don't want to talk about it."

"But please, there's so much at stake . . ."

"My dear, you are young and you are beautiful. Take my advice. This is the stuff of corpses. You will find nothing but pain. It's an old story and it's better forgotten. Much better. Nobody will benefit, and I will suffer. Please, leave me in peace. Everybody's dead."

"It's not true," Argyll said quietly from his vantage-point at the window. "There's one person left. If Flavia doesn't find out what's going on, there may well be another murder."

"What other person?" she said scornfully. "There's no one."

"There's someone called Rouxel," he said. "Jean

Rouxel. We don't know why, but he is a candidate for attack as well."

The statement had a profound effect. Mrs. Richards bowed her head once more, but this time when she lifted it her eyes were full of tears.

Flavia felt dreadful. She had no idea what was going on in the woman's mind, but whatever it was, it was giving her emotional pain; enough, temporarily, to blot out the physical suffering which she endured.

"Please," she said. "The last thing we want is to cause you any distress. If it weren't important, we wouldn't be here. But if you really feel you can't tell us, we'll leave you in peace."

It was murderously hard to say it, of course; like it or not, this frail old invalid was their last hope of working out what had been happening in the past week or so, and it was formidably difficult to give up any possibility of a solution. But as Flavia uttered the words, she meant them. If the woman had said, OK then, go away, she would have stood up and left. Then they could have gone back to Rome and confessed their failure. Argyll, at least, would be pleased about that.

Fortunately her offer was not accepted. Mrs. Richards wiped her eyes, and slowly the mournful sobbing ebbed away and then stopped.

"Jean?" she asked. "You know this? You're certain?"
Flavia nodded. "It seems so."
"If he's in danger, you must save him."
"We can't do much if we don't know what's going on."

She shook her head.

"If I help you'll promise?"

"Very well."

"Tell me about these others first. This—what are they called? Ellman? Muller? Who are they? And what is their connection to Jean?"

"Ellman is a German who apparently changed his name from Schmidt. Muller also changed his name; he was originally called Hartung."

If mentioning Rouxel had been like hitting Mrs. Richards, the name of Hartung had a similar effect. She stared at Flavia silently for a few seconds, then shook her head.

"Arthur?" she whispered. "Did you say Arthur was dead?"

"Yes. He was tortured, then shot. We now think by this Ellman man. For a painting stolen from Rouxel, as far as we can tell. Why—well, that's what we were hoping you could tell us. How did you know his name was Arthur?"

"He was my son," she said simply.

Both Flavia and Argyll were stopped in their tracks by this one; neither had the slightest idea of what to say. And so they said nothing at all. Fortunately, Mrs. Richards wasn't listening anyway; she was off on her own path now.

"I ended up in England by accident, I suppose you could say. When the Allies liberated Paris, they found me, and evacuated me, to England for treatment. They did that for some people. I was in hospital for several years, and met Harry there. He treated me, did his best to put me back together again. As you see, he didn't have much to work on. But eventually he asked me to marry him. I had no ties anymore to France, and he was good to me. Kind. So I agreed, and he brought me here.

"I didn't love him; I couldn't. He knew that and accepted it. As I say, he was a good man, much better than I deserved. He tried to help me bury the past, and instead let me bury myself in the countryside."

She looked at them and gave them a little smile, a sad little effort with no amusement behind it. "And here I've stayed, with death eluding me. Everybody I've ever cared for had died first, and they deserved it much less than I did. I've earned it. Except for Jean, and he should live. Even poor Arthur is dead. That goes against nature, don't you think? Sons should outlive their mothers."

"But—"

"Harry was my second husband. My first was Jules Hartung."

"But I was told you were dead," Flavia said a little tactlessly.

"I know. I should be. You seem confused."

"You could say that."

"I'll start at the beginning then, shall I? I don't suppose you'll find it at all interesting, but if there's anything that can help Jean, you'll be welcome to it. You will help him, won't you?"

"If he needs it."

"Good. As I say, my first husband was Jules Hartung.

We married in 1938, and I was lucky to have him. Or at least, that's what I was told. I was born into a family that lost everything in the Depression. We'd had a good life—servants, holidays, a large apartment on the Boulevard St-Germain—but with the collapse, it all began to disappear. My father was used to high society and gave it up unwillingly; his expenses always exceeded his income, and progressively we got poorer. The servants went, to be replaced by lodgers. Even my father ultimately saw the need to get a job, although he waited until my mother had got one first.

"Eventually I met Jules, who seemed to fall in love with me. Or at least, he thought I would be a suitable wife and mother. He proposed—to my parents, not to me, and they accepted. That was that. He was nearly thirty years older than I was. It was a marriage without any passion or tenderness; very formal—we used to call each other *vous* and were always very respectful. I don't mean that he was a bad man, far from it. At least to me, he was always correct, courteous and, I suppose, even devoted in his way. You see I am telling you my story without the benefit of hindsight.

"I was eighteen and he was nearly fifty. I was exuberant and I suppose very immature, he was middle-aged, responsible, and a serious man of business. He ran his companies, made money, collected his art and read his books. I liked to go dancing, to sit in cafés and talk; and, of course I had the politics of youth whereas Jules had the outlook of the middle-aged industrialist.

"I found myself visiting my parents more and more often; not to see them, of course, they were as dull as Jules and not half as kind, but to spend time with the lodgers and students who increasingly filled up their house.

"My father, you see, had assumed that once I was married, a nice flow of money would pour from my new husband and restore him to his accustomed style of life. Jules didn't see it like that. He didn't like my father and had not the slightest intention of supporting someone who openly despised him.

"He was an odd man in many ways. For a start, I wasn't Jewish, and for him to marry me was something of a scandal. But he went ahead anyway, saying he was too old to worry about what other people thought. He was also quite easy-going; wanted me to go with him to functions and act as his hostess, but otherwise let me be. I liked him; he provided everything I needed, except love.

"And I needed that; I needed to be in love. Then the war came.

"We were going to leave, the moment that it became clear the whole thing would be a disaster. Jules saw it; whatever his limitations, he was perceptive. He knew the French had no stomach for a fight, and knew that people like him would get rough treatment. He'd prepared for it, and we were about to head for Spain when I went into labour.

"It was a bad birth; I was bed-bound for several weeks in dreadful conditions; everybody had left Paris, the hospitals weren't working properly and were overflowing with wounded. Few nurses, fewer doctors, little medicine. I couldn't move and Arthur was so fragile he would have died. So Jules stayed too, to be with me, and by the time we could go it was too late; you couldn't get out without permission and someone like him couldn't get it.

"And life sort of drifted back—not to normality, obviously, but to something which seemed understandable and bearable. Jules became wrapped up in trying to preserve his business, and I went back to my life with students. And we sat and decided we should do something to fight back. The government and the army had failed us, so now it was time for us to show what being French was all about.

"Not everyone thought like us; in fact very few people did. Jules, as I say, merely wanted to keep out of trouble; in the case of my parents—well, they had always been on the right. Bit by bit the students departed, to be replaced by German officers billeted on them. They liked that, my parents. Getting in well with the new order. Their natural tendencies had been reinforced by Jules's refusal to hand over money; now it was encouraged, they became openly anti-Semitic as well.

"About a year after the armistice, there was only one student left, a young lawyer who'd been there for years. I'd always liked him, had introduced him to Jules, and they'd taken to each other like father and son. Jean was just the sort of son Jules had always wanted. Handsome, strong, honest, intelligent, open-minded; he had everything except a decent family, and Jules set about providing that. He paid his fees until he qualified; encouraged him in every way; introduced him to important people; set about giving him the chances he needed and deserved. Even gave him presents. They got on so very well. It was wonderful while it lasted."

"This was Rouxel, I take it?" Flavia asked quietly.

She nodded. "Yes. We were about the same age. He took a room at my parents' and I saw a lot of him. If it hadn't been for Jules, I imagine we would have been married; as it was, we had to content ourselves with being lovers. The first man I loved. In a sense, I suppose, the last as well. With Jules—well, what passion he had was used up shortly after we married. And Harry was a good man; but not like that, and it was too late then anyway.

"I imagine you find that—what? Surprising? Disgusting even, to look at me now. An old wizened cripple as I am. I was different then. Another person, you might say. Do you smoke?"

"I beg your pardon?"

"Do you smoke? Do you have any cigarettes?"

"Ah, well. Yes, I do. Why?"

"Give me one."

Somewhat surprised by this departure from the way the conversation had developed thus far, Flavia fished around in her bag and pulled out a packet of cigarettes. She handed them over and gave one to the woman, who tugged it awkwardly from the packet with her gloved hands.

"Thank you," she said when it was lit. Then she broke

into an appalling hacking cough. "I haven't had a cigarette for years."

Argyll and Flavia looked at each other with raised eyebrows wondering if they'd lost her for good. If she drifted off the subject now, it might be impossible to steer her back on to it.

"I gave up when I was in the asylum," she said after smelling the burning cigarette with interest for a while. It was strange; her voice had become louder, more solid in tone now that she had begun to talk.

"Don't look like that," she went on after a while. "I know. No one ever knows what to say. So don't say anything. I went mad. It was simple enough. I spent two years in there, in between operations. Harry did his best to look after me. He was a very good man, so kind and gentle. I missed him when he died.

"I got the best of treatment, you know. No expense spared. I have no complaints at all. The finest doctors, the best private asylum. We were looked after as well as possible. Many soldiers got much rougher treatment."

"May I ask why?"

"I will tell you. As the war went on, Jean began to become more enthusiastic about the Resistance, more convinced the Germans could be beaten. He became the effective leader of this group called Pilot; established links with England, worked out targets and strategies. He was a wonderful man. He lived in the most appalling danger constantly. And yet he was always there to reassure, encourage. Once he was picked up by the Germans and held for a few days, then he escaped. It was Christmas Day 1942, and the guards were lax. He just walked out and had vanished before anyone noticed. Extraordinary man; he had real style, you know. But he was changed after that: very much more serious and wary. He guarded us carefully, often refusing to sanction operations he judged too dangerous, always keeping at least one step ahead of the Germans.

"Of course they knew we existed, and they were after us. But they had no success. At times it was almost like a game; sometimes we ended up laughing uproariously about what we were doing.

"And all the time he was there: calm, assured and utterly confident that we would win. I can't tell you how rare that was in Paris then. We would win. Not a wish, or a calculation, or a hope. Just a simple certainty. He was an inspiration to us. To me particularly."

She switched her attention back to Flavia, this time with the faintest shadow of a sad smile.

"When I was with him, in his arms, I felt superhuman. I could do anything, take any risks, court any danger. He strengthened me and would always protect me. He told me that. Whatever happened, he said, he'd look after me. Sooner or later something would go wrong, but he'd make sure I got a head start.

"Without him, it would have been so different. Someone would have slipped up and been caught much sooner. And eventually it was too much even for him. He was too caring. That was our downfall.

"We needed places to hide, money, equipment, all that sort of thing, and we had to approach people on the outside, hoping they could be trusted. One of these was Jules. He was worried about our activities, and even discouraged them because he was afraid, but Jean tried to persuade him to help. Jules agreed, but very reluctantly.

"Jules was terrified about what would happen if the Germans ever discovered him. He was Jewish after all, and many of his people had vanished already. He survived— so he said—by paying out massive bribes, and slowly giving up his possessions. A fighting retreat, he called it. Of course he had his final option of running, but he didn't want to leave until he had to. So he said.

"Anyway, things started going wrong. We were being betrayed, and it was clear it was coming from inside. The speed and accuracy of the German reaction was just too neat. They had to have inside knowledge. Jean was desperate. For a start it was clear we were all in danger; him in particular, as he felt he was being followed. Nothing concrete, but he had this strong feeling of a noose tightening around him. Then when he finally accepted we had a traitor, he took it personally. He couldn't believe a friend of his, someone he trusted, could do such a thing. So he prepared a trap. Bits of information given out to different people, to see where the leak was coming from.

"One operation—a very simple pick-up of equipment— went wrong: the Germans were there. Only Jules had been told about it."

Here Flavia wanted to break in, but she was transfixed

by the story and dared not interrupt in case the flow was broken. The old woman probably wouldn't have heard her anyway.

"Jean was devastated, and so was I. Jules had been playing his own survival game and kept his distance—for our sake as much as his, he said—but nobody ever suspected he might sell us to preserve himself. Doubt remained, but one evening, after a confrontation with Jean in his little lawyer's office, he fled to Spain and the Germans swooped down on us.

"They just rolled us up. Fast, efficiently and brutally. I don't know how many of us there were, maybe fifty or sixty. Maybe more.

"I remember that day. Every second of every minute of it. In effect it was the last day of my life. I spent the night with Jean and got back home about seven in the morning. Jules had gone. It was a Sunday. The twenty-seventh of June 1943. A beautiful morning. I thought Jules had just gone to the office or something, so I had a bath and went to bed. I was still asleep an hour or so later when the door was kicked in."

"And Rouxel?"

"I assumed he'd been killed. He was too courageous to last long. But apparently not: it seemed that by mere good fortune he slipped through their net. Unlike most people he stayed in Paris rather than run, and began to reorganize.

"In a sense I was lucky, if you can call it that. A lot of

them were shot or sent off to a death camp. I wasn't. For the first three months I was treated quite well. Solitary confinement and being beaten up alternated with good food and gentle persuasion.

"They wanted everything I knew, and to make sure I gave it, they told me everything they did know already. There was little I could add. They had a complete picture. Drop-points, meeting-points, names, addresses, numbers. I couldn't believe it. Then they told me how they'd got it all. Your husband, they said. He told us everything. Jules must have been spying on us and listening and reading scraps of paper for months to have accumulated it all. It was a systematic, complete and cold betrayal. And he got out, scot-free."

"Who told you all this?" Flavia said with sudden urgency.

"The interrogating officer," she said. "Sergeant Franz Schmidt."

Another pause greeted this remark as the old woman coolly assessed how they were taking her story, and whether it was being believed. Eventually she felt able to go on.

"I never said anything, and they were prepared to take their time. But at the start of 1944 that changed. They were getting more panicked. They knew the invasion was on its way soon and they needed any result fast. Schmidt stepped up the pressure."

She stopped, and in the half-light of the room pulled

off the glove from her left hand. Flavia felt her throat rising in protest at the sight. Argyll looked, then turned away quickly.

"Fifteen operations in all, I think it was, and Harry was the best there was. They wanted to give him a knighthood for his expertise. This hand was his greatest success with me. As for the rest . . ."

With enormous difficulty, she pulled the glove over the hand again. Even when the scarred, brown claw with its two remaining misshapen fingers had vanished underneath its covering, Flavia could still see it, and still felt sick. Nothing could bring her to offer any assistance.

"But I survived, after a fashion. I was still in Paris at the Liberation. They couldn't be bothered to send me east, and didn't have time to shoot me before the troops arrived. As quickly as possible, I was shipped to England. To the hospital, the asylum, and finally here. Then you come; to remind me, and tell me it's not all over yet."

"I'm sorry," Flavia said in a whisper.

"I know. You needed information, and I've told you what I know. Now you must repay me by helping Jean."

"What happened afterwards? To your husband?"

She shrugged. "He got let off lightly. He came back to France after the war, expecting that nobody would know what had happened. But Jean and I had survived. I didn't know what to do, but I knew I couldn't see him. Jean was behind the push to get him brought to justice. Not for revenge, but for the sake of the people who'd died. Despite everything, he felt it was like condemning his own father.

The commission wrote to me; very reluctantly, I agreed to give evidence.

"Fortunately it wasn't necessary. When he was confronted with the facts and the promise of our testimony, Jules killed himself. Simple as that."

"And Arthur?"

"He was better off where he was. He thought I was dead, and he had a good family to look after him. Better he didn't know. I wrote to his foster-parents, and they agreed to keep him. What could I do for him? I couldn't even look after myself. He needed to start afresh, without any memories from the past, of either his father or mother. I asked them to make sure he knew nothing of either of us. They agreed."

"Rouxel?"

She shook her head. "I didn't want to see him. His memory of what I was like was all I had left. I couldn't bear to have him come into my hospital room and see his face change into one of sympathetic horror the way yours did. I know. There's nothing you could do. It's an involuntary reaction. People can't help it. I loved him, and he loved me; I didn't want that destroyed by his seeing me. No love could survive that."

"Did he not want to see you?"

"He respected my wishes," she said simply.

Something unsaid there, Flavia thought. "But surely . . ."

"He was married," she said. "Not to a woman he loved, not someone like me. But he married when he thought I was dead. After the war he discovered the truth; he wrote to me, saying that if he'd been free . . . But he wasn't. It was better like that. So I accepted Harry's offer as well."

"Do you know anything about Hartung's paintings?" Argyll asked, changing the subject somewhat dramatically.

She looked puzzled. "Why?"

"All this started off with a picture which belonged to him. Called *The Death of Socrates*. Did your husband give it to Rouxel?"

"Oh, that. I remember that. Yes, he did. Just after the armistice. He decided that the Germans would probably take them anyway, so he gave some pictures away to friends for safe-keeping. Jean got that, to go with one he'd already been given. A religious one, that was. Jean was quite perplexed and didn't really want it, I think."

"Did Hartung know about you and Rouxel?"

She shook her head once more. "No. Never a murmur. I owed him that. Within his limits he was a good husband. Within mine I was a good wife. I never wanted to hurt him. He never had the slightest idea. And I was always careful with Jean as well. He was a hot-blooded, passionate man. I was terrified he might go to Jules and tell him, hoping he'd divorce."

She'd begun to cry again, at all the memories and the lost joys of life. Flavia had to decide whether to stay and offer comfort or just leave. She wanted to know more.

What did she mean, she'd been careful with Rouxel? But she seemed to have had enough, and any comfort offered was not going to do much good. Flavia stood up, and turned to face the bed. "Mrs. Richards. I can only thank you for your time. I know we've made you remember things you want to forget. Please forgive us."

"I will forgive you. But only if you fulfil your side of the bargain. Help Jean, if he needs it. And when you do, tell him that it was my last gift of love to him. Will you do that? You promise?"

Flavia promised.

*G*OING back out into the cool fresh air and feeling the soft warmth of the sun was like waking up after a nightmare and finding that the horrors were not real after all. Neither of them said anything as they walked to the car, got in, and Argyll started the engine and drove off.

A mile down the road, Flavia grabbed his arm and said: "Stop the car. Quickly."

He did as she asked, and she got out. There was a break in a hedge near by, and she walked through it into a pasture. On the far side there were some cows grazing.

Argyll caught up, to find her staring across the field at nothing, breathing heavily.

"You OK?"

"Yes. I'm OK. I just wanted some air. I felt I was suffocating in there. God, that was horrible."

There was no need either to comment or even to agree with her. Side by side they walked slowly around the field in silence.

"You're thoughtful," he said eventually. "Something beginning to make sense?"

"Yes," she replied. "Not there yet, but it's coming. I wish it wasn't."

"Come on," he said softly after a while. "Let's get going. You'll feel better once we start doing something."

She nodded and he led her back, then drove to the hotel where he steered her into the bar, ordered a whisky and made her drink it.

In all, it took her nearly an hour plunged in thought before she was able to lift her head and say, "What do you think?"

And Argyll wasn't concentrating on anything, either. "I think it's the first time I've ever met anyone where I could honestly say she'd be better off dead. But I suppose that's not what you meant."

"I didn't mean anything. I just wanted to hear someone talk normally. Anything. Even you seem to have lost your flippant style."

"All I know is that we now have another good reason for working this mess out. It's not going to make much difference to her life, but someone owes her a little. Even if it's just guarding her memories."

17

VERY tired and downcast, Argyll eased Edward Byrnes's unscratched Bentley into a parking-space outside the art dealer's house at about half-past seven, then they went and rang the doorbell.

"Flavia!" came a booming voice from the direction of the sitting-room as the door opened. "About time, too."

Following the voice after a second or so came the body of General Bottando.

"My dear girl," he said solicitously. "I'm so pleased to see you again."

And, with a most unprofessional lapse into emotional-ism, he wrapped his arms around her and gave her a squeeze.

"What are you doing here?" she said in astonishment.

"All in due course. First, you look as though you need a drink."

"A big one," Argyll added. "And some food."

"And then you can tell us what you've been up to. Sir Edward here delivered your message, and I thought it was time I got on a plane to have a chat. You seem remarkably unwilling to come back home," Bottando said as he led the way into Byrnes's sitting-room.

"How about *you* telling me what *you've* been doing?" asked Flavia, following him in.

Bottando said calmly, "Do you want some of Sir Edward's gin?"

"Definitely."

Byrnes, who had been standing in the background looking on approvingly and with some pride at his ability to host reunions, duly poured the drinks, considered the possibility of discreetly retiring, rejected the idea on the grounds that he was too curious, and sat down to listen.

The pair of them sitting there, Flavia's boss and Argyll's former boss, had more than a passing resemblance to Tweedledum and Tweedledee. Both portly, both benevolent, both wearing dark, well-cut suits, one with dark grey hair, the other with light grey hair. A very reassuring couple they were; after the events of the past few days, from murders to pursuits to distressing interviews with old ladies, they were the very embodiment of a return to the normal world, where paternal authority existed and was, on the whole, well disposed. Byrnes's comfortable sitting-room and opulent glasses of gin confirmed the feeling slowly building up in Flavia's mind that she could now relax a little.

Not that her delivery was smooth and well rehearsed; instead, the story came out with unusual hesitations and interruptions.

"She's his mother," she started off.

"Who is?"

"This woman in Gloucestershire."

"Whose mother?"

"Muller's. She sent him out of France in 1943 and stayed behind. When the Germans swooped, she was picked up. She decided he'd be better off where he was so left him in the care of those Canadians."

"Are you sure?" Bottando began, then retracted when he saw her frown. "I mean, how interesting."

"And she was Hartung's wife and Rouxel's mistress. Isn't it a small world?"

"Indeed. Does this assist us in discovering why Muller was killed? Or why Ellman was killed?"

"I don't know. Did I tell you that Ellman's real name was Schmidt?"

"You did. And I have badgered the Germans mercilessly for information. I asked what they had on anybody of that name and asked why he would have changed his name. To give them a hint I suggested that they should look at army records. Specifically Paris."

"Yes, well . . ."

Bottando, having something to contribute, was not prepared to be put off. "Seemed worth a try. I was quite proud of the idea. Anyway, it took them some time; poor people, working their way through every Franz Schmidt in the German army must have been a fair old task. However, they produced the goods. He was in Paris in 1943 and 1944."

"We know that."

"But he was no pen-pusher. The man whose name he adopted was a desk-man; Schmidt was in an Abwehr Intelligence unit. Specifically there to counter the Resistance."

"We know that too. Mrs. Richards told us."

Bottando looked irritated. "I do wish you'd tell me these things. Then maybe I could stop wasting my time on things you already know about."

"We only found out this afternoon."

"Hmmph! Did you know he was wanted for war crimes?" he asked hopefully.

"No."

"Good. Well, he was. The wheels of justice go slowly but they seem to have caught up with him in 1948. They were about to arrest him when . . ."

"He vanished, went to Switzerland, changed his name and was never heard of again," Flavia said helpfully, earning herself another hurt look from Bottando.

"Anyway," he said, a little disappointed. "So he knew all about Hartung."

"He was the one who broke the good news to the man's wife," she said. "While he was torturing her."

Bottando nodded. "I see. And, of course, he would have

been well practised in the sort of techniques used on Muller. In fact, I think that we can reasonably conclude beyond much doubt that he did kill Muller. The torture and the gun. Sort of adds up."

"But we still don't know who killed *him*."

"No."

"But do we really care?" Argyll asked wearily, resuming his old theme of wanting to go home. "It sounds as though whoever it was was doing a public service. If I happened to have a gun, met this Ellman/Schmidt character and found out what he'd done, I might have shot him as well."

"That's true," said Bottando. "But who *did* know what he'd done? Besides, I'm afraid that from an official point of view we're not allowed to look at it like that. And, of course, there is always the problem that whoever shot Ellman might not be finished. Rouxel. Do we know if he's been approached by anyone?"

"No."

"You realize, of course, that this Europa prize presentation takes place in ten days? If Rouxel is under any threat it has to be fended off. And to do that we have to know what that threat is."

"But how could he possibly be under any threat? Who could be threatening him?"

Bottando cocked his head. "This man with the scar, for example?"

"I've been thinking about him," Flavia replied. "And concluding that he may well be what he says he is. He said he was a policeman. When he was chasing us."

"And when he phoned Mr. Argyll in Rome, assuming it was him."

"And the connection with Besson indicates the same. Janet says he isn't, but somebody removed documents from that deportation centre and told the director not to help me much, and Janet was the only official who knew I was going there. And in Rome, this man rings Argyll and says he will come round at five. Argyll tells us and you ring Janet, telling him about this murder. And this man doesn't show up. I think Janet sent him a message saying, in effect, get the hell out of there."

"It's most unlike Janet, though," Bottando said reluctantly. "He's normally quite scrupulous."

"And so are you. But there are times when you've been leant on as well. What I can't work out is why anyone is leaning on him. But I suspect it'd be no good asking."

Bottando thought about this for a while, not at all happy. Murders and things were all very well; but he did not see why the smooth running of his department should be disrupted by them. His easy co-operation with the French had been an important factor in his department's limited success for years; the prospect of its being wrecked by this case was becoming extremely worrying.

"You're going to have to sort this out quickly," he said glumly. "I'm not having years of friendship and careful work wrecked by one stupid picture. Do you have any idea what is going on?"

"Yes," she said simply.

Argyll was roused from his reverie by this comment. He

had been staring into space most of the time, not really paying attention to the conversation. There was something in the back of his mind, and he couldn't quite pin it down. Indeed it had been there for days; and, rather like a very small stone in the bottom of a shoe, it was causing increasing irritation. The fact that, try as he might, he couldn't work out exactly what was bothering him made it all the worse.

"You do?" he said. "You might have told me. What is it?"

"I said I had an idea," she replied. "I didn't say I had proof, or that the idea was right."

"I'm not impressed," he said.

"Nor am I. But we still don't have enough information. General, did you, by any chance, have any luck with the Swiss over that phone call? The one to Ellman that sent him to Rome?"

"Ah, that," Bottando said with a frown. "Indeed. You might not like the answer though."

"Try me."

"It didn't come from Paris at all; it came from Rome. The Hotel Raphael, to be precise."

"The what?"

"As I say."

"Whose phone?"

"Alas, we can't find that out. But we can conclude certain things ourselves, can we not?"

He looked at her with that faint smile that he adopted when he had reached an answer before she had. A bit unfair, really, as he'd had longer to think about it. Even so, she wasn't that far behind.

"Oh, dear," she said. "This was Monday, right?"

He nodded.

"And that was the day I could get no work out of anyone at the Interior Ministry because there was some international delegation in town. Financial liaison and supervision, or something."

He nodded again.

"And Rouxel's granddaughter told Jonathan that he was on the French delegation of some committee dealing with financial supervision."

Bottando nodded again.

"Rouxel was in Rome that day?"

A further nod.

"He made that call?" she asked, pursuing the matter with what she thought was fine logic.

Bottando shrugged. "No," he said, spoiling it. "It seemed a reasonable presumption. But at the time he was in a meeting, which he never left. A further snag is that when Muller was killed Rouxel was at an official dinner, and when Ellman was shot he was already on a plane back home. I checked and double-checked. There's no doubt. He didn't kill anyone or phone anyone."

"Which leaves this putative policeman with the scar."

"It does. And if you're right, then we're delving into very muddy waters indeed."

"Oh, God," she said, suddenly disgusted with the whole business. "What do you think?"

"As far as evidence goes, I don't know," Bottando replied.

"Damnation," Flavia said crossly. "All our leads have gone dead. Or at least, we've made progress, but it hasn't got us anywhere. All we've uncovered is long-dead detail that doesn't mean much. I wish Muller had been right. If there had been something special about that last judgement, we would at least have had something to go on."

And over in a quiet and almost forgotten corner of the room, cogs whirred. Old, rusty levers clicked over. Synapses, sluggish with disuse, flickered into hesitant life. The half-formed idea in the back of Argyll's mind leapt suddenly and boldly into full and well-focused shape.

"What?" he said.

"This painting. If we could—"

"You called it the last judgement."

"Yes."

"Ah," he said, leaning back in his armchair with an air of profound relief and satisfaction. "Of course. Do you know, you've never told me I'm brilliant as well as beautiful."

"And I'm not going to unless you earn it," she said a little testily.

"Logic. Hartung's letter referred to the last judgement; Muller assumed it meant *The Death of Socrates*, the last one to be painted."

She nodded.

"One of a series of four."

She nodded again, trying to be patient.

"The sales list of Rosier Frères listed Hartung's purchases. One picture by Floret of Socrates. And another. Sent to an address on the Boulevard St-Germain. The street where Mrs. Richards' parents lived. And Rouxel lodged. And Mrs. Richards said Hartung had given Rouxel a picture. A religious one."

"So?"

"The series was the judgements of Alexander, Solomon, Socrates and Jesus. We knew where three are; *The Judgement of Jesus* is missing. We assumed it referred to a representation of Jesus' trial. Before Pilate. But is that so?"

"Jonathan, dear—"

"Hold on. Hartung gave Rouxel the Socrates to go with the other one. Right? Mrs. Richards said so. And he still has the other one," he went on with mounting enthusiasm. "I saw it. I recognized the style, not that it registered. Heavy colour, slightly wooden. *Christ Enthroned with the Apostles.*"

She looked at him blankly.

"That's the advantage of living with art dealers of the more educated variety. At the end of the world, Christ will sit enthroned with his disciples, and he will judge Man from the Book of Life. And he shall separate them one from another. Some routine like that, anyway. Also called, as you know very well, the Last Judgement. Muller hadn't thought it through. He was after the wrong picture."

He sat back once more looking awfully pleased with himself. "If there is anything at all to be found, that's where it will be."

Flavia considered this carefully. "I wish you'd thought about this before," she said.

"Better late than never."

"I hope so."

"Does it help?" Bottando asked.

She thought about that. "It will confirm—or refute— my general idea. If there's anything there. I think, you know, it's time to bring this case to an end of some sort. One way or another."

"Can you do that?"

"I think so. Yes."

"Isn't she clever?" Argyll said admiringly. "Whatever did you do before she worked for you, General?"

"Oh, I just had to struggle along," he replied.

"I'm so glad we're getting married," he continued. "Such a smart person to have as a wife."

Bottando thought this was getting irrelevant. "Congratulations," he said drily. "I hope you'll be very happy. Not before time, in my opinion. Now, Flavia, dear. Are you sure you can wrap this up?"

"Let me put it like this. I can either find a solution, or make sure no solution will ever be found. Whatever, the case will come to an end. Do you want me to do that?"

Bottando nodded. "It would probably be best. Ideally, I would like to bring a murderer or two to book. But if that's not possible, I want it off our hands. How do you propose to go about it?"

She smiled faintly. "I think first of all we have to consult. That is, we go through tried and trusted channels. We will go back to Paris."

18

WHATEVER happened, this had better be over soon, Flavia thought to herself as she trooped wearily on to the plane. She couldn't keep this up much longer. Some businessmen, it seemed, could do this sort of thing perpetually. Three countries a day, airport-hopping. She couldn't. She could barely even remember what day it was. All she knew was that the moment she thought she'd reached a place where she could lay her head and have a quiet, uninterrupted night's sleep, the opportunity was whisked away again. She'd had one decent night's sleep in the last week. She was haggard, confused, upset and thoroughly miserable. A short fuse. A little time bomb waiting to blow.

Argyll, who recognized the signs all too well, left her

alone throughout the flight, lost in his own thoughts. He knew perfectly well that to try conversation, or even to attempt to brighten her life with his little jokes, would be counter-productive to say the least.

Besides, he wasn't feeling like little jokes either. He didn't know what was going on in Flavia's mind, but he did know he was mightily sick of this business. People trotting around stealing pictures is one thing. Even murder wasn't so bad, once you got used to it. But this case involved too much long-term unhappiness for his taste. Argyll liked people to be content; however naïve it made him appear, he had always considered contentment to be the most basic of human rights. And this case was full of people who had missed it. Muller, living all his life with the desolation of being virtually parentless, of having to deal with his family heritage. At least he was spared the anguish of knowing his mother was still alive in such a condition. And his mother, leading a shady half-life, a sort of hobbling corpse for forty years or more. Even Ellman's son had been corrupted by it all, effectively blackmailing his own father and justifying himself by saying it was all in a good cause. Only Rouxel and his family were untouched. The distinguished man, the beautiful granddaughter, sailing serenely through life, unaware of the misery swirling all around them. Perhaps they were about to be enveloped as well. Something had reached out of the past; Rouxel was the only one it had left untouched. So far.

Dear old Byrnes had driven them to the airport, lent them money and even paid for their tickets, saying that he was certain that the Italian state would take care of it eventually. Even his frosty wife had recovered from the early-morning affront to make them sandwiches for the trip. As Argyll had tried to explain, she wasn't so bad really. English ladies are occasionally like this: hearts of marshmallow, heavily protected by a covering of solid titanium. They can be quite kind, as long as no one notices and points it out. Then they get brusque and insist that they're nothing of the sort. An odd national characteristic, really.

Bottando had stayed behind, nattering to Elizabeth Byrnes. These two had hit it off quite nicely, and as Flavia and Argyll dragged their weary steps to the car, they'd left Bottando in the kitchen drinking wine and watching his hostess potter around doing the cooking. Of course the General would stay for dinner and stay the night. No trouble at all.

Hmmph. This was approximately the thought of both Flavia and Argyll as they'd driven off. Somehow the division of labour seemed a touch unfair. They ran around like beheaded chickens, Bottando settled down for a comfortable night. His mentioning the privileges of rank as they'd left hadn't helped either. Nor did his contribution— ringing Janet to tell him they were on their way—seem exactly like overworking himself. Argyll had protested about this, saying Janet's track record for being helpful hadn't exactly been exemplary, but Flavia had insisted. That was the point, she'd said; besides, this time she thought Janet would turn out to be useful.

But, as Bottando had said, this was Flavia's case. She'd started it, she should finish. See it as a mark of trust, he'd said. Besides, she knew all the ins and outs; he didn't. And of course, she was the one who wanted to show Fabriano a thing or two.

Charles de Gaulle was relatively empty, and they got off the plane fast, making their way along the mechanized walkways quickly to the exit. Then to passport control, and the line for holders of EC passports. Generally this is simple: frequently the immigration officials don't even bother to examine passports. Especially in the evening, a gruff nod and a bored look at the cover is about as big a welcome as a traveller can expect.

But not in this case. Whether he was young and enthusiastic, or had just come on his shift or whatever, this one was insisting on doing his job properly. Each passport was opened, each face scrutinized, each person sent on his or her way with a courteous "Thank you sir, enjoy your stay."

Whoever heard of a courteous immigration official at an airport? Everybody knew there was an international training-school somewhere which drilled them in basic offensiveness and advanced sneering.

"Madame, m'sieur," he said in greeting as they handed over their documents, Flavia feeling ever more like a lamb being led to the slaughter.

The feeling was strengthened when he looked intently at the photographs, studied their faces with care, then referred to a book of computer printout on the desk.

"Bugger," said Argyll under his breath.

"Don't worry," she said.

"Would you mind coming with me, please?" said the official.

"Not at all," she replied sweetly. "But we are in an enormous rush. We have no time to waste at all."

"I'm so sorry. But it will only take a few seconds. I'm sure you understand. Routine checks."

Like hell, she thought. But there was no chance of doing anything but march off dutifully as instructed. She'd noticed the four armed policemen earlier. Perhaps the guns weren't loaded; she didn't know, and had no intention of finding out.

She had the feeling that the little cubicle they were ushered into had been deliberately designed to be depressing. Dingy white walls, no windows, uncomfortable seats and a metal and plastic table all combined to create an atmosphere that reduced you to being an administrative problem, best solved by ejection.

There were two doors, the one through which they entered, and the other which opened shortly after they had come in and sat down in uncomfortable and worried silence. So this is what it feels like to be an illegal immigrant, Flavia thought.

"Surprise, surprise," Argyll said as he saw the person who came in.

"Jonathan. Good to see you again," said the man who, in recent days, had been tackled, hit with bottles, thumped with handbags and tripped up. Despite the words, he didn't seem at all happy to see them. He had a large piece of sticking-plaster above his left eye. Flavia suppressed a slight snigger and decided not to mention their last meeting. No point in being provocative.

"The feeling is not reciprocated," Argyll said.

"I thought it might not be. No matter," he replied as he sat down. He then opened a bulky file of papers and studied some—more for effect than anything else, Flavia suspected—before looking up at them with a vaguely concerned air.

"Well, what do we do with you two now?" he went on, to take command of proceedings.

"How about a proper introduction?" Flavia asked.

He smiled thinly. "Gérard Montaillou," he said. "Ministry of the Interior."

"And an explanation? Like what's going on?"

"Oh, that's simple, if you like. You are a member of a foreign police force and require permission to operate in France. That permission is being denied. So you will go home. As for Mr. Argyll, he is lucky not to be charged with smuggling stolen pictures and he will go home as well."

"Piffle," she said sharply. "You never bothered to ask permission when you came to Italy."

"I was a civil servant attached to an international delegation."

"A spook."

"If you like. But I did nothing so awful that anyone is likely to object."

"Two people are dead, for God's sake. Or is that all in a day's work for you?"

He shook his head. "Too many spy stories, mademoiselle. I sit at desks and shunt paper around. A bit like you, really. This sort of thing is all quite exceptional for me."

"Which is why you're not very good at it."

He didn't like that very much. If he had been on the verge of relaxing a little, it reversed the process.

"Maybe," he said stiffly.

"So we go home, I put in an extradition order for you so you can be charged with murder?"

"I didn't kill anyone," he said. "As I say, I push paper around. And every time I've wanted to talk to you you've hit me. I can prove that when Ellman died I was back in Paris. And I never even met Muller. I went to his apartment, but there was no one there."

"I don't believe you."

He shrugged dismissively. "That's your problem."

"I can make sure it's yours as well."

"I don't think so."

"So what were you doing, then?"

"I don't need to tell you anything."

"What harm would it do? I'm going to raise an almighty stink about this when I get back to Rome. *You* convince me I shouldn't."

He considered this for a moment. "Very well, then," he said eventually. "You are aware, of course, that a painting belonging to Jean Rouxel was stolen."

"We had noticed."

"At the time, we paid no attention to this. As a member of a department that deals with the security of officials I was notified—"

"Why?"

"Because Monsieur Rouxel is a distinguished man, a former minister, and is about to receive an international prize. Prominent public figures are our—my—line of business. My job, mainly, is protection of politicians. It's all quite normal. It seemed unimportant, but about a week or so ago, the art police arrested a man called Besson. He confessed to an awful lot of things. One of them was stealing this painting.

"So I was called in to talk to this man. Eventually we did a deal. Besson was let go, and he told us what he knew."

"Which was?"

"Which was that he had been approached by a man over this painting, and asked to acquire it for him. This man Muller said that the price was immaterial, and he was to get hold of this painting at any cost. Naturally Besson pointed out that the picture was hardly likely to be for sale. Muller said that didn't matter. He wanted the picture and wanted it fast; if he had to steal it, then that was fine. Just get it, but make sure it was untraceable.

"Besson asked what was so important about this picture, and was told it belonged to Muller's father. He persisted, saying it was not a very good reason. Muller then said it contained important material about his father.

"Besson was paid quite a lot of money and, being the

sort of person he was, couldn't resist. He stole it, and routed it through Delorme, then apparently through you. That was when I came in; as far as I was concerned, you were just another illegal courier."

"So why not just arrest me?"

"We were in an awkward position. Clearly this Muller attached significance to the picture, we didn't know what that significance was, and the timing was very worrying. Rouxel was going to be awarded this prize in a week or so. A very big deal indeed, and it seemed something or other was about to pop up. Maybe it was something trivial, or untrue, or just the lunacy of a complete nutcase. It didn't really matter. My superiors decided the best thing to do would be to sit on the thing until we could find out what was going on. If we arrested you and Muller found out, he might say something; the idea was to get the picture back and get down to Rome before he worked out what was going on. On top of that, of course, I was very pressed for time."

Not convincing, Flavia thought as she scrutinized the smoothly talking man opposite. All very curious, this business. She knew that these spooks were not the brightest people on earth, but this was just ridiculous. Of course it would have been more sensible to descend in a posse on the railway station, arrest Argyll and take the picture. To act as he had was simply absurd. Amateurish. Even more, to expect her to believe this was plain insulting. Someone here was being less than perfectly truthful. And it wasn't her or Argyll.

She glanced to her side and saw Argyll fidgeting as well, looking unconvinced. So, as discreetly as possible, she poked him and gave him a keep-your-mouth-shut look.

"And you made a mess of it," she said. Just because she was going along with his story didn't mean she had to let him off easily.

Montaillou looked not at all embarrassed. "I'm afraid so," he said with an easy smile.

"And so to Rome, where you went to visit Muller."

"Who was out. I never saw the man."

"And phoned Argyll, asking for the picture back."

"Yes," he said with a much more convincing display of being honest. "That's right."

"And then your superiors contacted you, told you Muller had been murdered and told you to get the hell out of there fast."

He nodded.

"Thus hampering a murder investigation."

He varied the diet by shrugging this time.

"Did you phone Ellman in Basle? Tell him to get the painting?"

"I'd never heard of the man. Really. I still have no idea how he was involved."

"Rouxel knew what you were up to?"

"Not the details. That is, I talked to him, and kept his assistant informed."

"Ah," she said. "And, as far as you're concerned, there's nothing more to be said. That is, two murders in Rome are none of your business. The picture is back in place and Rouxel is not going to be touched by anything embarrassing."

He nodded. "That's correct. All that remains is for you to be sent home. Please don't think I'm being obstructive—"

"Wouldn't dream of it."

"If at any stage you come across real evidence identifying the murderer, we will of course act on it."

"Do you mean that?"

"Of course. But at the moment, your probing is just stirring things up. You have no suspects, I believe? No hard evidence to accuse anyone?"

"Not exactly."

"I thought so. I suggest you contact me when you have something a bit more substantial."

"Right," she said, as he got up, bade them a good evening, picked up his file of papers and left.

"You're very co-operative all of a sudden," Argyll said as the door clicked shut. Her sudden shift to contrite acquiescence he found something of a surprise. Not really like her.

"Go with the flow, that's what I say. What did you think of all that?"

"I think I was right all along. I told you phoning Janet wasn't such a good idea. Of course that man was going to be here to welcome us to France."

"I know," she said, a little irritated by his being so slow on the uptake. "That was the point. I needed to talk to him. How else could I get hold of him? I had to know what his role was. So, what do you think of him? What he said?"

"I thought it was a little bit peculiar," he said. "I mean, I know these people do make a mess of things from time to time, but they seem to have gone out of their way to make this whole business unnecessarily complicated."

"You reckon."

"Yes," he said firmly. "Dealing with this picture would have been all very simple. And they went out of their way to introduce all sorts of contortions."

"So you're inclined to the incompetence theory."

"Do you have something better to suggest?"

"Yes."

"What?"

"Don't you know?"

"No."

"That does make me feel better. I do."

"Stop being secretive. Just tell me."

"No. There isn't any time. We've got to get out of here."

"We will be out soon."

"I don't mean getting on a plane and going meekly back to Rome, either. I want to visit Rouxel."

"But they don't want us to," Argyll said. "At least, I assume that's what those men with machine-guns are there for."

"And it's not occurred to you that an armed guard is perhaps a little excessive?"

"I don't know. And you won't tell me. All I know is

that there's a man with a machine-gun on the other side of that door."

She nodded. "But probably not on the other side of that one. Come along, Jonathan," she added as she tugged at the handle of the door Montaillou had used. "We're in a hurry."

The little cubicle where they were confined was one of a series in which unfortunates trying to get into the country could be interrogated and kept waiting for hours. On the one side, a series of doors along a wall of the passport-control area admitted the would-be immigrants; on the other a parallel series of doors giving on to a corridor allowed immigration officials to come in to do their business. The corridor had a wall at one end, and at the other, blocking the way to freedom, was a guard with a gun.

"This doesn't look too hopeful, does it?" Argyll whispered.

"Shh," she said. Not that there was much point. The guard was not particularly alert. He didn't have to be, after all. They'd have to walk over his toes to get out. And as Argyll hinted, there wasn't much chance of his not noticing that.

"Come on," she said. "This way."

And, making sure the guard wasn't looking, she walked as softly as possible in the opposite direction, towards the blank wall at the far end of the corridor.

In slightly easier circumstances, Argyll could have pointed out the disadvantages of this move. But he managed to restrain himself; sceptical expressions do not make a noise, however, and his doubts were clearly visible.

Their cubicle had been more or less in the middle of a range of about a dozen. When Flavia reached the last one, she eased open its door and pushed her head in. She was unlucky: it was occupied. A worried-looking man, apparently Algerian or Moroccan, was staring glumly at a stiff official, who turned round when he heard the door open.

"Sorry," said Flavia in her brightest French. "I thought we were meant to be interviewing him."

"Who are you?"

"Police," she said. "We reckon this one might be wanted back home for a robbery."

"Oh, great. You can have him if you like. I was going to send him back anyway."

"Shall we take over? We'll give you a call when we're done. There's no need for you to hang around if you want a break."

"Fine by me. I could do with one. This is my twentieth today."

He stood up, stretched and, with a friendly smile at them, and a scowl at the man he'd been interviewing, strolled out of the room leaving Flavia and Argyll in charge.

"Come with me," Flavia said briskly to the immigrant, who now looked terrified. "And shut up," she added as he began protesting his innocence.

She opened the door on to the public area and looked

out carefully. The armed guards were still outside the door of their original cubicle, idly chatting to each other. More passport officers were in operation now; more importantly, the one who had nobbled them had vanished.

"Come on," she said, and marched confidently out towards one of the passport desks.

"We've got to take this one off to charge him," she said to the man on the desk. "All the paperwork's in order. You can have him back once we've done the fingerprinting at the station."

"OK. As long as you don't lose him."

"We won't. See you in half an hour."

And with Argyll gripping the man's other arm, she frog-marched the protesting Algerian through the immigration and customs sections and out into arrivals. There, she just managed to suppress a snigger.

"And with one leap, we were free," she said. "Oh, do be quiet," she said to their prisoner as she walked swiftly out to the taxi rank. "Do you understand me?" she added.

The man nodded, still deeply upset.

"Good. Now. Get in this taxi. Take this money," she went on, pulling out a bundle of Edward Byrnes's notes and thrusting it into his hand, "and go and have a nice life. OK? I don't advise going too near any police for a bit."

She told the driver to head for central Paris and watched as the cab disappeared along the ramp and into the night air.

"Now it's our turn," she said, heading for the next one.

"Christ," she added as they got in. "I accidentally gave him about six thousand francs. He must think it's his birthday. How the hell am I going to explain that to Bottando?"

"Where to?" asked the driver, revving up his engine.

"Neuilly-sur-Seine. That's where he lives, isn't it?"

Argyll nodded.

"Good. Take us there then," she said to the driver. "And as fast as possible, please."

19

IT was now after nine and the rush-hour traffic was easing off, allowing the taxi-driver to show what he could do. He drove a vast Mercedes, hopelessly uneconomic from a commercial point of view, in Argyll's opinion, but undeniably effective in rushing them into Paris as fast as was conceivable.

The only difficulty was that the driver wasn't all that certain about where they were going. Flavia and Argyll, neither of them exactly experts in Parisian geography themselves, had to lend a hand: Flavia with a map, Argyll with his memory of the last time he had visited Rouxel's house. With the three of them working together, they made a decent job of the trip; only two wrong turns and one of those not completely disastrous. The driver, feeling quite pleased with himself but not overjoyed to be leaving his fare in the middle of a residential district with no chance of picking up anyone else, dropped them in the next street along from Rouxel's.

Caution is a virtue, even when it is not necessary. She needn't have worried too much. No matter how many police would shortly be swooping down when they got their act together and worked out that their captives had fled the airport, no one had turned up yet.

This time the gate was not locked, and opened with a slight squeak.

"Flavia, before we go any further here, what is this about?" Argyll asked.

"Dates," she said.

"What dates?"

"The dates for the break-up of the Pilot network."

"I'm not with you. But no matter. What has that got to do with anything?"

"We'll have to ask Rouxel."

Argyll sniffed. "Have it your own way, then. Although I must say that if I didn't trust you so much, I'd be mightily tempted to go back to the airport."

"But you do. So shall we stop talking and go in?"

Cutting off further opportunity for dissent, she wheeled around and rang the doorbell. There was no answer. After waiting awhile and pressing it again, and tapping her foot with impatience, she decided that in the circumstances the social niceties could be disregarded. She turned the handle, found it open and pushed. Walking into other people's houses seemed to be becoming a habit.

There was a light on in the hallway, which gave on to three rooms, each with the door firmly closed. Under one, there was a faint chink of light. She picked this one to start off, and went in.

It was empty. But evidently someone had been there recently: there was a book open on the carpet and a half-empty glass of brandy by the hearth.

"I can hear something," Argyll said quietly. There was no great need to whisper, but it seemed appropriate.

"Well?" she asked, as they stood outside the room that the noise was coming from.

Although it was an absurdly fastidious piece of courtesy on the part of someone who, after all, had just barged uninvited into someone's house, Flavia knocked softly. There was no answer. So she again reached for the handle and pushed the door open.

"Who's that?" came a quiet voice from the corner as she opened the door and looked in. Rouxel was by a veritable forest of house plants, spraying the leaves with some unguent. Argyll had said he was keen on plants, Flavia thought unnecessarily.

The room was dark except for two pools of light, one by the desk, the other by a nearby armchair which contained Jeanne Armand. It was the study where Argyll had interviewed—or been interviewed by—Rouxel a few days previously. Dark wooden bookshelves lined with leather-bound books filled one wall. Heavy and comfortable armchairs were on either side of the fireplace.

Flavia looked around the room to try and gain a few moments to think. She was becoming confused about how to proceed. On the one hand was her certainty that she finally understood. On the other was a sudden and burning hatred for it all.

"Who are you?" Rouxel said again.

"My name is Flavia di Stefano. I'm with the Rome police."

He didn't seem very interested.

"I've been investigating the theft of your picture."

"That has been returned."

"And the two murders associated with it."

"Yes. I was kept informed. But it's all over now, I think."

"I'm afraid you're wrong. It's not at all over."

She walked over to the far wall, on the side of the room opposite the glass doors leading on to the garden. "Where is the picture?"

"Which picture?"

"*The Death of Socrates*. The one given to you by your mentor, Jules Hartung."

"Ah. Well, you know, it was so much trouble, I had it destroyed."

"You what?"

"It was Jeanne's idea. She burnt it."

"Why?"

He shrugged. "I don't think I have to explain to you what I do with my own property."

"Still, you have others left," she said. "Like this one." She pointed at the small painting hanging beside a mahogany bookcase. It was about the same size as all the others. Argyll's sort of thing. Christ sat in the centre of the Apostles, in a fashion derived from Leonardo's *Last Supper*; they all looked serious, but some of the Apostles had an air of sympathy, even sadness on their faces. Below them was a queue of people, with one kneeling and awaiting his verdict.

Again, there was no answer. Rouxel was not resisting her questions, not even resenting them or trying to stop them. Nor did he seem worried. He just wasn't very interested.

" 'And they were judged every man according to their works,' " she quoted. "Are you prepared for that, monsieur?"

At last she gained a response. Rouxel gave a bleak smile and stirred slightly. "Is anybody?"

"I wonder how long it will take for the cavalry to get here," she said, looking at her watch.

"Who?" Argyll asked.

"Montaillou and his friends. They should have arrived by now."

"And then what?"

Now it was her turn to look indifferent. "I don't really

care. What do you think, Monsieur Rouxel? Should I explain?"

"You seem like a young woman who believes things can be explained. Accounted for, understood and made comprehensible. At my age, I'm not so sure. What people do and why they do it is often incomprehensible."

"Not always."

"I think they're here," Argyll said, moving to the window and peering through the curtain. "Yes. Montaillou and a few others. One looks as though he's being told to guard the gate. Another is on the front door. The other two are coming in."

Montaillou and the other man, whom Argyll had never seen before, came through the front door and into the study. While the Intelligence officer had been polite at their last meeting, now he abandoned even a nominal attempt at courtesy.

The other man seemed more detached. In his late fifties, with close-cropped grey hair and a sharp nose, he had a look of alertness that was now masked by resigned concern.

"A few hours ago I said I would not charge Mr. Argyll or disrupt your career," Montaillou said in a clipped voice that barely concealed his fury. "I'm sure you'll understand if I say that I no longer feel able to stand by that."

Flavia ignored him. Possibly not the best way of disarming his anger, but what the hell? "Hello again, Inspector Janet," she said. "How delightful to see you again."

The grey-haired man nodded at her uneasily. Argyll gave him a quick look-over, at close quarters, for the first time. The man who was supposedly the only one they could trust. Whatever happened, he thought, Franco-Italian relations over art thefts would take a long time to recover.

"Hello, Flavia," he replied with an almost rueful, apologetic smile. "I'm really very sorry all this has happened."

She shrugged.

"But why did you come here?" Janet went on. "What was the point?"

"I know what the point was—" Montaillou began. But Janet held up his hand to silence him. Flavia noticed that. It was interesting. She'd always known that Janet wielded more power than his status strictly warranted; that unlike Bottando he was one of the cadre of officials who knew a lot of people; who could phone contacts and fix things by having a quiet word. But this was new. Montaillou implicitly accepted the man's greater authority. And Janet still seemed to acknowledge some sort of obligation, or connection to her and the Italian department. It gave her a chance that, at least, she would be heard.

"I made a promise," she said.

"You have any explanation? Any evidence?"

"I think I can give a good account."

"It will have to be good."

"I don't think so. I don't think we'll need any proof or anything. It's not that sort of case. I fear this is not going to end with anyone arraigned, or extradited or tried, somehow."

"Are you going to suggest that French Intelligence was behind the deaths, then? I do hope not," Janet said. "However inadequate Monsieur Montaillou's handling of this case . . ."

She shook her head again, noting the rift. That could be useful; no great love lost between these two representatives of the French state. "No. He—and you—merely made it more difficult to find out what was going on."

"So who did kill these people?"

"She did," Flavia said simply, pointing at Jeanne Armand. "Or at least, she organized the first murder and committed the second."

A complete silence greeted this, with not even the woman sitting in the chair breaking it with any protest. Eventually it was Argyll who reacted first.

"Oh, Flavia, really," he said. "What an idea! Does she look like a murderer to you?"

"Do you have any evidence for this, either?" Janet asked.

She shook her head. "Nothing conclusive. But Monsieur Rouxel was in Rome that day, heading a delegation to the Interior Ministry. The call which summoned Ellman to Rome was made from the Hotel Raphael. And in the next room but one to Ellman was a witness that Detective Fabriano interviewed. A Madame Armand. That was you, was it not?"

Jeanne Armand looked up and nodded. "Yes. But I told the truth. I heard nothing of any interest. It was a dreadful coincidence that I was staying in the same hotel, of course—"

"Dreadful," Flavia agreed. "And not entirely frank of you."

"I thought it best to protect my grandfather. I—"

"—didn't want his name in the papers just before the prize-giving. Yes, of course."

"But it was still a coincidence," Janet said quietly. "Unless you convince us otherwise."

"I say again, I have no proof. But I can tell you a story, if you like. You can believe it or not as you wish. Then I will quietly take the next plane home and forget it."

She looked around, but nobody either urged her on or told her to keep quiet, so she took a deep breath and began.

"We have a whole loose network of people, spread over several generations and several countries. Some dead, some alive. Jules Hartung, already fairly old when the last war began. Jean Rouxel, Mrs. Richards, Ellman, all the same generation and in their twenties in 1940. Much younger was Arthur Muller. Youngest of all is Jeanne Armand here. They came from Switzerland and Canada and England and France. But all of them were profoundly marked by that war, and in particular by what happened on the twenty-seventh of June 1943. The day that the Resistance network dubbed Pilot was broken up by German army Intelligence.

"If you want, we can talk about that later. First I want to tell you what happened. When Arthur Muller commissioned Besson to steal that picture, he was acting very much out of character. A more upright, honest and straightforward man could scarcely be imagined. He did not do things illegally. But in this case, he got involved quite deliberately in a crime. Why? We know he wanted to examine a picture, but why not write to Jean Rouxel and ask?

"The answer, I suspect, is simple. He did. And was fobbed off."

"That's not true," Rouxel said. "I had never heard of the man before last week."

"No. Your secretary screens all your mail. She saw the letters, and answered them for you. Initially, I imagine she thought Muller was potty; he had good reason for not being entirely frank and saying why he wanted to look at the picture. Whatever, she blocked all his approaches."

"You'll have a hard job proving that," Jeanne said.

"I know. When you killed Ellman, you made sure you took and destroyed the file of correspondence he'd taken from Muller's apartment. I imagine that contained all your letters to him."

"And maybe not."

"Indeed. As I say, I'm just telling a story. When the police arrested Besson, he was interviewed and passed on to Montaillou. He rang to enquire about the painting. You talked to Madame Armand, is that right?"

Montaillou nodded.

"So she knew the picture was heading for Muller, and she now had an idea why it was so important. She wanted it stopped, so she said that Muller was a complete madman, obsessed with revealing that Rouxel had bungled the inquiry into Hartung's guilt. It was she who pressed you to get it back before it left the country, warning of possible embarrassment."

He nodded again.

"And you failed. As far as she was concerned, by that time it was too late. Even if the painting was recovered from Muller, there was no guarantee that its contents had not been removed. Muller was dangerous and had to be taken care of. And before you interrupt, I will tell you why in a moment.

"It was a delicate matter, and she needed someone she could trust. So she called Ellman. Phoned him from her hotel, and told him what to do. He agreed.

"Ellman arrived in Rome and went to Muller. Muller denied having the painting, and was tortured to make him reveal where it was; when he said Argyll had it, he was killed and Ellman left with the documents.

"Ellman then met Madame Armand, who had stayed behind after Rouxel left for Paris. Perhaps he tried to be too clever; I don't know. But she shot him with his own gun, then left with all the papers he had in his room. I assume she destroyed them.

"A couple of days later, Jonathan Argyll returns the picture, free of charge, and Madame Armand, just to be sure, burns it."

She looked around to see how the audience was taking what was, after all, a pretty weak account. Much supposition, little substance. She could almost hear Bottando grumbling in the background.

The reactions fitted well with her expectations. Argyll looked faintly disappointed; Janet surprised that he had been dragged out late at night for such stuff; Montaillou was contemptuous, and Jeanne Armand seemed almost amused. Only Rouxel himself was unmoved, sitting quietly in his chair as though he had just heard some junior but enthusiastic manager expound something truly outlandish.

"You must forgive me if I say that this is very thin, young lady," he said after it became clear that no one else was going to break the silence. And he smiled, almost apologetically, at her.

"There is more," she said. "Except that I don't know whether you want to hear it."

"If it's as feeble as the first part, I imagine we'll survive," commented Montaillou.

"Monsieur Rouxel?" she asked with considerable reluctance. "What about you?"

He shook his head. "You are committed. You can't stop now. You know that as well as I do. You have to say what you think, however foolish it may be. My opinion scarcely matters."

She nodded in acknowledgement. "Very well. Now we turn to motive. Both of them. Montaillou for wanting to get hold of that painting so urgently. Jeanne Armand as well.

"Madame Armand first. A cultivated, intelligent woman. Who went to university, began a promising career then, gave it up to help her grandfather temporarily. Except that he could never do without her again, and persuaded her to stay when she wanted to get on with her own life rather than looking after his. Despite her abilities, she was treated as little more than his secretary.

"Monsieur Rouxel married in 1945, his wife died young and he never married again. His daughter died in childbirth. Madame Armand was his nearest relative, and was extremely solicitous of his welfare. Although how she managed it, considering the way she was treated I, for one, do not fully understand. But she worked for him, looked after him, kept the troubles of the world at bay. Is that correct?"

Rouxel nodded. "She's everything an old man could want. Entirely selfless. She's been wonderful to me, and I must say, if you are going to attack that, I shall begin to get angry . . ."

"I presume she is also your heir."

He shrugged. "Of course. That's no secret. She's my only family. Who else could possibly be?"

"How about your son?" Flavia asked quietly.

A silence so profound followed the question that she wondered if it could ever break. There was not even the slightest sound of breathing to disturb the quiet.

"Arthur Muller, the first victim in this affair, was your son, monsieur," she went on after a while. "The son of Henrietta Richards, previously Henriette Hartung. She's still alive. Your mistress for several years. Muller was born in 1940, at a time when, according to his mother, she and her husband had not had what she termed close relations for a couple of years. You had. She kept who his father was a secret. It would have damaged her son's chance of inheriting and, by her own lights, she wanted to be a good wife. Which meant being discreet where she couldn't be faithful. And she didn't want you going to Hartung to demand that he give her up."

Rouxel snorted. "There was no chance of that."

"Pardon?"

"Me? Marry Henriette? The idea never crossed my mind."

"You were in love with her," said Flavia, the hatred mounting now.

"Never," he replied contemptuously. "She was fun, and attractive and amusing. But love? No. Marry the penniless cast-off of Hartung? Absurd. And I never once told her that."

"She loved you."

Even now, in these circumstances, Rouxel gave a little shrug that was almost vain. Of course, he seemed to imply. "She was a silly girl. Always was. And bored and wanting excitement. I gave it to her."

Flavia paused and studied him more closely, breathing

carefully to control herself. As he'd said, she was now committed. No holding back any longer. She owed Henriette Richards that. She'd promised.

"But she didn't tell anyone about you, except her son. When he was shipped out of danger to Argentina and then Canada, she told him his father was a great hero. He was only small, but he understood and clung to that belief; even when he was told what had happened to Hartung, he refused to believe it. His adoptive sister thought he was living in a fantasy world. But he believed what his mother had said. It was certain that even before he was accused of treachery Hartung himself was not the stuff of heroism. Therefore his father must be someone else. When he read the letters from his parents, he knew his long belief had been correct, and began to search.

"He did the obvious thing; that is, wrote to people who were connected to his father and went looking around the archives himself; not that he was any sort of historian. He talked to the archivist in the Jewish documentation centre. His letters to Rouxel that Jeanne intercepted and read, other casual remarks she'd picked up over the years and a certain amount of reading the papers in your office to which she had free access allowed her to work out what he was after. She knew who he was; she knew he was after documents proving it; but she didn't know where they were.

"What Muller wanted was the evidence Hartung talked about. In 'the last judgement.' He identified it, so he thought, and stole it. It was the worst mistake of his life.

"When the painting was stolen, and Montaillou told her who had stolen it, everything fell into place. She moved fast. She killed your son, monsieur. Had him murdered in cold blood. Tortured to death by the same man who tortured and destroyed the life of your mistress. That is her repayment for the way you've treated her.

"Do you believe me?" she said after another, long silence.

"I don't know," he said, shaking his head. He believed her. The way his shoulders had slumped demonstrated clearly enough that, even if Janet and Montaillou might remain sceptical, Rouxel knew perfectly well that what she was saying was true. No proof; but any trial and punishment the legal system could hand out would be minor in comparison anyway.

"Henriette Hartung was your mistress around the time her son was conceived?" she continued.

He nodded.

"And you never suspected?"

"I worried, yes. But she told me not to. I was a student, and a poor one. Hartung had been good to me. I owed him everything. And I was having an affair with his wife and didn't want to stop. But I didn't want him to find out, either. It wasn't just that he could have destroyed my career before it had even started, I liked the man as well."

"Did you, indeed?" she said. "You have an odd way of showing your affection."

Argyll, sitting quietly and watching the proceedings, looked up at this comment. There was an edge to it: a tone of bitter sarcasm that was quite out of character for her. He studied her carefully; her face was quite impassive and controlled, but he—and knowing her best, he was the only one who was aware of it—was fairly certain that something nasty was about to happen. And it was all bad enough already, in his view.

"Considering he was someone who had helped you so much, whom you admired so greatly, you betrayed him pretty comprehensively."

Rouxel shrugged. "I was young and foolish. It was a bizarre time in Paris then."

"I didn't mean that."

"What did you mean, then?"

"Monsieur Montaillou knows, I think."

Montaillou shook his head. "No, I don't know. All I know is that you are causing a great deal of distress for no reason. We now know who killed Muller. Ellman killed him. You have no proof about who killed Ellman and I don't imagine anyone is really so concerned. Leave it be."

"No," said Janet with surprising vehemence. "I'm tired of all this. I want to know. I have been subjected to intolerable pressure and interference in the past week. I have had investigations closed down. I've been ordered by your people to obstruct a murder inquiry in Italy and caused enormous damage to relations with colleagues abroad in the process. I caught an important thief whom I've been chasing for years and you let him go with a virtual amnesty. I've had enough. I want to get to the bottom of this before I launch a major complaint against you, Montaillou. So you continue, Flavia. Explain all this."

"I don't know who Montaillou works for, but I'm damned sure it isn't some potty little organization to protect public figures. As you say, he's been throwing his weight around in recent days. You can't do that if you merely follow diplomats and politicians around to make sure they don't lock themselves in the shower.

"Montaillou's job was to prevent a major embarrassment. He and his department were manipulated, of course, by Madame Armand, just as everyone else was. But he was led to believe that the picture stolen by Muller contained incriminating documents which, if revealed at the right moment, might have involved a very public withdrawal of Monsieur Rouxel from accepting the Europa prize. For which he had been nominated by the French government. His job was to stop that happening.

"So we have to go back again. To Pilot, and its destruction. Someone was betraying it; operations started to go wrong. But who was it? Rouxel took matters into his own hands. Advance information was selectively given to certain people; if the operations in question went ahead without problems, then those people in the organization were probably in the clear. Others remained under suspicion until they were eliminated. A slow and difficult business, but one which someone had to do. Of course, I know nothing about wartime conditions, but I imagine there could be nothing worse than a slow suspicion eating through morale. The culprit had to be found.

"And he was. Information given solely to Hartung led to an operation going wrong. It was conclusive evidence, and almost convinced even his wife. So Hartung was summoned to an interview where, according to Mrs. Richards, Monsieur Rouxel accused him to his face. And then let him escape. Is that correct?"

Rouxel nodded. "Yes," he said. "When it came down to it, I couldn't do it. He was supposed to be taken away and executed. But I couldn't do it. Sentiment, I suppose, which I regretted immediately. It cost us dearly."

"Indeed. Hartung fled, and Pilot was wrapped up quickly. The obvious conclusion being that, knowing the game was up, he alerted the Germans as he left. And this was confirmed by the Germans themselves. Franz Schmidt tormented Hartung's wife by telling her that her predicament had been caused by her own husband's betrayal. He hadn't even tried to save her. Because of that, above all, both she and Rouxel were prepared to pursue him after the war. Is that a fair summary, monsieur?"

"Yes," he replied, "that's about right."

"And it's lies from beginning to end."

Rouxel shook his head.

"Hartung was always on the fringes of your cell, and yet he managed to betray it all, every single person in it? How could he possibly have known all that detail? You talked to him on the evening of June the twenty-sixth, round about ten at night, and yet at six-thirty the next morning the Germans swept up the whole lot in a large operation? Which they'd organized from scratch in seven hours? And if that was the case, how did you escape? The only person who really mattered, the leader, the man they were after most of all? The man who really did know the names and identities and location of everyone in the group?"

"I was lucky," he said. "And the Gestapo could move very fast when they wanted to. It was called Operation Razor; they were good at that sort of thing."

"Yes. Operation Razor. I've heard about it."

Rouxel nodded.

"To destroy Pilot. Organized on the basis of Hartung's total betrayal on the night of June the twenty-sixty. Which he did because he knew the game was up after he talked to you."

Rouxel nodded again.

"So how is it that the orders for Operation Razor were made out on June the twenty-third?"

"What do you mean?"

"The dossier about Hartung's art collection in the Jewish documentation centre. It states quite clearly that they were acting in accordance with instructions for Operation Razor given on June the twenty-third. Three days before Hartung was accused, before he fled and before, according to you, he betrayed you."

"So maybe he betrayed us before."

"And maybe he didn't. Maybe when he talked to you that evening he accused you of being the traitor. Maybe he said he had proof. Maybe you contacted the Germans to make sure he was silenced, but he escaped before they could catch him. And you ensured that Henriette was kept alive so she could be told her husband was the traitor and could give evidence against him later."

Rouxel laughed. "Purest fantasy, my dear woman. You have no idea what you are talking about."

"I'm not so sure. Let us think about it. This Schmidt character. A torturer, and a wanted war criminal. Known personally to your former mistress. When the authorities wanted to arrest him in 1948 he heard about it in advance and vanished, successfully changing his name. But in recent years a financial services company has been paying him sixty thousand Swiss francs a year. Services Financieres. Controlled by you, monsieur. Can you explain why? Did you feel sorry for him or something? Or were you buying his silence?"

"I don't know what you're talking about."

"Of course you do. Don't lie to me. A payment of that amount was made into Ellman's account by a company called Services Financieres. Of which you are a board member and former chairman. And a major shareholder. Why?"

"I don't know."

"Nonsense." She paused after this comment, and regathered herself. The last thing she needed was to get herself into a slanging match. She had to proceed methodically and calmly.

"A last problem," she went on. "Hartung hanged himself in prison rather than face his trial. Why, though, if he was convinced he could clear his name? Is that a reasonable act for someone who believes he can prove his innocence? Of course not. The official account is that the prosecutor visited him, presented the case and Hartung, seeing no way out, killed himself. He was found in his cell the next day. You were the prosecutor in that case, Monsieur Rouxel. You visited him the night he died. And you hanged him to stop him denouncing you at his trial."

"Utter lies and fabrication."

"Fortunately we don't have to rely on your being truthful. There is proof."

Here she had their full and undivided attention; until then it had been a battle between Flavia and Rouxel. Now everyone else dropped the role of spectator and jerked to attention.

"What proof?" asked Janet.

"The only proof that remains," she said. "The rest has been systematically hidden, maybe destroyed. Muller's files. The classified ministry files. I told Janet I'd go to the Jewish documentation centre and someone swept down before me. You, I suppose, Monsieur Montaillou. And that leaves Hartung's evidence, the stuff he was convinced would clear him. The material all this has been about."

"I thought we'd established it didn't exist."

"Oh, it exists. Muller worked out it had been hidden in the last picture of a series of pictures on justice. Of judgements. *The Judgement and Death of Socrates, Judgement of Alexander, Judgement of Jesus, Judgement of Solomon.* I think those were the four. The Socrates was given to Monsieur Rouxel when he passed his law exams. But there was also the *Judgement of Jesus* bought and delivered when he was still living at Henriette's parents. That one there," she said pointing at the painting hanging in the corner. "*Christ and the Apostles in Glory. The Last Judgement.* Not Jesus being tried, but Jesus sitting in judgement. Which was hanging in the office where Rouxel and Hartung had their talk in 1943. The least likely place, Hartung said in his letter. And so it was. Do you think we should take it down and look?"

It was a gamble. After all, she didn't know that there would be anything at all. So she imbued the comment with all the force and conviction she could muster. The next few minutes would prove her correct, or see her make a complete fool of herself.

This time it was Jeanne Armand who broke the silence. She burst out laughing: a harsh, humourless laugh that was all the more disturbing for being so unexpected and inappropriate.

"What's the matter?" Janet asked.

"I don't believe it," she said. "All that work, all that covering of tracks for decades, to be finally brought down by something that's been in your own study for forty years. It's funny. That's what it is."

"Do I take it you accept my explanation?" Flavia said quickly, hoping to keep her talking.

"Oh, God, of course."

"You asked Ellman to get the painting back?"

"Yes. I knew who Muller was, and I was damned if he was going to sweep in here and deny me my rights. I've slaved for that man for years. He begged me to work for him, saying he needed me so much, an old man like him with no one else in the world. He's very persuasive, you know that. So I did; to honour the family hero. I gave up everything and all I got in return was reproach that I wasn't a grandson he could be truly proud of. To carry on the Rouxel name, as though that meant anything. And then this man turns up. I could see it: the tear-filled meeting, the formal adoption, the gracious welcoming into the family bosom. A son: the final crowning of a golden life of achievement. Oh, no. I wasn't going to be shoved out of my deserved place like that. I knew about this man Ellman."

"How?"

"I told you. I organized Grandfather's life. All his letters, all his finances. All his old papers. I knew about these payments but couldn't work out what they were for. So I stopped them a year ago. A month or so later Ellman turned up. He told me a great deal about my heroic grandfather. I did a little looking around in Grandfather's papers; enough to know that Ellman was the sort of person who could do a job like that and would have good reason to keep quiet. I didn't think Montaillou would do it for me. What if Montaillou visited this man, and got a full explanation? Do you think he would have destroyed the evidence about who Muller was? Not a chance. That wasn't what his job was. He would have considered that a harmless domestic matter and left it alone. I needed someone who would get the evidence and destroy it. And

I didn't know that he was going to commit murder. I never wanted that. I just wanted Muller's proof."

"So why was he killed?"

"Because I underestimated how nasty a man Ellman was. He didn't want a rival muscling in on his territory, I think. He was worried Muller might be some investigator who'd go to the newspapers. And, of course, if that happened he might be discovered and prosecuted as well."

"And you killed Ellman in turn?"

"Yes, I did," she said perfectly calmly. "He deserved it. He told me he had recovered the painting and, if it was so important, I would have to pay a million francs. I had no choice. I didn't know he was lying and had found nothing. So I shot him with his own gun. So what? Does anybody here think he deserved to live? He should have been hanged years ago. Would have been, had the scourge of injustice here not protected him."

She nodded to herself, then looked at Flavia as though she was the only person who really understood. What else could any reasonable person do? she seemed to be asking.

"You say Ellman told you about your grandfather?"

"Yes. I couldn't believe it. The great man, you know. So upright and honourable. And the government had never done anything about it . . ."

"They knew, of course," Flavia said. "That's why Montaillou was given *carte blanche*."

"I knew nothing of the sort," Montaillou said stiffly. Good. He was wavering as well.

"There I believe you," Flavia replied. "I don't think you did. Your superiors probably did, though."

"Schmidt, Ellman, whatever his name was," Jeanne continued, "told me that in 1942 or something, Grandfather was arrested and threatened with torture. He caved in immediately. Didn't even try to put up a fight. Ellman held him in total contempt. Said he would have done anything to be let go. And did. In return for his freedom, he offered to hand over the names of everybody he could think of.

"The more I thought about it, the more it made sense. And now you tell me there's proof. Good. I'm glad of that. At least it clears up any uncertainty. I can be sure I didn't do anything so wrong. Not in comparison with everyone else."

Flavia breathed an enormous sigh of relief. But she got no satisfaction from having proven her case. "Monsieur Rouxel? If you want to prove me wrong, you can."

But Rouxel had abandoned the struggle as well. He knew as well as Flavia that it didn't matter now whether there was any proof or not. Everybody in the room knew that what she'd said was correct.

"One mistake," he said wearily after a while. "One failing. And I've spent the rest of my life trying to make up for it. I have, you know. I've worked hard—tirelessly, I might say—for this country. That's what this prize was for. And I earned it. I deserved it. You can't take that away."

"Nobody is—"

"It was the pain. I couldn't stand it. Even the idea. I was arrested by accident. Stupid bad luck, that was all. And I was handed over to Schmidt. He was a terrible man; a monster. Really, I'd never dreamt that people like him existed. He liked hurting people. It was his natural calling. I think it was realizing that interrogating me would give him pleasure that I couldn't stand. And I knew I'd break eventually. Everybody did. So I gave in. They let me go— pretend to escape—in return for information."

"There was no need to co-operate quite so fully, was there?"

"Oh, yes. They knew where I was. If I hadn't, they could have come and got me at any time."

He looked around him to see if what he was saying was having any impact. Evidently he decided he didn't care one way or the other. "Then the war began to turn. The Americans had come in and everybody knew the Germans were going to lose. I met Schmidt, and he offered a deal. Not that I had any chance of refusing. He'd keep my secret, and I'd keep his. He knew that when the Allies won he'd be a wanted man; we needed each other.

"It was a mistake. It was the meeting, I think, that Hartung heard about. How he knew I never discovered. But he got hold of something: a photograph, a diary, whatever. He began treating me strangely, and so we came up with this idea, Schmidt and I. Solve all our problems in one go. We concocted a scheme in which Hartung would be told about an operation, it would go wrong and I could place the blame on him.

"Just as everything was ready, he came to my office and accused me to my face of being a traitor. Of course, I denied it, but he must have guessed something."

"Was he ever alone there?"

Rouxel shrugged, co-operative, even helpful now. "Perhaps yes. Maybe that was when he concealed his evidence. Next day he fled, and the Germans missed him. I don't know how he got away, but he did. They caught everyone else.

"After the war he came back. That was easy. I was working for the commission, so it was simple to have him arrested and to prepare the case. My own testimony, that of his wife. Watertight. But when I visited him in jail to interrogate him, he said he was looking forward to the trial. Then he would produce his evidence.

"Did he have some? I didn't know, but he seemed confident. I had no choice again, you see. I couldn't let him make a statement in court. So he was found hanged. It was the same with Schmidt; I couldn't allow him to be tried either. So when I heard the Germans were looking for him, I tipped him off, and helped him get a new identity. He started blackmailing me properly about ten years ago. Said his son was expensive. Of course I paid.

"And now it comes to this. I discover I had a son, and that my own granddaughter had him murdered. I can think of no more severe punishment you could mete out."

Then he lapsed into total silence, and everybody looked around wondering what to do next.

"I think we ought to have a little talk," Janet said. "I'm sure you realize this creates problems far beyond a mere murder, however serious that might be. Montaillou here can take Madame Armand away to the police station for further questioning. And you, Flavia, I would like to talk over a few matters with you."

She thought quickly and looked at Rouxel. If there had ever been any doubt in her mind, the sight of him dispelled it. He was a broken man. All his defences and protests had crumbled into nothing when Jeanne Armand began to talk. He was a man whose life had come to an end. There was not much danger of his running away. And what would it matter, really, if he did? So she nodded.

"Fine. Shall we go outside?"

And while a very deflated Montaillou led the woman away, Janet and Flavia, with Argyll in attendance, stood in the hallway and talked quietly.

"Firstly," the Frenchman said, "I hope you'll accept my apologies. I really had little choice."

"Don't worry. Bottando's feathers are a bit ruffled, but I'm sure that won't last long."

"Good. Now, the question is, what do we do now? I don't know about you, but I think that proper tests might well indicate that Madame Armand is mentally unbalanced."

"Which means you want to put her in a hospital?"

"Yes. I think that would be best."

"No trial? No publicity?"

He nodded.

"Part one of a cover-up? What's part two?"

He shifted uneasily on his feet. "What else can we do?"

"Bring charges against Rouxel?"

"Too long ago. No matter what evidence is in that painting, it's all far too long ago. Besides, can you really imagine the government sanctioning charges against a man they themselves nominated for this prize? When there's a danger it will come out that they knew about him all along? How damning is this evidence?"

She shrugged. "We'll have to see. I doubt if it would be so good now. Backed up by the testimony of others it might have been enough to acquit Hartung fifty years ago, but now . . ."

"So there's probably no solid evidence? No proof? Almost nothing for anyone even to build a rumour on?"

She shook her head. "I doubt it. But you know it's the truth, though. So does he in there." She gestured towards the door leading into Rouxel's study.

"What we know and what we can prove are different."

"True."

"Shall we go back in again?"

She nodded, and opened the door. "I think it's time," she said quietly.

She heard Janet's gasp as it swung open to reveal the scene inside. Rouxel was dying, tormented by agony but bearing the pain with dignity. On the floor beside him was a phial that had dropped from his hand. It took little intelligence to realize it had contained poison: the insect-killer he had been using on his plants when Flavia and Argyll had arrived. His skin was pale and his hand, clenched into a fist, hung loosely towards the ground.

It was his face, though, that grabbed the attention. The eyes were open and glazed, but it had a dignity and tranquillity. It was the face of someone who knew he would be mourned.

Janet stood still to take in the scene, then swung round on Flavia with sudden anguish. "You knew," he yelled at her. "Damn you. You knew he would do this."

She shrugged indifferently.

"I had no proof," she said.

Then turned to go.

20

"DEAR me," said Bottando. "What a mess. What was this evidence after all that?"

"A couple of photographs and some notes slipped between the canvas and the lining. Hartung must have suspected so he had Rouxel followed. The man witnessed and noted down Rouxel's movements. Including a late-night visit to a German army headquarters and a meeting in a café with Schmidt."

"And you let Rouxel kill himself? That, if I may say so, was unusually callous. Are you becoming an angel of vengeance in your old age?"

She shrugged. "I didn't know he'd do that. Really, I didn't. But I can't say I was so upset. It was the best thing that could have happened. In a way Hartung was heroic.

He knew Muller was not his son; his reference in that letter to the foster-parents suggests that. But he stuck by his wife in 1940 when he could have escaped. And he continued to encourage Rouxel despite the affair."

"I don't know whether to congratulate you or not," he said.

"Frankly, I'd rather you didn't," she said. "This has been a nightmare from beginning to end. All I want to do is forget it."

"Difficult. The reverberations will go on for some time, I'm afraid. On the one hand we're now exceedingly unpopular with Intelligence. Relations with poor old Janet will take some considerable time to repair themselves. And, of course, Fabriano will never talk to you again."

"Every cloud has a sliver lining."

"Still, I feel sorry for him. He's not going to get much credit for this, even though we will have to keep our nose out. More to the point, it's been such a nasty case we're not going to get a great deal of applause either. And I'm sure this has been simply awful for Janet as well. You saw the papers?"

She nodded. "I gather they're going to go the whole hog. A massive funeral. President of the Republic in attendance. Medals on the coffin. I can't say that I could bring myself to read it."

"I suppose not. So, my dear. Back to work? Shall we try to pretend again that you take orders from me?"

She smiled at him. "Not today. I'm taking the afternoon

off. Domestic crisis. And first I've got to write a letter. Which I'm not looking forward to."

*I*T was surprisingly easy to write it, once she'd got started. But deciding what line to take took nearly an hour of beginning, crossing out, starting again and staring out of the window indecisively.

Then she just emptied her mind and wrote.

Dear Mrs. Richards,

I hope you will forgive me for writing, rather than coming to see you in person, to tell you of the outcome of our meeting.

As you may have seen in the newspapers, Jean Rouxel died peacefully in his sleep a few days ago, and will shortly be buried with full honours as befits a man who served his country well. His contributions to France, and indeed to Europe, were immense in almost every field—industrial, diplomatic and political. His courage and vision were an example to an entire generation. They will now continue to inspire others in generations to come.

I was able to talk to him briefly before he died. He told me what you had meant to him, and described the actions he had taken to save you. His feelings for you were unchanged despite the passing of the years, and he had never forgotten you.

I hope you find these words of some comfort. You suffered enormously, but your sacrifice protected a man who, through your courage, was able to go on and make an enormous contribution to his country. And, at the last, your intervention allowed him to die as he deserved.

With very best wishes,
Flavia di Stefano

She reread the letter, thought carefully, then put it in an envelope and sent it off to be posted. Then she picked up her bag and left, glancing at her watch as she closed the office door.

The appointment to see their new apartment was at three, and she was going to be late. As usual.